VENTURE SCIENCE FICTION SERIES

Series editors, Rog Peyton and Rod Milner

VENTURE
SCIENCE FICTION

CROSS THE STARS

David Drake

Hamlyn Paperbacks
Venture SF

A Hamlyn Paperback

Published by Arrow Books Limited
17-21 Conway Street, London W1P 6JD

A division of the Hutchinson Publishing Group

London Melbourne Sydney Auckland
Johannesburg and agencies throughout
the world

First published in Great Britain 1985

Printed and bound in Great Britain by
Anchor Brendon Limited, Tiptree, Essex

ISBN 0 09 943550 0

DEDICATION

To Jim Baen, for ten years of making me a better writer, and for acting as a friend.

ACKNOWLEDGMENTS

This novel began in discussions with Glenn Knight, while we were some thousands of miles apart. Jim Baen and Bernadette Bosky were of inestimable help in matters of direction. Karl Wagner—kindly old Doc Wagner—provided technical data as always. When my nerves were frazzled, Sharon Pigott spent an evening keying in the last of the rough draft and saving me a further day and a half of crushing work. And my wife, Jo, made friendly, dispassionate, enormously helpful comments on that rough.

Blessings to you all.

CHAPTER ONE

A hologram of a tank, bow-on as it plowed through a brushfire, filled most of the wall behind President Hammer's desk. Either by chance or through Hammer's deliberation, the tank was Two Star—Danny Pritchard's unit twenty years before, when he had been a sergeant in the Slammers and not Hammer's chosen successor.

"Hey, snake," the President called cheerfully when he saw it was Pritchard who had entered the office unannounced.

Hammer tilted away the desk display which he had been studying. He had not let age and the presidency blunt all the edges of his appearance. If Hammer's hair was its natural gray now, then it was still naturally his own. His shoulders and wrists would have done credit to a larger, younger man. There was a paunch below desk height that had not been there five years before, however. No practical amount of exercise could wholly replace the field work of the lifetime previous. "Had a chance to glance over the proposal from Dominica?"

"Glance, yes," Danny said, perching himself on the arm of an easy chair instead of the seat. The fabric responded to his weight, squirming in an attempt to mold itself to his contours. Pritchard preferred a solid bench, so he gave as little pur-

1

chase as possible to the luxury with which Hammer disarmed visitors. "I like the idea of having somebody else pay for part of our army, sure . . . and, well, train it while things are quiet here on Friesland. But I think Dominica's too far if we—needed the guns back in a hurry."

Danny popped the rolled notes he held against his knee. It was a sign of the nervousness which he otherwise controlled. "Thing is, Alois," he continued to the older man, "that isn't what was on my mind right at the moment." He smiled. "Even though it should have been."

Hammer snorted. He spun his desk display toward his Adjutant and heir presumptive. "Teitjens sent this over as background before he briefs me on the slump in heavy equipment export projections. I'd sooner listen to you, on the assumption that I'll at least understand your problem when you've finished."

"Yeah, well," the younger man agreed. "The problem's easy."

He slid down into the cup of the chair after all. The office walls were a slowly-moving fog-blue, almost a gray. Pritchard slitted his eyelids. The hologram behind the President could have been a real tank on a skyswept plain. "We got a homeworld query on one of our veterans. Do you remember Captain Don Slade?"

Hammer nodded calmly over his clasped hands. "Mad Dog Slade? Sure, I remember him. He was the one man I really wanted who insisted on retiring when he heard his father'd died. Home to Tethys, wasn't it? The Omicron Eridani Tethys, I mean. I offered him a duchy here on Friesland, too, Danny."

"Via, he was a duke back home, Colonel," Pritchard said to the blurred man and to the tank. "He was the next thing to a king there if he'd wanted to be." The Adjutant opened his eyes again and sat as erect as the cushions would permit him. "We were—well, he did me a favor. We were friends, Don and me. Tell the truth, he didn't much like to be called Mad Dog."

"Well," Hammer said with a laugh, "if he'll come back, I'll call him Duke Donald or any curst thing he chooses. Not because he's a friend of yours, Danny—though that too—but because you can't have too many people like Slade on your side." The President did not precisely frown, but his face lost most of its laughter. "Among other reasons, because if they're on your side, they aren't on the other guy's."

"I think Don had had about enough of sides when he left here," Pritchard said. He looked up at the ceiling and remembered his big, black-haired friend in the spaceport at their last meeting. "He said he was ready to spend the rest of his life fishing like his grandfather."

"*Fishing?*" Hammer repeated in angry amazement. "He was going to go from one of *my* tank companies to fishing?"

It was his Adjutant's turn to laugh. Danny gestured with his notecards and said, "Well, fishing on Tethys isn't that different from the sort of jobs we gave M Company, Alois. There's a lot of water there, and the things that grow in it are pretty much to scale, from what Don told me. . . .

"But the thing is," Pritchard added, sobering, "Don didn't get there. We got a query from—" he checked the uppermost card from habit rather than from present need— "Marilee Slade, asking if Don were still on our establishment."

"Not in two years," Hammer said with a frown. "Mother? Or Via! Not his wife, is she? Don didn't take home leave in, well, at least the ten years since I promoted him to ensign."

"Seems to be his sister-in-law," the younger man said. Hammer had already swung the display back around. The President's fingers were calling up Slade's personnel file and planetary data on Omicron Eridani II—one of a trio of worlds named Tethys by their original settlers. "Brother's widow, I'd guess, from the way the query was worded," Pritchard continued. "Never talked much to Don about why he'd joined the Slammers, but I sort of gathered this lady had something to do with it. Also he was the younger son, that sort of hereditary nonsense." The Adjutant's eyes met those of the childless President. There was iron in the grin of each man.

Hammer grunted approval at whatever he saw on his display. "Council of Forty runs the place," he muttered. "Hereditary oligarchy. You know, I like the look of some of these average metal prices. Might be worth our while to ask for quotes, especially on the manganese. Either they sweat their workers like I wouldn't dare, or they've got a curst slick operation."

He gestured over the desk with an upraised palm. "But I don't suppose you thought you needed me to clear a trace on Don Slade, did you? Shoot."

"He left here on a tramp full of hard-cases. He was in a hurry and he wouldn't listen to reason," Pritchard said to the ceiling. "Golf-Alpha-Charlie Five Niner. I located a survivor on Desmo and got the story. Fellow'd gotten to Desmo on an Alayan ship. Don had been aboard the Alayan, too, but he'd gotten off at a place called Terzia. Produces medicinals. Place got one or two tramp freighters a month, so it shouldn't have been a bad place to trans-ship."

Pritchard shrugged himself out of the chair again and began to pace the large, austere office. "No question of coercion," he continued. "The survivor says Don tried to talk them all into working their butts off in the jungle or some such thing. Don was free to go, just like the others he was with—and *they* all lifted off."

Compared to Hammer, the brown-haired Adjutant was tall. He slapped the notes on his left palm. "What the problem turned out to be is that Terzia's refused landing rights to every ship that's approached it since the Alayans lifted off. It could be chance; but chance or not, the result's the same. For over a year, Don's been caged there as sure as if he was behind bars . . . and he may be that, too, for anything we know otherwise."

Hammer was playing with the controls of his display again. "Terzia's got real-time commo," the President said in the mild voice that he used when his brain was busy with something besides the words he was speaking.

"Yeah, and that's funny," said Pritchard. "I got the impression that the place was virtually pre-industrial. Exports some high-purity natural medicinals, but nothing in quantity. No quantity that there'd be a Stadtler Communications System, unless the economic pyramid comes to a pretty sharp point."

The President nodded. "One projection system, one Transit launch, one of a lot of things. One Don

Slade right now, though that wasn't going to show up on a Commercial Movements Summary, was it?" Hammer's fingers tapped the surface of the display gently. "Though that may be a flaw in the compiler's outlook, not Terzia's."

Hammer got up from his chair also. He ambled past the hologram. Beyond that wall of his office were the grounds of the Presidential Palace, lushly beautiful and maintained for no purpose but the President's enjoyment. Hammer did not object to the gardens, but it was at his orders that the crystalline window giving onto them had been replaced by the hologram. He saw the palace grounds only through the windows of his armored limousine as an incident of travel. "Right now, it's the projection system that matters," he said aloud. "You'll have Margritte handle it?"

Danny nodded at the reference to his wife. "We've got a few other people supposed to be trained on the Stadtler rig," he said. He rubbed his lower back and ribs absently with both hands. "Sometimes it works for them, sometimes it doesn't. With Margritte, it works, and I hope to blazes there's somebody on Terzia that good too. . . ."

Danny Pritchard had made a point of wearing civilian garments ever since the day of Hammer's inauguration. His present suit was as soft and smooth as the creamy shimmer of its color . . . and it was acutely uncomfortable on a body that suddenly felt the need for battle-dress again. "Alois," the Adjutant continued, "that leaves a couple questions."

"Margritte has a blank check," Hammer said. "If they won't listen to reason about Slade until she threatens that we'll land a Field Force regiment, she can do that."

"Terzia's a full seventy Transit minutes away from us," Pritchard said flatly. "They may think they're far enough away to be safe, so they don't have to listen to us."

Hammer turned. He was no longer the paunchy ruler of a complex industrial world. He was a commander whose troops had stormed Hell a score of times before and might do it again.

"If they won't listen to *us*, they'll listen to our guns, won't they?" Hammer said. His voice was as hard and sincere as the bow of the tank behind him. "Slade broke up a Guards Regiment with one tank company and a battalion of half-trained militia. If the Guards had taken the port behind us, Danny, you and I wouldn't be standing here, would we? Though our skulls might still be on poles out front."

Pritchard shrugged like a dragonfly beginning to pull free of its cocoon of soft, cream fabric. "I'd roughed out some contingency plans," he said as he turned to the door. "I'll work on specific movement orders while Margritte tries to get a connection with Terzia."

"Tell them," Hammer called to his Adjutant's back, "that I don't know if we can release Don Slade alive by force. But I'll promise to burn their planet for his funeral pyre if we can't."

For some moments after the door closed, Hammer continued to stand where he was: silhouetted against the bow of the tank.

CHAPTER TWO

The Citadel was a spike in relief against the mottled turquoise sky. There was no bulky starship on the landing platform beside the tower.

Don Slade swore very mildly, his voice as leaden as his heart. He stepped aside to let the work gang pass him as the trail dipped back into the jungle.

This was the one vantage point on the trail's length. Slade had cradled the short barrel of his powergun in the crook of his left arm as he marched ahead of the column. Now he held the weapon vertical for safety. The butt was against his hip, and the muzzle touched at eyebrow height the tree against which the tanker leaned wearily.

Bedyle, the foreman, stopped beside his superior. "Problems, sir?" the lightly-built humanoid asked in Spaceways English. The language differed radically from the version of English Slade had learned to speak as a boy on Tethys, but it—Spanglish—provided a medium of trade throughout the human universe . . . and beyond that universe, as on Terzia. Though it was sometimes difficult for Slade to remember that he and the Terzia herself were the only two humans on the planet.

"No problem, Bedyle," Slade said. "Nothing new, at any rate. There's just no ship. Still."

Slade's black hair was cropped short on his head

and jaw for comfort. Hair coiled like strands of honeysuckle over his bare chest and splashed down his limbs to the backs of his hands and feet. From a distance, he had a bestial appearance which the calm of his expression belied. Slade was taller by forty centimeters than the tallest of the work gang; taller and stronger besides than most of the humans whom he had met in a life of knocking about the universe.

"You know, Bedyle . . ." the big man said. His eyes were on the distant spire, but his mind was much farther away. "You'd think after nine days in the copper-pod jungle, that place would look good. But . . . if there was a Palamede slave-ship docked there, I'd ship out in its hold before I'd take another step through the gate of the Citadel."

"Your life is so very bad, then?" the foreman asked softly.

The workers were filing past, chanting something melodious and without meaning. Slade had been unable in a year to learn a word of the native language. The Terzia swore that when her ancestors had landed on the planet, the autochthones already spoke Spanglish. There was no reason to believe that she was lying . . . or that she was telling the truth, for that matter. Slade had no way to judge the Terzia's statements.

The locals, males and females alike, carried fifty-kilo burdens of copper-pods without signs that their frail-looking bodies were being strained. They were nude. Only in the greenish cast underlying their brown skins, and in the lack of external genitals in the males, were they demonstrably inhuman.

Slade had personal experience of the human characteristics of some of the females.

"Bad?" Don Slade said, echoing the foreman.

The sounds of lesser animals seeped from the jungle and merged with the voices of the work gang. "Via, no, Bedyle. Life isn't bad. I've got every luxury I could dream of, and the most beautiful woman I've ever met. I've got a job I'm needed at—" he nodded toward the workers he supervised and protected—"and it keeps me on my toes besides. I don't even get bored, what with all the different habitats we crop. I'd have to say my life is perfect."

The man paused. He turned to scan as much of his surroundings as he could see through the broad-leafed, ten-meter plants that made up the basic vegetation of this spot. A train of colorful, multi-legged creatures chased itself around one fleshy stem. The joints of the beasts' exoskeletons clattered softly.

"The only problem is," Slade went on, "its not the life I want to live. And there's not a curst thing anybody can do about that until another ship sets down."

The sucking sound of a tree being pushed up from beneath was overlaid by the scream of the worker caught in the first pair of pincers.

Slade pumped the fore-end to charge his weapon as he pivoted the butt to his shoulder. The monster's emerging head was toward the back of the file. It curved from the ground, dripping loam from its compound eyes and from the agate-melded segments of its broad carapace. A workman, streaming blood where the knife-edged pincers entered his body, was being transferred to the maw that gaped sideways to receive him. Slade had no time to pick his shot there, however. The real danger lay at the other end of the carnivore's rising body.

Along ten meters of the trail, pairs of pincer-tipped legs slashed out of the soil like sprouts in time-lapse. Three other workmen had been caught and were being swung toward the head end for ingestion. The survivors of the file screamed and leaped into the jungle. Their burdens tumbled in the air behind them.

At the further end, toward the Citadel, waved the tail and the slim, meter-long cone of the creature's sting. Slade fired at the base of it.

The carnivore lay ambushed on its back beneath the trail. As the pincers struck upward, the tail arched toward its prey. Large prey would be dispatched by a sting, while numbers of smaller victims—like the file of laborers—would be immobilized by sprayed venom even if they had escaped the first thrust of pincers. Now the impact of the bolt caused the tail to spasm. It drove a stream of chartreuse venom from the sting a moment before it would have been properly aimed at the work gang.

Slade was turning toward the monster's head again even as the jet of poison splattered onto the foliage above. The ground beside the man was cracked and heaving. A jointed leg as thick as his wrist lashed toward him, pincers clicking. The carnivore was squirming to turn its body upright.

Slade fired, stepped sideways, and fired twice more in rapid succession. A drop of poison struck his right shoulder and splashed upward across his neck, ear, and biceps.

The first three bolts from the powergun had shattered the creature's armor. The sting hung askew, one of the foremost pair of legs had been blown from its socket, and the cyan flash of the third round had cratered the curve of the head shield. The bolts liberated their energy instantaneously, however. Despite the amount of surface damage the powergun did, no single shot could penetrate to the vitals of this huge, loosely-organized carnivore. Slade's fourth round was aimed at the ulcer left by the third. The bolt struck in a gout of vaporizing internal tissue as the poisoned gunman screamed and dropped his weapon.

Skin was already sloughing where the venom drop had struck. Over the areas of secondary contact the skin was turning gray and black. Slade slapped his chest injector plate with his left hand because his right arm and side had gone numb. Leaf mold steamed beneath the hot iridium barrel of the gun he had dropped. The injector dumped stimulant and anti-allergenic directly into Slade's anterior vena cava. Under its impact and that of the venom, he staggered. He fumbled a medicated compress out of the kit at his belt and scrubbed at the damaged area. The fire in Slade's blood damped down as the compress debrided, then covered, the swatches where the skin was dead.

Although Slade had not lost consciousness, his conscious mind was surprised to find that he was kneeling beside his gun. His torso felt as if it swelled and relaxed with every beat of his heart. There had been enough breeze to carry one droplet of the unaimed venom to him. It had almost been enough to be fatal.

The creature was dying with the noisy lethality of a runaway truck. It hammered its surroundings. The middle part of its body was still within the trench in which it had lain hidden, while both ends lashed the vegetation above. Across the trail and the heaving exoskeleton from Slade, a stunned laborer tried to drag himself further into the jungle. A pincered leg gouged the earth beside him. Slade cursed and tried to leap to the injured worker's aid.

Slade had forgotten the amount of damage done to his own system by the drugs and counter-drugs that roiled within him.

Instead of clearing the monster as he had intended, the man landed on the blotchy carapace. His feet slid out from under him. The carnivore was trying to arch its center segments from the trench. Its weight pinned Slade's shins to the soft loam. The laborer scuttled safely behind the bole of a tree. The leg whose wild thrashings had endangered the native now recoiled toward the man. The creature's optic nerves and central ganglion had been destroyed, but its autonomic nervous system was making a successful attempt to heave the great body erect reflexively.

The powergun would have been useless even if Slade still held it. The carnivore was dead, but only time or a nuclear weapon would keep its corpse from being dangerous. Slade grabbed the limb as it swung for him. His biceps swelled as they directed the pincers down onto the dirt a hand's breadth short of his chest. They dug into the soil like the recoil spades of projectile artillery. That gave the leg purchase against the massive thrust it exerted a moment later.

The creature squirmed wholly clear of the trench. Its meter-thick body carried Slade up with it as its weight released him. There were tiny chitinous projections where the carapace armor joined that of the belly. They flayed the big man's calves through the tough, loose trousers that had covered them.

Slade threw himself out of the way. He was limited to the strength of his upper body because his legs were still numb. The creature was squirming off mindlessly into the jungle like a giant centipede. One of the legs of a rear segment still impaled a laborer. The corpse's drag kept that limb out of synchrony with the fluttering fore-and-aft motion of the others. The body segment itself twitched out of the line the remainder of the creature was trying to take.

In the dirt behind the carnivore dangled its sting. The plates that should have held and directed the weapon were shattered. Chartreuse venom still dripped and left a dark trail on the ground. In the wake of the creature's clattering exit, the jungle came alive with the moans of injured laborers.

Slade staggered to the fallen bundle that held the main medical supplies. When he had an opportunity, he would do something about the bloody agony of his own calves. They would wait—would have to wait—for Slade to treat the laborers who were already going into shock from trauma or poisoning.

The Citadel was temporarily only a memory behind a curtain of sweat and adrenalin.

CHAPTER THREE

At the top of her tower, the Terzia shuddered because a human would have shuddered in reaction to the scene she had watched. The breaking earth, the pincers stabbing upward with enough force to penetrate wood ... the venom drifting forward in a haze, burning like lava the bare flesh it contacted. ...

Everything that happened was out of her control once it began. But the danger had to be real or the exercise was pointless ... as it seemed to be pointless anyway, to judge from the bleakness of Slade's remarks to Bedyle.

The Terzia's awareness extended across all the life forms native to the planet. She watched from her tower and through the eyes of the laborers in Slade's gang, both the hale and the dying. When the brain-blasted carnivore stumbled against the tree trunk, the Terzia felt the impact both through the chitin and through the bark. Sunshine and starglow, breezes and rain all over the world simultaneously, were as much a part of her consciousness as was her terror of a moment before.

Like the wind, the chime of the Stadtler Communications Device was a stimulus external to the Terzia in all her facets. The human simulacrum in the tower turned the unit across from her in the open room.

The Stadtler Device consisted of a massive chair which faced a niche surrounded by a bank of cabinets. The smooth surfaces of chair and cabinets covered electronics as sophisticated as any other array in the present human universe. There was, in fact, no certainty that the orginal provenance of Stadtler Devices was human at all. A glaucous light on one chair-arm pulsed in harmony with the three-note chime.

The Terzia stepped toward the unit without hesitation and without any dimming of her awareness of every other factor sensed by the planet's native life. Stadtler Devices were almost solely the prerogative of governments, and generally governments of the richest worlds and nations. The units, built on or at least shipped from Stadtler, provided instantaneous communications over astronomical distances—at astronomical cost. A planet like Terzia could scarcely have afforded such a bauble, were Terzia not capable of directing its entire volume of extra-planetary exchange in as narrow a focus as it desired.

The Terzia seated herself in the chair. She touched the light to end its pulsing and to activate the projection circuits of the device. Her garment swirled as she moved. The fabric appeared to be layers of diaphanous gauze, gathered and pinned at the shoulders by crystalline brooches. In fact, the layers were sheets of light polarized by the crystals, and there was no fabric at all in the ensemble.

An image was beginning to form in the alcove across from the chair, just as a more-than-physical simulacrum of the Terzia would be awakening in the caller's unit, parsecs or kiloparsecs away. The Stadtler Device could not be used to receive alone. Its principle, whatever it was, required balance: a biological intellect at either node of a communication.

It did not require a human intellect. That was why the link worked as well for the Terzia as it could have worked for the human she counterfeited.

A woman on a couch like the Terzia's own gazed from the alcove. The soft focus of the caller's form sharpened as the electronic cabinets, the room, and the world beyond the room blurred and disappeared. The universe of the moment had shrunk to a pair of facing couches and the females upon them.

The caller was shorter than the Terzia and dressed in a soft, one-piece garment. She leaned forward and said, "I am Life Baron Margritte Pritchard." That rank flowed from Margritte's duties as Minister of State for Communication. "I speak with the authorization of President Hammer and the State of Friesland. This is a matter of highest importance, both to our world and to your own. The information you are about to receive must be forwarded for immediate response by your chief executive."

The Terzia's hair was a rich brown, falling in waves to her upper back. It rippled as she nodded. "I am the chief executive of Terzia."

The statement was true in a way that only the Stadtler Device made possible. In the field of the communications unit, there was a being called the Terzia who was separate from all other beings on the planet. Separate from the being that *was* all other life on the planet. The Terzia's face had been modeled on a fine-boned hybrid of French and Southern Oriental. It began to glow with the arrogance of individuality.

Visual and auditory contact had been complete almost immediately. The two personalities, those of Margritte and the Terzia, were still integrating. That process would continue, had to continue, throughout the communication to prevent the link from breaking up into static and sheets of color. For the moment, however, all Margritte was aware of was the fact that Terzia's ruler acted as her own communications officer. That was not an uncommon circumstance for the few who could afford a Stadtler Device. "There is a man being held on your planet," Margritte said. "You must release him immediately or risk the anger of—" she paused "—of Colonel Alois Hammer. The man's name is Donald Slade of Tethys."

The Terzia had known what must be coming. The name was still a numbing blow. Like a spark in her mind popped an image of Don Slade, back from the field. *His gun lay on the table by the door. It was safe, with its magazine ejected beside it, but it had not been cleaned and put up until other business had been attended to. Slade's black hair was long enough to wave as his head tossed with his laughter. His shirt lay in the hallway and he was stepping out of his trousers. The blaze of his smile and personality flooded the Terzia watching him from the bed.*

The Stadtler Field was momentarily a bloom of mauve static. Then it was peopled by entities whose mutual sharpness was beyond their own self-knowledge. Both minds had recoiled for an instant, then merged. The memory that had flashed into

Margritte's mind was nearly identical to that of the Terzia. *A younger Don Slade, a shell crater and not a luxurious bed-chamber; a uniform spattered with the blood of the corpse at the crater's lip. But the same laughter and the same fiery intensity ... and the same sinewy hands loosing the trouser fly.* "Oh dear Lord," Margritte whispered. "Oh Danny." She looked at the Terzia, seeing and being seen as never before.

"So that is why you want him back," said the alien with human features and a bitter human smile. "Reasons of state."

"No!" Margritte shouted, angry and cold with a lower-brain fear. Intellectually she knew that the Stadtler Device was proof against eavesdropping. Nothing which did not merge with the field could withdraw information from it after the link was established. What she did not herself report would not exist to Hammer; or to her husband. But certain reflexes are much older than the human intellect. "It was only once, under fire. It didn't mean anything, except that we were alive."

"Yes, alive," the Terzia agreed. She would have stood and paced if the logic of the Stadtler Device had permitted it. Instead, images of Don Slade wandered around the edges of the field, visible to both communicators.

The big man walked along the jungle edge beside the tender on which he had arrived. He had a pair of imaging goggles, but they were pushed high on his forehead. With his lips pursed, Slade was trying to duplicate the notes of something that had called to him from the undergrowth. The song hung in the Stadtler Field. It was not sound but the shadow of a memory.

In a second ghost-like moment, Don Slade was making love to one of the members of his work gang, a girl with bright eyes and skin the color of oak bark. They were all Terzia, all objects tailored to the needs of the planet in a universe over which humans swarmed with their mechanical responses to questions and their violence toward threats and toward excessive strangeness. The autochthones were a part of Terzia's defense system. So were the plants that produced complex drugs in wild profusion. And so was the "human" mistress of the world; the Terzia, who dealt with human traders and who controlled the hardware which kept less peaceful wanderers at a distance. *The image of the man astride the alien girl shouted with joy as unexpected muscles clamped. It showed a delight which the merely-human exoticism of the Terzia had not aroused in him for many months; and which itself had soon palled into despondency.*

The third image which flickered and trailed the others into the neutral background was that of the present morning, Slade leaping the thrashing carnivore to save a laborer who was not a man. To Terzia, the workman was no more than a skin cell, a fleck of spittle voided during a charade. To the man putting himself at risk, the victim was his responsibility ... and even if someone had told him the truth, he might have reacted with the same furious determination, because his duty was not a matter over which Don Slade gave power to any other to determine.

The Frisian and the Terzia—the women—were alone again.

Margritte tongued her upper lip, dry with tension.

She said, "You have to release Don Slade. We order it."

"Do you think he's kept in a cage?" the Terzia blazed. "He has *everything*, luxury, excitement—love, damn you, love if you will, for a soul like a jewel in the sunshine!" She paused and added in a whisper, "I am very old, and that is ... useful to me."

"Bring Don Slade here," Margritte said. "Put him on line with me. Have him tell me himself that he doesn't see the bars."

The Terzia tossed her head as if the wash of her lustrous hair could wipe away the words she was hearing. Margritte continued inexorably, "Or else let him go, lady. You have no other choice."

"Do you think you could take him from me?" the Terzia demanded. Her voice and bearing were those of the arrogant queen whose whim made the planet a danger spot for roistering spacers, a world whose profits barely balanced the harsh justice of its ruler. On the edge of the Stadtler Field flashed gunpits. They were armed with high-intensity weapons that could rip a ship from orbit or scar the face of a moon.

Margritte Pritchard's eyes were as cold as her smile. "Do you think," she said, "that Hammer's Slammers haven't dropped on a hot landing zone before?" *The Stadtler Field went black and red and saffron. Through it all spiked the blazing cyan of powerguns. Landing craft sprayed the perimeter from their gun tubs as the blunt iridium bows of tanks slid through cargo doors to hunt in a burning city.*

"That was M Company clearing an LZ on Cronenbourg," said Margritte's voice through the flashing darkness. "Don Slade was in the lead tank." Then she added, "Our panzers will bring him out of here alive, lady. Or they will sear this world to glass. I swear it, and Colonel Hammer swears it."

Tears were a human thing, but the Terzia was almost fully human as the Hell-lit carnage cleared.

"He doesn't want to go back to you," said the Terzia as her throat cleared. She looked at her fingernails and not the face of her tormentor. "He left you. He says he wants to go home."

"Then send him home," said the woman on Friesland, with a garden unseen outside and an ache in her own heart.

The Terzia looked up again, amber eyes behind long lashes. "There's trouble there, you know," she said steadily. "Those who want to kill him."

It could have been a lie. Hammer himself had no data beyond the bare bones of the request, and there was no evident way that the Terzia would be better informed. But it fit, the Lord knew; and Margritte was by no means sure that either of them could lie to the other on a link as intense as this one.

"That may be," Margritte said at last. "Maybe he'd be better to stay where he is or to come back to Friesland. We want him, the Colonel wants him. But Don's an adult. He can make his choices, even if they're mistakes."

"All right," said the Terzia. Her muscles bunched to raise her from the chair, a motion that would have broken the contact. She was human enough to scream against fate, but not in front of this messenger, this rival.

Margritte raised a hand to hold the Terzia one final moment. When she spoke, it was not as Life Baron, not as the representative of Friesland—if it had ever been, since the link had been forged so strongly. "Lady," Margritte said, "others have planned to kill Don Slade, you know. And the mistake has always been theirs."

She nodded, and the gray envelope of the Stadtler Field brightened for both into separate living worlds.

CHAPTER FOUR

An armed man in the crimson livery of the Dyson family waved. His helmet speakers boomed, "All right, clear to land."

The air car sagged gratefully into the courtyard of Slade House. The vehicle's bright caparisoning had been stained by spray and perhaps a storm in its journey from one of the more distant of the Council Islands—baronies, in effect—of Tethys. There were more shouted orders from the man in crimson. The driver lifted minusculely and slid the car sideways. It joined the line of other cars parked along the courtyard's southern wall.

More than a score of Councilors had already arrived. Teddy Slade did not recognize the trappings of this vehicle, nor could he place the youngish man who got out of it with his entourage of flunkies.

"Wasn't used to be like this, Teddy," rasped Coon Blegan. The old man shifted on the skirt of the gun drone to take some of his belly's pressure off his belt. "If your great grand-dad'd learned a Dyson was giving orders in the compound, he'd have reached for his boat gun. And their tarted-up bully boys running things at Slade House, well. . . ."

Blegan morosely scratched his left armpit. Thomas Slade had ordered Blegan to stop wearing his illegal shoulder holster when he appointed the old retainer as servant to his son Edward. Increasingly since Master Thomas had died, the old man had felt the lack of a burden he had thought he had forgotten. "Didn't call the old man Devil for nothing, you know," Coon went on. "Devil Don. Always wondered how it came they named your uncle after him, Teddy. Wouldn't have thought there was any way to know how a little baby like that was going to grow up."

The youth's control was born of a lifetime's experience with Blegan. He said "Perhaps Uncle Donald had a chance to grow into a perfectly decent, useful human being like Father, Coon. Only he heard too much talk by old farts about the grand days of the Settlement, when a Slade could shoot a man for looking cross-eyed. I'd be obliged if nobody tried to repeat the experiment with me."

Three more cars were approaching over the perimeter wall; the Rices and the Mortons, trailed by a larger van carrying additional retainers for Madame Morton. Even when everyone arrived, however, the most noticeable livery would be crimson. The Dysons shared Main Island with the Slades—and the Port, which was supposed to be neutral ground for all the Councilors. Even if Beverly Dyson had needed to bring his men in from half across the planet, however, they would have been here in strength for the present occasion.

"It was never like that, Teddy," Blegan said.

"Via!" the youth shouted. "All the rest of the world can remember to call me 'Edward', Coon—at least part of the time. How come you can't?"

Belgan looked at young Slade reproachfully. "Perhaps I didn't think the rest of the world knew you the way I do, Master Edward," he said. "But I'm an old man and ready to be cut up for bait, I'm sure."

"Oh, Lord and Martyrs, Coon," Teddy muttered. He squeezed Blegan's hand. "What's a word matter? But I wish . . ." He looked up. A supply truck was balancing awkwardly in the air, waiting for landing permission from the man in crimson. The truck's color was weather-beaten blue-green, Slade Blue. "But I wish. . . ." the youth repeated, and he let his voice trail off again.

"Things were hard during the Settlement, they tell me," Coon Blegan said. He did not look at Slade, just squeezed the lad's hand and released it. "I'm not that old, not even Coon, but they told me. These—" he patted the skirt of the gun drone. For all the old man's apparent flabbiness, the metal rang with authority. "These weren't for men, they were for the orcs and the knife-jaws. I know you don't believe it because they steer clear of Council Islands by now, but I myself saw an orc come right over this wall."

Coon waved toward the three-meter perimeter barrier, then back up at the gun of the drone the pair of them leaned against. "Ten centimeter bolts cooked her just fine, same's they did during Settlement when the orcs came in packs."

"Those days are over, Coon," Slade said quietly as he watched liveried hangers-on rumaging through the provisions truck. They were squabbling, each of a dozen parties trying to snare any special delicacy for the Councilor whom they served.

"Ooh, aye," Blegan agreed, "and glad I am, too, an old man like me doesn't need excitement." He paused. "But I didn't need to carry your father back dead from the Port, either, with a knife through his belly and half his ribs. He'd not have gone there alone had he an ounce of sense, not the way things are now."

Teddy swung in front of the old servant and took him by the hands. "Don't you see, Coon?" he demanded. "It won't make this a better world to live in if people like *us* help tear down civilization the way the thugs at the Port do. We need order here, but we won't get it by the two of us buckling up like vigilantes and getting ourselves killed too. If the only way to keep decent men from dying in the street was to make Beverly Dyson the President, then—I'm glad of that too."

"*That* one," said Coon Blegan, but he smiled and did not spit as young Slade had expected. The youth did not recognize the smile any more than he had recognized Coon's gesture toward his armpit for what it was.

Blegan was watching the crowd around the truck. A knife had flashed, then gone sailing through the air as a coda to the crack of wood on bone. Men cheered as the group broke apart. Durotige, a big man in Slade coveralls marked as well with a crimson stripe, roared triumph. He was swelling in the congratulations of liverymen who stayed clear of his artfully-spinning nunchaku. Durotige fed the chain-linked batons in a figure-8, between his legs and over his shoulders alternately.

His opponent of a moment before wore shabby green and scarlet livery. He was hunched over, holding a right forearm that was probably broken. The injured man backed and cursed as the outward arch of the nunchaku snapped just short of his nose. Durotige had been a Slade Under-Steward a month before. That his constituency had now changed was shown by the stripe on his trousers—and by the enthusiasm with which the crimson Dyson claque supported him.

"Beverly Dyson," the old servant repeated grimly. "That one wants to piss with the big dogs, but I don't think he can raise his leg high enough. One of these days Master Donald'll come home . . . and there'll be some to learn why your Uncle was nicknamed what he was."

CHAPTER FIVE

"Oh, come, Marilee," said Beverly Dyson in a reasonable tone of voice. "Why shouldn't I call him Mad Dog? It's what his own father called him, isn't it?"

Councilor Dyson touched the base of a stim cone to his left wrist. The disposable injector wore the black and gold striping of a powerful euphoric. In fact, the stock which Dyson carried was loaded with a mild stimulant. It did nothing to disturb the Councilor's plans or the ruthless speed with which he could execute them.

"Don's father hated him, as you well know," snapped Marilee Slade as she stared through the window. The family apartments were on the third floor of Slade House. The Trophy Room in which she sat with Dyson looked across the broad courtyard to the Council Hall beyond. The truck which had for all practical purposes been looted in the courtyard was just getting under way again. It would stop at the service dock behind the House for proper unloading. Ever since a driver had been beaten within an inch of his life, the provisions vehicles touched down in the courtyard first. "That's why," Marilee continued on a rising inflexion, "his father falsified the birth records thirty years ago to make it appear that Thomas was the elder twin."

"Marilee, my dear, we've been over this," said Dyson in a patronizing sing-song. It rasped the woman's nerves like wind on an aspen. Dyson knew that, and his smile was all the broader for that fact. "Legally, your late husband was the Slade Councilor—as your son Edward will be when he comes of age. There's no point trying to overturn a Council decision, especially a decision made so long ago. And after all, if you claim your father-in-law, lied to the Council, why do you presume his dying words to his son were the truth? That's not logical, my dear."

"Well, it's the curst truth!" the woman blazed. She turned. Her heels clacked on the mosaics of imported marble which overlaid a floor of sand-finished concrete dating back to the Settlement. The widow was tall, man-tall, though most of her height was from the waist down. The garment she wore had legs when she strode, but it was a single glittering cocoon when she chose to stand straight. The fabric shaded from black at the lower gathering to a flame-shot scarlet on the woman's slim neck. "Listen, Dyson," she snapped along a pointing finger, "even if—"

"Beverly, my dear, please," the handsome man interrupted. "After all, we've known each other all our lives." He too stood, dropping the flaccid stim cone back into the waist pouch from which he had taken it. There was a trash chute in the pedestal table beside him. Using the chute would have permitted others to examine the container, to penetrate a facet of the disguise in which Dyson wrapped himself.

"*Councilor* Dyson," retorted Marilee Slade. "Look, if you want me to treat you as a human being, then you've got to stop this nonsense about appointing yourself guardian for Edward. He's not a child, he's almost twenty—and if he *needs* a guardian, it can be me!"

The tall woman pivoted back to the window. Beverly Dyson permitted his face to lose the mobility he maintained when others were watching him. "I don't appoint anyone guardian, Marilee," he said. "That's what the Council meeting is being held to discuss. Though of course I won't deny that many of the Council do believe there should be— a—I'm sorry, but facts are facts—a strong male hand at the helm of the Slade Estate during these troubled times."

When the woman did not respond, Dyson stepped carefully closer to her. He had been beautiful as a child and as a youth. When he reached adulthood, Dyson had been wise enough to eschew the cosmetic treatments that would have frozen that youthful beauty. Twenty-odd years of natural ageing had left Councilor Beverly Dyson ruggedly handsome. He was as attractive to men as to women, and he had none of the smooth cuteness that destroyed respect when power was being discussed.

There was a mark on Dyson's left forehead where age had begun to undo some expensive plastic surgery. The skin there was a trifle shinier than the rest, and there was a path that could be traced back in whorls along Dyson's short-cut hair. "You know, my dear," he went on in a carefully modulated voice, "there's a simple solution. We were friends when we were younger. I still want to be your friend, and more than friend." His hand reached out toward the woman in a gesture that deliberately stopped short of her arm.

The curving crystal surface of the window had been treated during extrusion to permit no reflection on the inner side. There was obvious awareness of the outstretched hand in Marilee's voice, however, as she said, "If you want a strong male hand running the Slade Estate, then wait for Don to return. It can't be long, now that Friesland says they've traced him."

"Marilee," said Dyson sadly. "Even if I believed that weren't one of your little games to delay the Council, my dear, I scarcely think that Mad Dog Slade is what is required on a world already having difficulties with violence among the *lower* orders." He had difficulty keeping his tone light, and his arm lowered slowly.

"Mad Dog," the woman repeated with seeming amusement. She continued to face the activity in the courtyard below. "You know, I knew Don Slade pretty well, Bev . . . and I never knew him to lose his temper."

"I'm the wrong one to tell *that* silly lie, lady!" shouted Councilor Dyson. His fresh, bubbling anger drew Marilee's gaze as his attempted tenderness had not. Dyson touched the scar on his forehead. "I'm not going to forget, you see, what he did to *me* for a childhood prank!"

Marliee smiled. His rage was her victory. "I haven't forgotten that either Bev," she said. "It must have been quite a surprise when Don popped to the surface after you thought you'd bolted the escape hatch over him. But I really don't think he lost his temper when he came for you with the wrench. I think he had just decided the world would be a better place with you dead. Don was never the one to leave dirty jobs for other people when he could handle them himself."

Laughter pursued Councilor Dyson as he strode from the room.

CHAPTER SIX

"We had a bad one," Don said without preamble as he opened the door of the Terzia's chamber. "I left all the harvest so we could get back quicker with the wounded. Brought the dead; I know it didn't matter, but I did and I don't care cop what you think about it."

The big man paused for the first time since he entered the room. He swallowed and said, "There were two missing. We searched, but there's two missing."

"That doesn't matter, Don," said the Terzia from the bed itself. "Come—come sit by me while I talk."

The poison burns on Slade's upper body were white with the SpraySeal which now covered them. Besides the sweat-streaked dust on his skin and trousers, Slade's hands had a black patina. He had changed the barrel of his powergun as soon as he entered the Citadel. The one he had used on the giant carnivore was by no means shot out; but there was no reason to skimp on equipment, and a millimeter's tighter focus on a bolt might mean a life.

"Lady," Slade said, "the harvest's all over the trail and beside it. I'm going out with another gang. I'll be back as soon as we've gathered up the copper-pods—"

"They don't matter, Don. Sit down."

"—and found the bodies; Terzia, it matters to me," Slade concluded. His weariness was no veil over the angry determination in his voice.

The Terzia lay on a glade-green spread in a pool of light muted to duplicate forest shadows. Slade had never been sure of the process by which Terzia controlled the light. At other times, it had seemed to him to be extremely sensual.

"Don," the Terzia began. Then she lowered the hand with which she had beckoned him. In a changed, business-like voice, she said, "Both the bodies are with the carnivore, as you call it, some three kilometers from where it was shot. A party of workers has been sent out to retrieve the remains from the seventeenth-segment limb on the animal's right side and from its gullet. That business does not require you. This does. Sit down, please."

Slade's lips worked—silently, because he could not decide quite what words he wanted them to form. His left hand, smudged already with carbon and metal, touched the fresh and gleaming barrel of his powergun for reassurance. "I don't . . ." Slade said without the haste or hostility of a moment before.

"Don, come here if you think you might ever want to leave Terzia," the other said. She held out her hand again.

Slade moved as he would have moved to mount his tank in an alert: quickly, but with the caution that kept haste from being a danger. He laid his weapon on the table that had held it in the past and stepped toward the bed. He wiped his palms nervously on the dirty fabric of his trousers. Slade was not fit to see a woman, to make love on a sleek, resilient bed to a beauty herself so sleek and as capable of innovation as of response.

He did not hesitate, because he knew by more than words that the Terzia cared for the customary graces only as it pleased her lover to provide them. Slade had made love in alleys and in trenches, once even on his own stretcher in the casualty holding station as an affirmation to himself of his intention to survive. The Terzia was a jewel, not some fellow-swimmer in the maelstrom as those other partners had been. Or again—

Slade's groin was quickening with new excitement as he slid onto the bed.

"Is . . ." he said as his hands cupped her left shoulder and right buttock, calluses over smooth skin and the muscles supple beneath each. "Is there word of a ship coming in?"

"And any ship would be enough," said the Terzia sadly. Her arms circled him, drawing her naked chest against the big man's. His body quivered with a vibrancy she had not drunk from it in months. "You want to leave me so badly."

"Lady," Slade said. He squeezed her tighter in unconscious reaction to the words he was framing. "I don't want to leave you, but I want to go home. I'd. . . . You're a princess here, a queen." He arched back slightly so that he could look at the Terzia's face. "It'd be crazy for you to leave all this to come to Tethys. Gravel and sea, that's all it'd be to you. But it's my home."

"No, I couldn't leave my world, even with you," the Terzia said. Her eyes were on Slade's chest, on the black, springy delicacy of the hairs that doubled by their shadows on his skin. "I'll arrange for you to leave, then, Don. I think you should know—" she looked up to meet his puzzled expression—"that matters on your homeworld are very unsettled. You might find yourself safer—and happier—if you chose some other destination in which to settle down. If not here, then—" the assumed humanity of the Terzia caused her voice to catch— "perhaps back on Friesland. Your friends there have not, have not forgotten you."

Disbelieving, as tense and as careful as when he disarmed booby-traps, Don Slade said, "Lady, I thank you, but . . . it's been a long road to get here, and I don't think I'll turn back now. If there's trouble on Tethys, then I guess there's trouble anywhere, one way or the other. I'm as used to it as the next man. And I'd—" he bent forward again and nuzzled the Terzia's hair— "really like to go home."

"You will," said the almost woman. She shifted her body to free Slade's trouser catches. "You will very soon, my darling."

CHAPTER SEVEN

There was a bay concealed in the Citadel's flank. Its doors slowed, then latched open. Slade stared at the vessel hangared within. Then he looked back at the Terzia. He was not sure whether she had made a mistake through ignorance or whether he was the butt of a joke grim even by the standards of mercenary soldiers. "Terzia," Slade said in a voice that he worked to control, "this is only a lifeboat. It can't carry me back home."

"Not directly," agreed the Terzia off-handedly. For the first time since Slade had met her, she had not dressed before leaving her chamber. Intellectually, Slade knew that there was no more reason to dress for the autochthones than there was to dress before being seen by so many dogs . . . and there was no more reason to dress for one's lover than for one's mirror. Terzia's nonchalance surprised Slade, however, and the fact that nudity was a change bothered him. "It has a range of forty-five Transit seconds, though," she continued. "That will take you to Elysium."

Slade had stepped into the bay to touch the boat's nose. The hull's spongy coating was perfectly fresh. The only marks on the vessel's white surface were consistent with jostling during loading and shipment. The boat had very clearly never been moved under its own power. "I don't recall an Elysium in this sector," the man said as he paced cautiously along the vessel's seven-meter length. Like "Tethys," Elysium was a name of some frequency among the scattered human settlements.

"It's not in your indices," said the Terzia. Something she did caused a motor to whine. The lifeboat began to ease out of the bay on its docking cradle. The low sun stained the ablative coating a pinkish color as the nose inched into the light. "The inhabitants are human, though they have no open traffic with the rest of the galaxy. They'll help you home for my sake; and perhaps for your sake as well."

Slade let the vessel slide past him. He stepped around its stern. He continued to examine the boat, even though his expertise would scarcely have let him discover gross damage to the structure. Slade was no rocket jockey. The thought of leaving in this contraption frightened him even against his hopes of escape from plush captivity. Only the fact that lifeboats were designed for use by the ignorant gave him any confidence at all in the coming operation.

The Terzia stood in the open. To Slade, she was framed between the bulk of the vessel and the doorpost. Her waist tucked in above hips that felt firmer than their fullness suggested. The shadow of one breast lay across the cone of the other. Her nipples were dark and still erect, though the Terzia's face was in repose as she met Slade's eyes.

The motor's whisper died back into silence. The lifeboat halted, now clear of the bay.

A tendril of vine squeezed a switch in a control box. The boat's hatch began to clamshell open.

The Terzia had no non-mechanical control over machinery or other inanimate objects. Mechanical control was not limited to that exerted by her humanoid body, however. The result had to it a touch of magic or implanted electronics. It was new to Don Slade; and it was being shown him now only because the whole mime was ending.

"It's programmed to Elysium," the Terzia said. She was facing Slade, smiling at him as he walked slowly out of the building. "Food and water for twelve, there'll be no difficulty that way. You will have to bring her down yourself, though; there aren't any over-ride docking facilities on Elysium."

"I . . ." said Slade. His eyelids lowered as he stepped back into the sunlight. "Lady, I've never landed one of these. I guess you're sure that there'll be no freighters down soon?"

"That's beyond my control," said the Terzia coolly. "I can prevent ships from landing, but I can't make them come. And I can't be sure how much time I have. How much time your friends will permit me. I must consider the risk to Terzia now, you see."

"Of course," said the man, though the words made only grammatical sense to him. Something had changed, but Slade could not imagine what.

A year on Terzia had not rotted Slade's mind, but the year had its own parameters, as did any long time spent in a habitat. Slade was somewhat disoriented by being faced here with a sort of urgency that was familiar when he was a mercenary soldier. "Well, I've hit dirt on the likes of these before, so. . . ."

"At first I thought the ship itself was alive," said the Terzia with her face turned up to the sky.

It was still blue in the west, but it shaded imperceptibly to magenta on the further rim of the horizon. A few bright stars waited there, above the gently-waving jungle canopy. "Then I learned it was the men, not the ships; but it was very long, very long indeed before I realized that the men were different among themselves in such a way."

"I'm not—Via, I don't understand what you mean," Slade said.

A ladder began to extend from the open cockpit. It was swinging wide enough to clear the hull's soft coating. Half-deployed, the ladder began to jerk as the motor protested. Burrs on an untested cam or lubricant congealed in the step-down gears were hanging up the system. Slade jumped, caught the bottom rung, and let his weight jerk the ladder over the rough spot before he let go.

The Terzia had still not answered him. It was becoming clear that she did not intend to do so; and the man's words had not precisely been a question, anyway. "You will be able to land it?" she asked.

"Sure," said Slade. He rubbed his palms together, the one slick with grime of some sort from the ladder. "I, I'll just get some of my gear together, I guess."

"No," said the Terzia. "There is clothing aboard, and the Elysians will provide you with whatever you need there. Tell them I sent you, to help you go home. You had nothing of particular note with you when you decided to—visit here, did you? Your wealth is still on Friesland, waiting for a bank transfer?"

Turning to the open hatch and not to the Terzia's rich, dark hair, Slade said, "Ah, I wonder if I could, ah, buy one of the guns in the armory. I know there can be some problems with arms shipments, and you don't know when you'd raise another freighter, like you say. But I'd be obliged—"

"Oh, Don," the Terzia said. Her arms encircled him from behind. Her hair and perfume flowed over Slade like the love that was back in her voice. "You could have the planetary defense battery if you could carry it, but not to Elysium. They would be offended, and you won't need a gun anyway, not there. . . . Not here, either, except for the sake of your own wants. I'll keep the guns you used so well, and perhaps there'll be another visitor who will want them and want me . . . and whom I will want in turn. I don't think you can imagine how rare—"

Slade turned. Her breasts were warm against him; a runnel of perspiration on his own chest dammed and spilled sideways as the two embraced. "I wish," Slade whispered before their mouths met. There was nothing more he could have said in any event.

It was the Terzia who gave the extra squeeze, then stepped away. "You are welcome here," she said. "You will always be welcome here, while you remain—the Captain Donald Slade that you are. While you live." She turned and began to walk briskly away from the open lifeboat.

Slade licked his lips, then nodded to no particular purpose. The ladder was ten rungs to the hatch, but he mounted them with only six long, deliberate movements of his arms and legs.

At the rim of the hatch, the man looked back and found the Terzia was watching him again from an open gateway of the Citadel. "You must remember," she said distinctly, "that I am not really human, Don Slade." Then she disappeared within the black, towering building.

It seemed somehow to Slade that the Terzia had been talking to herself; and in the softening light, he could not really have seen tears on the lovely cheeks anyway.

CHAPTER EIGHT

"Number two thruster has failed to trip," said the console, in Spanglish and with a decidedly cheerful tone.

"Via!" Don Slade said. The boat's control console was supposed to have brought them out of Transit space with momentum calculated for a feather-light thruster landing on Elysium. "Why—" Wrong question, save it for later. "Cancel. Does the other thruster have enough power to bring us down safely?"

"The other two thrusters," the console said, supercilious now as well as cheerful, though Slade could imagine a programmer thinking the correction might be useful to the pilot, "have more than enough power to execute the landing within the original parameters."

Praise the Lord, even if the initial announcement had taken a year off Slade's life. He didn't have much head for heights, and the rate at which Elysium was swelling in the analog displays did nothing for his heart rate, either. The planet appeared blue in the onrushing holograms. Tethys would have been gray at the same distance; though on Tethys' surface, the moaning seas were blue and green and sometimes a maroon like an emperor's robe, when the sun and the life within the waters were just right. "What happened to Number Two?"

"An error in assembly," the console said. "A three-oh-three-seven board was installed in the control circuit instead of the four-oh-three-seven board proper for this model."

"Via," Slade repeated. The vessel was beginning to shudder now with the atmospheric buffeting he recognized from a score of light-craft insertions. However, Slade did not usually have a display to remind him of the terrifying height and speed.

"The feed valve in number two thruster did not shut off when the unit failed to trip," said the console's happy voice. "We are losing reaction mass at the maximum rate of flow for that unit. We will be at approximately twenty-one thousand meters above the planetary surface when thrusters one and three shut off for lack of reaction mass."

"Blood and death," said Don Slade in open-eyed horror.

"Unless there is a failure in those unit controls also," the console added in a caveat which it might have programmed into itself during the past seconds.

"All right," said Slade. He rose from the pilot's seat in front of controls he did not understand and could not in any case have used as effectively as the console itself had done. "Run through recommended procedures for this emergency—and if you say there isn't one, I'll come through a bulkhead to find you!"

"Unlock and press the red lever on the underside of your right chair arm," the console said. "The chair will drop into the escape capsule. I will deploy the capsule when thrust ceases. I am broadcasting a Mayday, giving course and altitude particulars on five bands carrying local communications traffic. I am adding the information that the Terzia has asked that you be afforded aid."

Slade interlaced his fingers behind his neck and jerked back, cracking stiffness out of his shoulder muscles. Then he sat down again in front of the console. The short hop from Terzia had required three weeks of perceived time, because the boat's instruments were not powerful enough to lop off large chunks of Transit space. During that time, the console had gotten on Slade's nerves badly. Its cheerful voice had seemed to sneer at all his questions as at those of an ignoramus ... as Slade indeed was, in the craft of space-faring.

But the machine's exposition now reminded the man uncomfortably of his training officer long years before. The officer was Major With, an Academy graduate from Friesland and a professional with no sympathy for recruits who had not grown up with organized warfare the way he himself had done. Major With had discussed failures in target practice or personal hygiene in a dispassionate voice that cut a recruit like a trip to the flogging block.

With's voice had remained just as cool, his appraisals just as accurate, the night enemy commandos hit the Operations Center because local traitors had sabotaged the perimeter warning system. None of the commandos survived after they wiped out the headquarters cadre. With precision, Major With had disposed his half-trained recruits by radio even as the commandos blasted through a wall of the room in which he was barricaded.

Control consoles were not human, of course. But Slade hadn't been sure that Major Frikki With was human either, before that night he saved so many of the trainees he had scorned.

"Dust to dust," Slade muttered as he sat down again. He threw the concealed lever. His stomach lurched with the drop, and the light went out. Something slammed shut overhead.

The lifeboat had bunks for twelve, but it did not surprise Slade to learn that there was only one escape capsule. Spacers and those who built to spacers' specifications had a tendency to regard outsiders as cargo, not humans. This boat had been intended for an immigrant ship in which a single crewman would have commanded a load of lay freight.

The lurching darkness in which Slade was now confined was oddly comforting. He no longer had displays and meaningless controls to worry him. What waited on the ground did, sure, but it wasn't a hot LZ. The familiar state of mind excluded the other concerns over which he had no control. Slade's right palm sweated for a gunswitch to rest on, but that was no great lack.

Ejection was downward and sudden, sharp enough to lift Slade against the restraints that had wrapped him to the seat without his will or notice. The capsule was not blind, as he had thought and secretly hoped. Screens, black because their pick-ups had been shrouded in the belly of the lifeboat, flared when the capsule spat free. Three digital displays and a horizon with arrow came to life at the same instant of uncoupling. The shock of the

drogue chute deploying snapped Slade back into
the seat. His feet and the base of the capsule jerked
up against the drag. Then the main canopy banged
open, forcing Slade's weight through the cushions
and against the metal backing of the seat.

That was the point at which everything went to
hell again.

It was probably nobody's fault that the boat's
fuel-starved thrusters cut out a half second apart
instead of simultaneously. That skewed impulse
was enough to send the vessel rumbling at 90° to
its programmed slant away from the capsule. If
the timing had been slightly worse, the separated
objects would have merged again and reached the
planetary surface as an amalgam of metal and extruded flesh. Instead, the lifeboat rotated through
the capsule's parachute with the motion of a hawker
winding cotton candy onto a cone. Then the vessel
passed on, releasing the chute with a last playful
tug. The fabric streamed behind the capsule. It
was a shroud for Slade's corpse and no longer a
canopy that could slow his impact to a safe degree.

The castaway had a brief hint of what must
have happened. The display whose pick-up had
shown the canopy's black fabric across the violet
of space suddenly changed. It filled with the
streaked white coating of the lifeboat's belly. Then
the black was gone and the white was a spark.
Images spun to match the sudden fury of the capsule from which they were observed.

The digital displays went wild. The attitude arrow blurred from its own spinning and from Slade's
failing consciousness. He never wholly blacked out,
but there was no task he could have accomplished
had one been set him. Slade was at the point of a

high-speed corkscrew. Centrifugal force darkened his face and hands with blood. Across him played the light of the downward screen. The screen was verdant with the image of a meadow through which the capsule would crush its path.

The first hint of relief was a tug too gentle to have been noticed, even if Slade had his full faculties. The canopy had been stopped from spinning, but it was some seconds before that stasis was transmitted through the line to brake the capsule's own rotation. Even before that happened, there was a shift of perceived weight downward as Slade's body translated deceleration into gravity. The unread altimeters that had been clicking off a descent of over fifty meters per second began to slow at an increasing rate. The capsule was being controlled as an angler controls the rush of a fish against a light line. The attitude arrow steadied into a sway that matched the way the globe rolled in the lower screen.

In the upper screen was a daisy-chain of four air cars, each with a line of the canopy looped over a stanchion. The cars were so light that even under full power they should not have been able to halt Slade's plummeting descent. With intelligence and equal care, they had re-extended enough of the canopy to take the initial shock of deceleration. The cars must have dived nose-first to make the pick-up, but now their bellies were to the capsule and their fan modules were directed straight down. It would have taken skill and great strength to control such a vehicle with one hand and with the other to reach out into a two-hundred kph airstream to snag the canopy.

Now that the descent was slow and controlled,

the drivers leaned over to peer at the capsule between their vehicles and the black curve of the canopy. Either the pick-up lied, or Slade's rescuers were a group of young girls.

CHAPTER NINE

Because the capsule was supported by four separately-controlled vehicles, it lurched the last hand's-breadth to the ground. That was still a softer landing than many that Slade had made behind professionals . . . and only seconds before, he would have traded his hope of salvation for the chance to awaken in a hospital, much less to walk away from the capsule. There was a quick-release lever in the center of the panel in front of the seat. Slade was still searching for it when his rescuers turned the dogs from outside and the walls fell away. Slade was surrounded by nymphs on a sunlit meadow.

Slade's first thought was that they were girls and very pretty. A moment's further consideration showed that in fact, his four rescuers were women and beautiful—but there was a level of truth to the initial impression as well. Three of them were dark-haired and stood nearly as tall as the man's shoulder. The fourth had the same elfin features, but she was fifty millimeters short of the others' height and her hair was red. None of them were as old as eighteen standard years, so far as the castaway could judge. The red-haired girl reached to hand Slade out of the capsule. If the others were nymphs, then surely the fourth was a pixie princess.

51

A girl giggled. "Lord have mercy!" Slade muttered. He had been too logy until that moment to remember that he was still as naked as he had been during the long, lonely Transit from Terzia.

All of his rescuers were laughing, now, though it was not a cruel sound. "Here, you've come this far," said the red-haired one as Slade tried to hide back in the capsule. She gave his hand an encouraging tug. "We shouldn't laugh," she said. "Liet, toss me my wrap from under the seat."

Slade swallowed. He should have learned more about Elysium before he left Terzia, but Lord! he'd been launched and gone before he really had time to think about what was happening to him. You don't really cross cultures when you have a gun in your fist and orders to execute. Your culture is that of your unit, and what surrounds your unit is so much glassware—to be spared where practical. This was different; and a gun, while intrinsically useless, would have made a useful pacifier for Slade's soul.

"Thank you, lady," he said to the girl who handed him the wrap. It was just that, a cape with a brooch fastener. The metal was a copper alloy, hand-worked and very delicate. With the cape upended, what would have been the lower hem for the owner could be pinned around Slade's solid waist. The rest hung down as a tawny apron, a natural wool of some sort, and quite adequate for modesty. Slade had soldiered too long to have any personal taboos about nudity. He had, however, a lively appreciation of how the parents of these girls might react to the naked man who suddenly appeared with them. He stepped carefully out of the capsule.

Flustered, Slade had last spoken in his birth
tongue. In Spanglish, "lady" would have been replaced by "donya" in the vocative. It was in the
same true English that one of the girls now said,
"But how are we going to carry him, Risa? He
must weigh two hundred and—" She flicked her
eyes back to Slade in a glance that appraised more
than his weight, correcting the phrase already
begun. "A hundred and ten kilos at least."

"Oh, that'll be all right, Sare," said the red-
haired girl, the leader as the castaway's instincts
told him. "He'll ride with me. We'll stay low and
slow. If the drain's still too much for my power,
you can jumper me."

"Ah, ladies?" Slade said. "You're going to take
me to your government? I was sent here by the
ruler of a neighboring world—" Via! The Mayday
had mentioned Terzia, and they must have heard
it or they couldn't have snagged him out of his
streaming plunge. Think! "Ah, I was sent here by
the Terzia, who thought your rulers could help
me."

The air cars, though light, showed a heartening
sophistication that belied the wool wrap and the
hand-crafted brooch. Dainty bronze-ware wasn't
going to get Don Slade home in his lifetime.

Liet giggled again, but Risa said, "We'll take
you to the city, of course. There aren't many visitors here on Elysium, not many people know about
us; but I'm sure we'll be able to help any friend of
the Terzia."

They were all looking at Slade in some wonder.
He had suspicion that Risa's "not many visitors"
was an understatement. "It's not in your charts,"

the Terzia had said of this Elysium, and Slade had
no reason to believe that she was wrong.

Certainly the cursory navigational data supplied
with the lifeboat did not mention the place. The
girls' eyes made Slade feel something like a side of
meat, but he had at least the consolation that it
was pretty good meat.

Slade was past his first youth, but he had no
inclination to have become inactive. He had seen
too many line officers leave a tank turret for a
desk and go to seed with appalling suddennness.
Slade's build would permit that if he let it, the
great ropes of muscle growing marbled with fat,
the hard belly beginning to sag to match the wob-
bling buttocks. The tan of Terzia's sun had faded
somewhat during the voyage, but improvised exercise had kept up the muscle tone of his big body.
Sare's estimate of his weight was short by five
kilos, perhaps because so much of Slade's bulk
was dense muscle.

Also . . . early in his service with the Slammers,
before a former nickname had resurfaced, Slade
had been known as "Tripod". He knew quite well
that in love-making, as in any other craft, the
workman's skill is more important than his tool.
From the way their eyes flickered to Slade's groin,
it seemed that these girls were not aware of that
as yet.

"Well, I think we'd better get back," Risa said.
"If you wouldn't mind, sir, we'll trim better if you
sit sideways in the luggage space instead of in the
other seat. I'm afraid you'll have to put your knees
up."

Risa was leading the way to the open car. She
stretched back an index finger as if to draw Slade

physically along. The other three girls scattered at once to their own vehicles. All of them were landed neatly beside the collapsed parachute. The chute's monomolecular fabric should have been of interest to locals who seemed to wear no synthetics. The girls scampered over the canopy without a glance down, and Slade knew enough to doubt their disinterest stemmed from ignorance.

The hull of Risa's car was molded in pastel swirls. The pattern was not quite garish up close, and at any distance it would mute into a blur more natural than any equal expanse of a solid color could be. The meadow's vegetation was more varied than the screens could suggest, but only an occasional stalk was more than a meter high. There were no thorns to jab Slade's legs or bare feet.

The car was little more than two seats and, behind them, a cargo space narrow enough to be a strait fit for Slade's chest sideways. "Lord and Martyrs," he exclaimed as he seated himself gingerly. "You dived this at two hundred kays?"

"We had to," said Risa, hopping into the driver's seat. "Nobody else was anywhere around, and we couldn't just let you fall."

The car staggered a little on a sliding lift-off, but its fans had a surprising amount of power for an open vehicle. Risa trimmed them manually at three meters, then slipped upward to ten where there was a better view of the rolling landscape.

The planet was not entirely open meadow as Slade's subconscious had been trying to convince him. Mountains were now visible astern in the near distance, and the broad band of darker green to the left was surely a forest fringing a watercourse. In addition, mixed herds of animals, none of them familiar to Slade, cropped the vegetation. Occasionally, the whine of fan blades or the shadow of one of the cars flitting above would spook a whole section of the plain. Hundreds of beasts, the largest species up to half the size of the lifeboat, would rush off across the sward like dark surf. They showed no signs of being domesticated.

It was a matter of increasing concern to Slade that, apart from the cars, there were no signs of civilization at all.

"You settled here recently?" he asked. That would explain both the low population and the Terzia's remark about the planet being uncharted.

The car was traveling at fifty kph or less, so wind noise was no impediment to normal speech. Risa glanced back at her passenger and gave him a broad smile. "We've been here longer than you might think," she said. "But if you mean Elysium doesn't show—signs of much development, well, that's true. Our ancestors picked this world to settle because it seemed to them a paradise, a—" she dimpled— "an Elysium. They were determined to keep it that way, and every generation since then has agreed. There aren't many of us on Elysium—that's part of why the planet has stayed, well . . ." She took her left hand from the controls to gesture in an evocative semi-circle. "But we're happy with our world and happy with our lives, almost all of us."

Slade nodded and tried to keep the questions behind his eyes. Early migrant ships did not pick and choose planets. They had drives which frequently failed, leaving them between stars with no way to re-enter Transit space, or—and this could only be surmised because it left only negative evi-

dence in the human universe—stranded them forever in Transit, in an envelope crushed slowly
inward by a palpable grayness.

Risa either read or deduced the doubt in the
castaway's mind. "Our ancestors were slow-ship
colonists," she said. "That wasn't working for many
reasons, so they found a way to escape from their
vessel. But I guess it'd be better if you heard the
details of all that from my parents."

"This seems a very lovely world," Slade said
carefully, "and a very peaceful one." He did not
know whether the girl was lying to him or if she
were merely retailing the lie which had been told
her in the guise of history. That was not important,
but it *was* crucial for Slade to learn enough of the
present situation for him to tailor his own lies to
meet it. He was a lone traveler, and his hopes of
getting home depended on the impression he made
on the people he was about to meet.

"Oh, very much so," Risa agreed with another
bright smile. "That's the main reason we don't
mix very much with other, well, cultures. There'd
be problems—sometimes not even everybody here
on Elysium agrees about what to do or how. If we
opened ourselves to the rest of the galaxy, some of
the problems might become violent. Avoiding violence was very important to our ancestors, and to
us."

"Well," said Don Slade, "a merchant like me
who's bounced around on a lot of planets sees
violence, I'm afraid. And I can only respect the
way you folk have managed to avoid it." There
was, Slade realized, as much truth to that statement as not.

Risa had not called her base, home, whatever, so

far as Slade could tell. He had noticed that the girls in the accompanying cars were speaking. Though there were no microphones evident, it was obvious that they were reporting to someone. Six or eight kilometers ahead, on the shore of a lake that reflected the clouds above it, was a settlement of a few hundred houses and a probable public building or two. None of the structures looked particularly impressive, though that opinion might be affected by distance and the way the walls managed to blend with their surroundings. "This is the nearest town, then?" Slade asked.

"This is the town," Risa said, "though we call it the city." For a moment the girl's smile was replaced by something gentle but wistful. "We've seen real cities, you know," she said. "But none of us have visited one."

Risa touched a plate in the dashboard. It glowed green, reassuring her about the state of the power-pack. The car's instrumentation was unobtrusive but very slick, certainly nothing some farmer had cobbled together during a long winter. "This isn't everyone," the girl said. "Lot of families like to live alone or with just a few neighbors. But there aren't very many of us, as I said."

"Well, the . . ." Slade said, frowning now in open puzzlement. "These air cars. They are made on Elysium, aren't they? Or do you—?"

"Oh, the machinery!" Risa said delightedly. "Oh, my goodness, you thought you'd see that! All of that is underground, right here, most of it, under the houses and some distance beyond, I believe. I'm sure they'll show it to you if you'd like, but it isn't the sort of thing we—on Elysium—wanted in the open. My goodness," she repeated, her laughter bubbling into the sky as an image occurred to her. "You must have thought you were on a planet where you'd have to grow a long white beard and learn to card wool. Really, I'm sure my parents can help you get home."

"Risa," said some undifferentiated part of the dashboard in a bass voice, "why don't you bring our guest by the house first. We have some clothes for him. After he's had a chance to bathe and change, your mother and I will walk him over to the Hall for dinner."

"All right, Dad," the girl replied. Slade could not see how she was keying the mike, but there could have been a button on the control stick. Risa made a moue over her shoulder at the man. "I hope you like red," she said. "Kelwin dearly loves it, and I doubt anyone else in town has clothes to lend that might fit you. Not that you're as *heavy* as Kel. . . ."

People were standing on porches or against vine-covered fences, watching the car approach. The individual yards were separated by walkways, but there did not seem to be any provision for ground vehicles. That was not completely inexplicable, but the only air cars Slade had seen were the quartet that had rescued him. Additional transport should have been parked in the yards, even if none of it happened to be airborn at the moment.

Then Risa guided her vehicle—a trifle too fast at first, because she was unused to compensating for Slade's considerable mass—around a house of weathered stone. An older man and woman waved from where they stood, well clear of the opened back wall. Risa tilted the fans forward to balance momentum with their thrust. Then she drove neatly into the building and parked beside two very similar cars.

The garage was well lighted. Slade had expected the floor and walls to be stone or concrete. It was with a sense of surprise that he realized these were some synthetic which glowed without any external light source.

The older couple had walked in as Risa shut the fans down. They could have passed as Slade's age or less, but the castaway's instinct was that they were much older. The man had Risa's hair and features, while the woman was nearly blond and somewhat less fine-drawn. Both smiled warmly at the girl and her passenger. "I'm Nan," said the woman as she stretched out a hand to Slade, "Risa's mother; and this is my husband Onander. I'm sure our daughter has welcomed you to Elysium, but let me assure you that the welcome was from the whole community."

The hull and seat-back flexed beneath Slade's weight when he levered himself out of the space in which he had ridden. He touched Nan's hand as he stepped from the vehicle, though he was careful not to put any strain on her. "Lady," he said, conscious of his image but able nonetheless to be sincere, "your daughter and her friends saved my life. I can't think of any welcome better than that one. And if there's any way you might help me get home, the way the Terzia thought you might, I—well, how could I owe you for more than my life? But I would appreciate it."

"Of course we'll help you," said Onander. He clasped the bigger man, hand to biceps, in a gesture that brought their left wrists together as if they were mingling blood. "But I hope you'll ac-

cept a night of our hospitality here. We dare allow
few visitors, but someone the Terzia recommended
is welcome not only as a guest but also as a font to
slake our curiosity. But you will—" he glanced
down at Slade's garment with a smile and not
censure—"be more comfortable in proper clothes,
won't you? They're right upstairs in the bathroom."

Nan and Onander were already leading the way
around the parked cars to the staircase in a corner.
The outside door had pivoted shut unnoticed. That
was the sort of effortless control to be expected in
a room with smoothly-gleaming surfaces; but the
stairs took Slade aback again. They were of dark
wood, old enough to show wear in the gentle bowing of the treads. Each tread was pegged, not nailed
or glued, to the stringers. The fit appeared flawless.

"Via, this is a fine piece of work," Slade said
aloud as he let his fingers brush the balustrade. He
felt that he had to be as careful with it as he had
been with his hostess, though the dense wood barely
flexed beneath his foot. It struck him that the
Elysians themselves might be less fragile than his
nervousness seemed to be warning him.

Nan glanced back at the big man. "My mother's
mother built it," she said. "To replace the extruded one. I'm told that it was almost six years
before she called it finished—not that she was working on it full time."

Nan paused at the stair head and rapped the
balustrade. The sound had a life that masonry or
synthetics would not have duplicated. "They were
both, this and the plastic, utilitarian in that they
permitted people to walk between the garage and
the first floor," the woman continued. "But this
had a utility for my grandmother while she was

working on it, too . . . and for us, to remember her every time a step sounds on the tread.''

As he mounted the last step himself, Slade glanced over his shoulder and smiled. Risa still waited at the foot of the stairs, watching the play of the castaway's muscles. When his eyes caught hers, the girl blushed before she grinned back.

CHAPTER TEN

"The seat of honor, Mister Slade," Onander said as he pointed to the chair at the center of the cross table. The chair to either side of the central one was empty also. Nan took the guest's hand lightly to bring him forward, much as her daughter had led Slade to the car.

There were about thirty adults already sitting at the two side tables and at the seats to either end of the table that crossed them into a square-based U. They clapped lightly as the castaway entered the room. There were decanters and covered dishes on the tables, but the meal had waited for Slade's arrival.

Slade's tunic and shorts were red, as he had been warned. The garments were comfortably light in the warm evening, and they were loose enough to give him occasional twinges as he remembered his garb on landing. Other Elysians were wearing similar clothing, though mostly of printed cloth. There was no certain cut or style. One man was nude at least from the tabletop to his cap of iridescent feathers.

Nan sat in one of the flanking chairs. Onander pulled out the central one and gestured Slade into it. Before the Elysian himself sat down, however, he called, "Friends? Our guest would probably be better for a meal in him. Afterwards, we hope he'll join us in the other room and tell us something about himself and the things he's seen; but for now, let's all eat in peace."

There was another patter of hands beneath a rainbow of Elysian smiles.

The Slammers were normally fed with ration packs, standardized food. It might once have had a Dutch emphasis, but when reconstituted it tended to be as featureless as a hooker's thirtieth trick of the night. The mercenary troops themselves came from worlds as varied as those on which a contract might station them. It was better to accept the cost and inconvenience of standardized rations than to lose thirty percent of your effectives to diarrhea or constipation every time you shifted planets.

Slade, however, had made a practice of eating on the local economy wherever possible. He hadn't joined Hammer to be bored, and he'd always figured he pulled his weight even when he had the runs. The big man therefore appreciated the meal before him as few of his fellows would have been able to do.

Not that the food was exotic in any normal sense. There was roast meat, vegetables both raw and cooked—nothing Slade recognized, and nothing particularly striking except a dish that looked like cole slaw and tasted like napalm—and bread, which was almost certainly baked from Terran wheat. The wine was probably better than Slade had a palate to enjoy. He had grown up on Tethys with stim cones, not alcohol. His introduction to the latter as a low-ranking trooper had been regimental stash, valued for reasons apart from its piquant subtleties of flavor.

"You know," he said around a bite of roast—from the end, where it was cooked gray, not pink—"I sort of thought you might be vegetarians. It, well, I thought you might."

"Some of us are," Onander said as he forked more meat from the tray between the two men. "Down at the far end," he noted, with a gesture toward one of the side tables, brief enough to be unobtrusive. "We haven't a large population on Elysium, but neither is it a monolithic one. You wouldn't prefer, ah, vegetable protein, would you? Really, I should have checked."

Slade had not been conscious of being the center of attention. The other people in the hall had been eating and chatting in normal fashion. Now, however, the big wood-paneled room had noticeably stilled. "Oh, not at all," the castaway said in embarrassment. "It's mostly seafood of one sort or another . . . a lot of it compressed and textured plankton, but animals to start out even if they were little ones."

He grinned and looked around the room. "Tell the truth, a lot of what I was raised to eat was about as bland as regimental food." He raised a bite of roast on his fork. "Nothing as good as this," he closed, putting an obvious period to the explanation by eating the morsel.

Slade had not done any physical labor since his last bout of exercise on the lifeboat. The tension of the landing, however, had itself kept his metabolism cooking at a high rate. He plowed on through repeated servings, vaguely conscious without focusing on it that those around him continued to eat though at a much lower rate. When Slade finished, covering a belch with his hand, there was almost simultaneous movement among his hosts to push their plates away and lean back.

Nan stood. "I think," she said, "that if we've all eaten, we can adjourn to the Assembly Room to listen to our visitor. If he wouldn't mind?" she added, looking down at Slade. The question was real and hopeful, not a rhetorical exercise.

"Ah, I'd be delighted," said the big man. When he got up, he found that his muscles were wobbly with exhaustion and the pleasant burden of food being digested. Natural courtesy aside, Slade owed these friendly people a duty for their hospitality. It did not occur to him to shirk his duties simply because he was tired.

"Of course everyone couldn't gather to meet you directly tonight," said Onander as he opened the door behind his own chair. A two-meter long hallway, open at the further end, lay beyond. "But from the Assembly Room, we can broadcast and share your talk with the whole community."

Slade had noticed that the dining room into which he had first been ushered was only half the exterior size of the building. The Assembly Room filled the remainder, save for the length of the hall between them. Too narrow for a kitchen, he would have thought . . . and none of his business; Slade wasn't searching this city for contraband.

The Assembly Room took his breath away with its abruptness.

They had dined beneath bare rafters, seated on wood and eating from hand-thrown pottery. The Assembly Room was by contrast as technically advanced as anything Slade had seen. It was of a style that was wholly new to him as well.

Elysians who passed as Slade stepped aside were reclining on what seemed to be a bare floor. The surface rose and mounded, not only beneath their weight but by meeting their bodies at comfortable angles. The feet of those walking to places to sit did not affect the floor in any visible manner.

But it was the walls that made Slade pause just inside the doorway. They held his attention in growing horror. The covering material had its own light as had that of the air car garage. This time the wall was not a wash of blank color but rather a mural painting with life and depth and movement.

"It's a scene from our history," Nan said with quiet dignity. "Our ancestors were slow-ship colonists. There was a higher level of radiation aboard than the designers had allowed for, or perhaps they just failed to allow for the passage of time on a closed system. There was, at the end, fighting between our ancestors and other passengers who had—deviated further from the original stock."

More than Slade's eyes were absorbed. He could not have seen the objects on the black background more clearly: rusty iron, the golden gleam of a join brazed instead of welded, the silvery polish of the lands against the shadowed grooves of a gun barrel. To another man, they would have been crude steel boxes, crawling their way one at a time through narrow darkness. But Slade was a tanker. His palms sweated and his heart began to race. "No," he whispered. It was not only other men in those tanks, it was him again.

The lead vehicle disintegrated. There was a spark

on the glacis, then a globe of orange fire. Fuel and
ammunition had exploded. For that brief instant,
the surroundings were more than hints in shadow:
girders interlacing, reaching far beyond visibility.
Nowhere in sight was there a longitudinal connection except the catwalk down which the armored
boxes struggled.

"The main drive was in East Section," Nan was
saying. All the others who had dined with Slade
were now seated on the floor. "For generations,
our ancestors had used auxilliary units in West for
power, but at the end it was necessary to tap the
main drive."

The next vehicle clumsily shoved aside the remains of the first. Glowing fragments slipped over
the edge of the catwalk and pirouetted, as softly as
thistle seeds, toward the black that swallowed them
and their warmth. Flashes lighted slots in the bulkhead at the walk's far end. Projectiles rang and
splashed from girders, from the walkway, from the
armored targets waddling forward.

"You can't just bull your way in!" Slade said.
"Not if they're waiting, not if they're hardened
and you give them time to pick and—"

The leading vehicle had been firing toward its
goal with three automatic weapons. Now a pale
amber beam threaded through the girders at an
angle and touched the vehicle's flank.

"—choose, it's—"

Another orange explosion.

—"*suicide!*"

"There was no choice," the Elysian said. Her
firm hands held one of Slade's to keep the castaway from gouging himself with his cropped nails.
"There was only one vehicular connection between

East Section and West. The crews knew what they were doing."

The third vehicle might have been lighter than its fellows, or perhaps even machinery could feel and react to desperation. The tank rocked through the wreckage at speed. The laser touched it but did not bite out the vehicle's heart. The beam left only a scar that glowed white, then red, as it cooled. As the tank neared its goal, the guns in the bulkhead fired at an increasing deflection. Shots still hit. The weapons replying from the vehicle's bow fell silent. But there were not so many hits, and they did not have the seam-splitting accuracy of moments before.

"At the time this was going on—" Nan continued. A white flash beneath the lumbering vehicle scattered the three iron road-wheels on the left side. They spun off the catwalk as the tank lurched the other way. Their edges glowed and disappeared.

"—a team was entering the power room from outside, unnoticed by the inhabitants who were concentrating on the bulkhead."

A door from somewhere ahead of the disabled vehicle spewed others onto the catwalk. The remaining gun on the tank fired until the barrel shone. Weapons from West Section itself must have joined, because the flecks of projectiles ricocheting patterned the vehicle's quarter for the first time. It made no difference. The others were over the tank like maggots on the third day's corpse. They were humanoid, but they had huger bodies and fewer eyes than men. They began to devour the vehicle's crew even as they dragged them through the prized-open hatches.

"If they had known, you see," Nan said as the

mural faded to swirls of dark pastel, "they would have cut the connection. The power had to be on for three full days before all the passengers in West Section could escape to Elysium. All the survivors."

Slade shuddered to bring himself out of the waste of fear and memory where he had lived for the past moments. Music of some sort was a soothing undercurrent in the hall. Patient, friendly faces were turned up to his. "Dear Lord have mercy," the tanker said. He released his hand from the woman's. He managed a smile. "I'm Don Slade," he said. "I was a merchant. . . ."

CHAPTER ELEVEN

"I think we've got a balance," said the blonde technician. Her voice whispered out to every human on Elysium except for Don Slade. "We're going to begin coupling in." Her fingers played over the banks of rocker switches before her.

"A little up in the thirties, I think," said her bald companion. The blonde's fingers replaced a nod. They touched controls and sharpened the color of the images forming in her mind, her companion's mind, and in those of the other thirteen thousand Elysians with right-brain implants.

The bald technician rubbed his temples. "Blessed Lord," he grumbled. "That spike almost took the top off my skull. And just the mural, not something he'd been through himself."

"How's this?" asked the blonde as the images firmed.

"Perfect," said her companion. He touched one of his own controls, minusculely changing the attitude of the hidden probe aimed at the back of Slade's head.

"I had the controls set down, just cracked enough to get a reading, I thought. Really."

"I'm not blaming you," the bald technician said. He had closed his eyes. "I never knew an affect to peak like that either. I just hope the shunts catch the next spike the way they're supposed to. Or—" he smiled, covering a wince of remembered pain— "our guest is going to be very surprised when his audience starts to scream just as he gets to the good part."

Then the two of them relaxed behind their instruments. With the ease of long experience, they let Don Slade's words and the thoughts like sharks beneath those words hiss simultaneously through their own minds.

"The ship on which I hired passage," the speaker was saying, "had a lot of military types aboard. There'd been a lot of fighting on Friesland in the recent past. Hard-cases had signed on with one side or another. Now that things had settled down, they were leaving; and sometimes one step ahead of the White Mice, the authorities. Passes weren't being checked very carefully. The Colonel—ah, President Hammer, the new executive, seemed to figure that it was as cheap to ship the trash out as it was to cull them and shoot them.

"Or just shoot them, I guess—" A vivid image of bound figures collapsing against a shot-burned wall; a smile on the speaker's face that matched the image much better than it did his merchant persona. "I hear that might've been discussed before a fellow named Pritchard, close to the President, put his foot down."

Elysium watched the men with the uniforms and bearing of military men who filled a small, tense room. Young men in battle-dress stood beside the door. The seated men had the age and rank. They were scowling, several of them ready to jump to their feet. Danny Pritchard in civilian clothes was clicking off, coldly as an abacus, the long-term effects of a present resort to terror.

Don Slade was not a figure in his own vision. The scene was tinged red with suppressed violence. Beneath the physical details ran an awareness of the weight of Slade's pistol holster and the smooth hardness of the mini-grenade concealed in his left hand. The big man was poised to clear the room if Hammer ordered his friend's arrest.

"I wasn't too worried about the other passengers," Slade was saying. His voice was a pleasant tenor, sharply at variance with the jagged images in his mind. It was always the striking memories that remained, of course. But what the subject found striking depended on the life that had brought him to them.

"I'd turned all my, ah, wares to cash, and I figured to arrange a bank transfer when I got home to Tethys. The others aboard the ship, a tramp with just the registry number GAC 59, weren't the sort of folks I'd have wanted to go to sleep with if I'd had anything worth stealing. But I didn't, and they knew it, and I figured I could handle minor annoyances about as well as the next guy." The smile again, and the great, scarred fingers of one hand caressing the knuckles of the other.

"Thing is," Don Slade continued, "there *was* one thing I had that the others turned out to want: my—trading experience, for the venture they were planning. . . ."

CHAPTER TWELVE

"Nice of you to come see us, Slade," said the leader of the men with their hair dyed blue.

"Hello, Blackledge," said Don Slade in a voice as cold as his expression. The tanker did not know why he had been called to the bridge. Likely it had something to do with the fact that the most recent Transit had been four hours ago, far too long for a normal computation.

It did not concern Slade to find that there were four other passengers on the bridge, along with the normal trio of crewmen. What Slade disliked was the fact that the four were Reuben Blackledge and three of his henchmen from Aylmer's Guards. That unit had been known for its members' blue hair and the abnormal brutality with which it conducted its affairs. Hammer had proscribed the Guards as soon as he thought he could spare their manpower. Individual soldiers had shaved or re-dyed their hair. The smart ones found passage off Friesland while the going was good. It was a bad sign that the outlaws were sporting their old color. It was worse that they lounged on the bridge as if they now owned it.

"Hey, hang loose, trooper," Blackledge said, tense to his own surprise when the tanker looked at him. All four of the outlaws had guns. The detector at the bridge hatchway had shown that Slade was unarmed . . . but no one with hands and a mind like Mad Dog Slade was really unarmed. "Look," Blackledge continued, "this isn't any hijacking or anything like that, is it?"

He looked around for support. His fellows nodded. They too had been shocked by the physical presence of the tank officer whom they had expected to overawe. The crewmen nodded also. Levine, the Captain, said, "These are hard times, Mister Slade. I have responsibilities, too, to do what's best for my crew and my backers."

"There's the matter of responsibility to your passengers, too, Levine," Slade said. He walked over to the bulb of the navigational display which was now dark and empty. It looked like a harmless motion, because Slade's back was to four of the Guards; but everyone on the bridge was now within reach of the tanker's arms. "There's three hundred of us who've paid to be hauled home on schedule and in order, right?"

"Happens the rest of us," said Blackledge, "want to change the schedule a little, Slade. Look—" his voice rose in nervous anger, though Blackledge was not a small man either— "it's fine for you, the fares pay the cost of Transit and the ship makes its profit off odds and sods of cargo it picks up on the way. But there's a lot of us aboard, your highness, people who spent their last sparkler to cheat the hangman one more time. You get off and transfer a fortune back into your pocket. But what d'ye think happens to most of *us*?"

Slade turned slowly to face the outlaw leader. Well, he'd never really believed he was meant to die in bed, for all his determination a month ago that he would go home and live as quietly as a shore-side mussel.

Blackledge's face was suffused. In that state it was marred by a scattering of white, hair-thin scars. "I don't suppose," said Slade in a reasonable voice, "that you called me here to see if I'd split my pay—" he had more than that, but less than the fortune in loot that Aylmer's Guards would have expected from someone with Slade's opportunities— "with everybody at our first landfall."

If Blackledge said they *did* intend such extortion, it was going to get tense. Slade doubted that these blue-haired clowns had the subtlety that would be needed to actually break Slade to their will; but he did not care to be around for them to practice on, either.

"Naw, we don't want your money," the outlaw said. Slade relaxed, and the outlaws relaxed. The ship's crewmen looked quizical, but they did not realize how close they had been to a maelstrom of bodies and gunfire. Blackledge was trying to find an alternative to the bantering superiority with which he had opened the interview and to the frightened hostility into which his tones had degenerated. "We're all mercs, right? We don't rob each other."

Which was a lie, but one whose telling was an olive branch that Don Slade was willing to accept with a smile. "There's a lot of us, you see," the outlaw continued, "who didn't figure on Hammer getting holier than thou once he'd shot his way into the presidency. We figure we're owed something, and there's plenty of places out there just waiting to pay us."

Places like Tethys, Slade thought as he nodded

false approval. Places that hadn't had an internal war since they were settled. Places whose emergency alert system was cob-webbed from disuse. The chances of this lot getting away with significant loot were slim, but Via! the damage they'd do before the locals mopped them up!

Via. . . . If Slade grabbed the submachinegun of the nearest outlaw, he could empty it into the control panel before they stopped him. "I don't know, though," the big man said as if he were considering. "Three hundred effectives won't give you much of a perimeter. I suppose everybody's pretty well agreed on this, though?"

Another man with scarcely a stubble to dye nodded furiously. It was Blackledge, however, who answered by saying, "This is just one ship of twenty-two, Slade. Isn't that right?"

"That's right," agreed Captain Levine with a bob of his head. "Ready and waiting. It's hard to make it on unscheduled loads, stony hard. I owe it to my backers to take a chance when it offers. . . ."

A chance to be slagged down with your rusty hull, the tanker thought. But he was accustomed to the ravening bite of powerguns, and to the short shrift they gave any but the most refractory armor. Levine did not have that experience; and the outlaws, who probably did understand, would not dwell aloud on the vulnerability of the chariots hauling them to fantasy loot.

But it meant that whether or not GAC 59 survived, the raids were going to occur. Good soldiers have to be willing to die, but suicidal men have little purpose in a well-run army. They just leave you with another damned slot to train for. "Sounds like you've thought things through pretty well," said Don Slade. "Now I'm just waiting for the other shoe to drop, hey?"

"We want you to command us," said Blackledge. He vomited out the words with a forward thrust of his head. The outlaw's hair waved above his scarred, red face.

Slade was genuinely surprised for the first time since he stepped onto the bridge. He jerked away from the words.

"Look, I don't mean we'd make you God," Blackledge continued hastily. He gestured toward Slade with his left hand. "There's a Ship's Meeting, same as there's a Fleet Meeting. You won't have cop to do with that, it's us that plan things. But after we hit ground, well—" The outlaw frowned across the company of his fellows. "Look, we've heard of you, you're used to commanding things. Most of the other ships, they've got their own officers, they left as formed units. Us here don't. We're bits and pieces from twenty outfits, and nobody the rest'd listen to. We *know* we're headed for some heavy traffic, Slade. You're going the same place. If you're smart, you'll be willing to help steer for a triple share of the loot."

Slade began playing again with the navigation bulb. It gave him a look of aimless placidity. "Whatever happened to Aylmer?" he asked. "General Aylmer, I think he called himself, didn't he?"

One of Blackledge's companions began to snicker. Blackledge hushed him with a punch on the shoulder and a molten glare. "Aylmer thought he'd make a deal for himself that'd leave some people hanging," said the outlaw leader. "Some people got to know about that. I think they may've greased Aylmer before they bugged out themselves."

A stubble-haired outlaw broke the silence he had maintained until then. "It's the same thing you've been at," he said. His lips flicked saliva. "Only we don't have tanks, is all. And don't worry about what your buddies who stayed on Friesland with the cushy jobs might say. *They* knew about this. We kept it quiet as we could, but there's no way a deal this big could have been put together without their high and mightinesses learning, was there?"

"All right," said Don Slade. His skin felt as though he were being crushed by an avalanche of needles. But choose Life, even when Life has a gun-stock. "It won't work, because I don't think any of your lot have the discipline to make it work. But I'll give you as much leadership as you're ready to take."

CHAPTER THIRTEEN

Slade was the first man through the cargo hatch, because there was no one else aboard he had trusted to lead the rush on the gun position. In fact, half a dozen of his thirty-man assault company were pounding across the rammed-earth field as more pirate freighters roared in to land and the personnel of Desireé Port reached for weapons they had forgotten.

The field was defended by a pair of heavy powerguns on opposite sides of the perimeter. The ball-mounted weapons were hardened, but not to the point that Slade would not have preferred to take them out with bursts from a tribarrel. None of the ships in this rag-tag assemblage would admit to having more than small arms aboard, however.

Levine had landed a full seventy-five meters from the gun Slade was to assault. The chill air and icy footing effectively doubled the distance that was already too long. Shots were being fired, some at random, some in the attack on the control tower that another vessel had been told off for. A bolt ripped a long gouge through the snow near Slade. One of the pirates following the tanker threw away a pistol and began to run back toward the ship.

The door to the gun turret was flush-fitting and

locked. One of the pirates fired at it from a meter away. Steel crashed and sprayed. The gunman howled as he danced back. He began swatting at the sparks that had ignited his tousled hair.

"Back, Via!" Slade shouted. The oval gouges in the door surface were bright orange, but the lime core within still glowed white and smooth. Gimbals squealed above the attackers as the gun tube shifted from its vertical alignment. Slade wore a set of back-and-breast armor, too small for him and so joined along the right side with leather straps. The armor prodded him over the collarbone as he slapped the home-made limpet mine over the lock plate of the door. The tanker had a helmet but no commo. He was point-man, not commander, might they all burn in Hell!

The gun fired above them. It was a sharp crack and a cone of heat that fanned across the snow. A pirate freighter, fifty meters up and settling on thrusters, collapsed inward around a cyan flash. The ship hit the field hard enough to bury half of itself before it blew up.

"Fire in the hole!" Slade shouted into the ringing pandemonium. He was unreeling the four meters of wire between the battery pack and the blasting cap in the mine. That length should take him safely around the curve of the gun emplacement. "Fire in the hole! Fire in the hole!"

Somebody in the Control Tower blew divots from the concrete to either side of Slade's head. The tanker threw the switch, knowing that if he ducked he would be back in the blast cone. Two of the outlaws who had followed Slade did duck. They were hurled sideways as the mine blew in the door. Slade was through the gap while the smoke still roiled. His submachinegun hosed a long burst as if the bolts were a knotted cord dragging the big man into the gun emplacement.

There were three men in civilian clothes within. One was on his back, unconscious. Two were screaming and frightened, with their hands rising even as the bolts savaged their torsos. . . .

"But after we traded on Desireé, they decided to touch down on a place called Mandalay," Don Slade said to the Elysian citizens before him.

The castaway's nails were tight against his palms because of his memories of the raid. The initial butchery, and then the savage counter-attack which the locals were able to mount because no one would listen to Slade shouting they should cut and run before Desireé had time to organize. Looting and raping . . . and then, for many of the outlaws, dying. The universe was better for that result, of course.

"I was against it," Slade's mouth said, "but all I could get was a delay for GAC 59. We held a light-minute out while the rest of the fleet landed."

"This is crazy!" Blackledge cried. He threw up his hands for emphasis. The outlaw was careful to speak toward the commo screen and not toward Don Slade who sat against a bulkhead on the edge of a plotting can. "There's five *thousand* of us, that's more'n in the whole settlement down there. They're not going to ladle cop on us, even if we weren't allies, like to say."

"The fact they're a bunch of bandits and you—we're a bunch of bandits," said the black-haired tanker, "doesn't make anybody allies. Besides—" He absently fingered the fresh scab on his biceps,

a memento of concrete flying during the Desireé
raid. "I could tell you stories about allies."

The main bridge screen was slaved to one of the
exterior pick-ups on the flagship. An Awami League
hasildar named Al Husad styled himself Fleet Admiral now. He was accepted as such in much the
same way that Slade was a captain. Al Husad
owed much of his position to hints that his vessel
mounted ship-killing guns in one cargo bay. The
Admiral had denied that loudly during planning
for the Desireé attack; and Slade's duties had not
kept him too busy to see that the flagship landed
on Desireé after both gun emplacements were in
pirate hands.

The digital signal feeding the screen was riddled
with static. The view of the spaceport and the
ships landing with various levels of skill was made
pale by the white static flares of individual receptors.

"Curse it, they'll have all the women," moaned
one of Blackledge's henchmen, with him on the
bridge. The outlaw would have muttered about
liquor, but Slade had reprogrammed the waste
processor. The unit could now turn out ethanol,
diluted by its own hygroscopic tendencies to about
95% but otherwise chemically pure.

"You think they're going to grow shut, Dobler?"
Slade gibed. Dobler's blue hair looked particularly
silly because it fringed his bald spot. Many of the
mercenaries aboard GAC 59 had taken up the
Aylmer fashion when they turned pirate. A few
had changed back after the raid, though. Seal rings
like the one Don Slade wore were having a certain
vogue. "I tell you, if any of you had the sense to
really listen to me, we'd wait here three days

instead of three hours. We'd be the only suckers on Mandalay with money to spend—and you'd be amazed how much cheaper you can go around the world, then."

"What is this cop?" demanded a crackly voice. Mandalay Control was talking again to Al Husad. The weak signal was rebroadcast by the flagship, but the static was amplified as well. "You say twenty-one and there's only twenty."

Service vehicles of some sort were flitting through the field of the vision blocks feeding the screen. Steam and dust drifted from the score of vessels. Anyone who had been present at a landing could imagine besides the hiss and pinging as metal cooled.

"They'll flood the market, though," said Captain Levine dolefully. None of the ex-mercenaries save Slade had an appreciation for the economics of being first to port. "Because you're afraid, we'll get cop for our cargo."

"Nope," said Slade. He had convinced the wrangling leaders of his vessel to go along with the delay. Now, faced with the fact of it, there was a chance that the only consensus left would be to lift the tanker's head. Slade held to his wrist the last of the cache of stim cones he had looted during the raid. "Our cargo's thrusters from the Desireé repair docks, not jewelry and trash like most of the others loaded. Our price won't go down."

"Had one drop its navigational computer," said Al Husad's voice. "If it don't get on line in a couple days, maybe we'll send help. But say, what about clearance? You come on with all this cop about staying sealed till you clear us, and then you sit on your thumbs. I got boys been in Transit three weeks, ready to tear the roof off this little burg."

"Do you?" replied Mandalay Control. The audio link roared into garbage. The image on the vision screen rocked, but it still showed bombs blowing in the hulls of every ship in sight.

Men with grenade projectors and full atmosphere suits leaped from the beds of the service vehicles which had earlier set the explosives. The grenadiers began firing projectiles into the jagged openings. From the way the Mandalay troops were dressed, Slade was sure they were lobbing gas rounds into the pirate fleet.

"B-b-but God in heaven!" babbled Captain Levine. "They aren't, I mean—Mandalay's a pirate haven, *everybody* knows that, they *trade*, they don't—" His circling hand indicated the carnage on the screen.

The local forces were not very numerous, probably no more in total than the few hundred men carried by any ship in the fleet that had just landed. That was quite large enough a force for the present purpose. The outlaws of the fleet were trapped like so many sheep in a slaughter pen.

The cargo hatch of one of the ships began to rise slowly on its hydraulic jacks. It had opened a little more than a hand's breadth when a trio of directional mines went off in the gap. The hatch continued to rise. Shrapnel had painted the interior of the cargo bay with the blood and brains of the men huddled to rush through it. With an almost leisurely calm, one of the Mandalayan troops turned toward the bay and shot in two grenades. On impact they began to gush black fumes, one of the skin-absorptive nerve poisons like KD2.

"Remember how Al Husad was talking?" Slade

asked, from his corner. The tanker was calmer for being proven right. None the less, he had to hide the fact that the butchery on the screen horrified him as much as it did the gaping outlaws around him. It had not always been possible to be a Slammer and be choosy about the cause for which you were fighting. Slade was a civilian now, and in another context he could have laughed as he pulled the plug on the pirates the way someone on Mandalay had just done it.

But right now, there was nothing intellectual involved. Slade was watching his peers die in an ambush that had been meant for him as well.

Everyone on the bridge continued to stare at the screen. The tanker was not even sure any of the outlaws were aware that he had spoken. He went on anyway. "Like I heard here, as a matter of fact. 'Might just take the place over, nothing they could do with so many of us. Hell with using Mandalay just for trade.' They're hard boys here, friends, and it seems they're not stupid ones either. *They* know there were too many of us to be safe if they let us swarm all over the place. One ship, maybe three . . . but not twenty-odd together. So they did something about it, is all."

Slade pointed toward the screen. The suited attackers were beginning to clamber aboard the ships they had disabled. There would be some resistance, some casualties, but panic and disorganization would have exposed almost all the pirates to the touch of the gas bombs. KD2 needed little more than that. One touch and nerve cells would begin to die in shrivelled black traceries until the rot reached the brain stem.

"I'd as soon," the big man said, "be gone when

they come to finish the job." But his great, scarred hands were twisting as if they wished they held a weapon.

"Cunning has value," noted one current of the community.

"It's scarcely a virtue, though, is it?" demanded the other viewpoint. It was an amalgam like the first, of every mind; not a segment polarized against the rest of the body politic. *"A human virtue, that is."*

"Have we been wholly open with him, then?" rejoined the first viewpoint. It was hard to say which advocacy was the Devil's. *"Or are we being . . . cunning?"*

CHAPTER FOURTEEN

"With the S—" Don Slade caught himself. "With the large trading organizations," he continued, "there's a lot of information available. It's expensive, but mistakes can be a lot more expensive. You don't think about it, the—man on the ground doesn't. The poop's just there when he needs it. Not always right, and never a hundred percent up to date; but a lot better than fumbling in the dark.

"Which is what we were left to do on Levine's tub, of course," the castaway continued. The smile he flashed was a pleasant one, not his predator's grin. He looked a trifle rueful, but more engaging for that; the sort of fellow who tells you any catastrophe is an adventure when you've lived through it. "There was diddly-squat for background in GAC 59's data base. Tell the truth, I doubt there'd been anything much better anywhere in the fleet, which may be why their leaders decided to try Mandalay, of all places. They'd all heard something about it besides the coordinates.

"Be that as it may, some of the folks aboard had heard about a place called Toler. Supposed to be a funny culture, but peaceful and some attractions as a liberty port. We still had a cargo to unload and Via! I didn't have any better suggestions. The straight run to Tethys was more than our recycling system could have handled. And besides, these types weren't the sort I wanted to bring home with me; it's a quiet place, Tethys. So we landed on Toler. . . ."

"Three by twenty-kilotonne thruster units," said the tall port official. He was jotting notes with a stylus and paper instead of punching the data into a computer link. Toler—there seemed to be only one settlement on the planet—had a gritty, run-down look to it. It consisted of one-story buildings with courts surrounding snaky-limbed trees. Vegetation was sparse. Most of it had the same yellowish cast as the dry soil and the dust that the wind blew in curls across the flat landscape. "One by fifteen KT unit, five by ten KT, three fivers. That's all? Spares?"

The port official was blond and very thin. He was only two-thirds of Slade's bulk, though their eyes met on a level. "No spares," the tanker admitted, "but they're first-quality units, Goldstein & Trumpener, still crated." Slade did not understand why the official was making written notes. GAC 59's landing approach had been fully automated and flawless, so the port *did* have a master computer. Maybe the linking system was down.

"Passengers and crew?" the blond man said, making another notation. His voice sounded edgy, but he had displayed no more than professional interest in the vessel. A tic raised the local's right cheek fractionally.

"Two hundred thirty-seven," said Slade. Virtually all the men had poured out of GAC 59 as soon as the thrusters shut down. The attraction of dives and mere solid ground had something to do with

the exodus; but so did graphic retellings of what
had happened to the rest of the fleet, buttoned up
on Mandalay. "Ah, it's sort of a cooperative trading arrangement, a lot of veterans pooling our
severance bonuses. Won't be any trouble beyond,
you know, a little wildness. I guess most of the
boys are already anticipating their profits a little
in your bars and knock shops." Slade essayed a
smile. It was warm enough, even in the shadow of
the lifted cargo hatch, but there was something in
the local man's demeanor that made the tanker
shiver.

"Yes, we have those," the official said. His right
hand teased the stylus across the back of his neck.
Something flickered in his eyes, a moment's cloudi-
ness like the nictitating membrane of a reptile—
but over the surface of the mind, not the pupil.
"More of our visitors prefer the sorm once they've
tried it, though, the tree. Not expensive, and very
. . . satisfying." The man's stylus twitched again.

"Yeah, well . . ." said Slade. This was the only
ship on the ground at the moment. That wasn't
surprising—they'd known Toler was pretty much
of a backwater—but it didn't augur well for a good
price on the thrusters. "When I've got this business taken care of, maybe I'll give it a try. Ah, who
should I talk to about selling our cargo?"

"I'll take care of that," the official said with the
absent look in his eyes. "You'll be made a fair
offer, as soon as I have, have fed in the data." To
Slade's surprise, the man reached out and touched
the tanker on the wrist. "You should try the sorm,"
the local said in unexpected animation. "Not everyone can appreciate it, the rabble you've arrived
with. But—"

The blond man cocked and lowered his head so that Slade could see the back of his neck. At the base of the hairline, the skin puckered into a wrinkled mound as large as the first joint of Slade's thumb. A tiny droplet of blood and clear fluid leaked from the scab.

"I know what you think," the official said as he straightened. "I did too, at first. But there's no harm, no tissue damage, a trivial puncture. And it opens a universe, Mister Slade, that minds like yours and mine can appreciate." He tongued his dry lips, again a reptilian gesture and not a sensual one.

Abruptly, the local man shuddered. His hair danced like a spill of chalky water. "I have to get back," he said. He was already walking toward what seemed to be the port office. It was a low, inner-facing structure like all the other buildings. "Don't forget what I've said."

"Right," Don Slade muttered to himself. "No bloody fear of that."

Something was chirruping in the depths of the hold, a bird or lizard; probably neither, possibly not local to this planet, and Lord! how empty it made the ship sound.

The big man unsealed the hip pockets of his coveralls and thrust his hands in to occupy them. Nothing was moving on the earthen field since the official had gone inside. From the streets curving among the courtyard houses came raucous cries and an occasional glimpse of carousing outlaws on the way from one entertainment to another. Via, Slade had been on enough strange worlds not to get nervous about docking in on some backwater.

He was a man, a human being, whether or not he had the hundred and seventy tonnes of a panzer wrapped around him.

He began whistling under his breath; not a full song, just catches from a tune that had been old when space travel was a dream. He began to walk toward the sprawling settlement.

"If I was to leave my husband dear
And my two babes also. . . ."

Slade did not carry a weapon, not a hidden knife, not the pistol that had been part of his clothing during twenty years of service.

"Oh, what have you to take me to,
If I with you should go?"

The individual houses were as regular as could be maintained with the differing levels of skill with which they had been constructed. The streets which connected—and indeed, separated—the blank house walls seemed to be more what remained of the area when the building went up on it than part of a plan. Each of the buildings had a single outer door. There was nothing Slade could recognize as advertising or even identification, but all the buildings with an open door were devoted at least in part to the desires of the men who had just landed.

The tanker stepped into a house at random. The room beyond the arched doorway was dim. It felt less dry than the outside. There was a bar to the left where two mercenaries drank. Why they wanted to pay for something the ship offered free was beyond Slade. The door leading to the right was ajar, but the big man could hear nothing meaningful from beyond.

"Yes sir?" said the woman in the armchair facing the outside door. There was a glow-strip on the wall beside her, but it was faint enough that Slade could not be sure whether her hair was blond or brown or a pale, friendly russet. "Whatever's your pleasure, we have it. And the first touch of sorm is on the house." She gestured easily toward the door to Slade's right.

The outlaws at the bar shifted abruptly. They strode down the hall to the left and out of sight around one of the internal corners.

"There's women?" Slade asked. He was rubbing his fists in recollection and present discomfort.

"Of course," said the greeter. She stood up. Her age was as indeterminate as the color of her hair. She was no longer young, but the body she displayed as she raised her patterned smock was firm and attractive. Because her breasts had been small to begin with, they had not sagged noticeably with age. Her belly twitched with a shudder of ecstacy; faked, no doubt, but—

"Lord!" Slade blurted. There was a wire from the wall to the back of the woman's neck. Not a wire, a tendril, the sorm the official had talked about.

"The root bothers you?" the greeter asked without concern. "It's not necessary." She tossed her head forward. Her hair was indeed russet. The shudder that wracked her body for an instant now was neither ecstatic nor counterfeit. But it was brief, and the smile was back on the woman's face even as the tendril subsided to the wall through which it grew. Slade noticed, however, the change in the woman's nipples. They had been as erect as bullet noses. Now they were relaxing almost as suddenly as the root had dropped away from the woman's spine.

"You're a strong man," she said. She stepped toward the tanker with the front of her dress still lifted to shoulder height. "Your children would have fine, sharp minds, too, wouldn't they?"

"Maybe another time," said Slade. He dodged back into the sunlight. He was furious with his body because it insisted on shivering for several more minutes.

A heavy air-cushion truck was grumbling down the street. It was almost the first vehicle Slade had seen on Toler. It pulled up beside one of the closed buildings.

The building's door opened. People from within joined the two men on the truck in unloading sacks of vegetables and flour or legumes. They worked without expertise, but they seemed to be in good health. The locals glanced at Slade as he walked past, but their attention was primarily focused on their task. No one spoke. The tanker half expected to see roots trailing back into the dwelling, but there was nothing of the sort. All the locals bore the puckered scars of the sorm tree, but they were free now and functioning normally.

Slade walked faster. "He took her to the top-mast high," trembled the words in his mind. "To see what she could see."

Slade was whistling through his teeth, but the result would have been a monotone to anyone not inside his mind as well. "He sunk the ship in a flash of fire," snarled the ballad to its conclusion. "To the bottom of the sea!"

Three soldiers stumbled out of a doorway ahead of Slade. They were blinking in the sunlight. Two of them dabbed at the backs of their necks. "You don't *know*, Donnie-boy," said one of that pair.

Slade jumped, but the third outlaw was the subject of the address, not the tanker who stood unnoticed as the others approached. "The most beautiful girl in the world could lie there with her legs spread, and it wouldn't be as good."

"Listen!" snapped the third soldier, "I *watched* that thing poking into you. It ain't natural."

"Never put anything in a vein yourself, Donnie?" asked the other of the pair who had tried the sorm trees. Then the outlaw bumped into Slade, although the tanker had flattened himself against a building to give the others more room.

Instead of the curse and violence Slade had bunched his fists to respond to, the outlaw patted the bigger man on the chest. "Scuse, brother," the fellow said as he stepped around the human obstruction. Not only had the outlaw himself responded mildly, he seemed to have forgotten that such a collision on a liberty night could bring a savage reaction from the other party.

"But I don't care, man," the outlaw was saying as the three of them continued on their way. His fingers had spread blood in roseates across his neck, but there was no real damage, nothing an injection might not have left. "You're chicken, but it doesn't hurt anybody but you. And you'll never know how much you're pissing away. . . ."

Slade cursed, very softly. Then he stepped into the building the three soldiers had just left.

The interior was much like that of the first dive Slade had entered, though the greeter here was male. "Good day, sir," the local said from his chair. "How can we help you?"

The automated bar in this entry lounge was

unoccupied. Slade had been concerned that the
hundreds of outlaws would overwhelm Toler with
consequent disaster, but the cribs and dives were
in adequate supply. What they did in the long
intervals between landings was another question.
For that matter, most freighters would have a score
or fewer crewmen. Only fifteen of GAC 59's complement were actually Levine's men. "Stim cones?"
Slade asked through dry lips.

The greeter shrugged. "Sorry, not on Toler," he
said. He gestured to the bar. "There's alcohol, of
course. And the sorm."

"Yeah," said the tanker. He opened the right-
hand door and entered the sorm parlor he had
expected to find there. "I'm not a coward," he
said, but the sounds Slade's lips and tongue formed
were too soft for even the speaker to hear them.

"Yes, sir?" said a local, one of the two men
within the good-sized room. The other man wore
ship's coveralls. Blaney, Slade thought his name
was, one of the drive operators. The man lay on one
of six narrow couches. He was flaccid except for
rhythmic shudders moving from his torso to his
extremities.

"He's all right?" the tanker asked. His finger
traced the path of undulations. Slade was trying
desperately to keep his voice normal.

"Certainly," said the attendant without a sneer
or condescension. He was changing the covering of
the end couch. The cushion was overlaid with a
thin, hard sheet that might have been either vegetable or synthetic. A pair of used sheets lay crin-
kled on the floor. "The sorm makes his muscles
shudder at intervals to keep up their tone. Not
that there's any need for that in a short touch, but

the plant does its best for its clients." The attendant gave Slade a glass-smooth smile. "After a time," he added, "one can work perfectly well without uncoupling, you see."

The attendant's own tendril waggled back to the wall as he tucked in the sheet.

There was a grommetted hole in the cushion. It was at about the point where a man's neck would rest if he lay supine on the couch. The sheet covered that hole, but the material was too thin to stop a tendril probing up, through it and skin and into the base of the brain. "I see," said the tanker. He was sure his voice was squeaking. "How much does a touch cost?"

"The first is free," said the attendant. He gathered up the used sheets and stuffed them into a chute in the wall beneath his tendril. "After that—" the local man turned around. "You're from Friesland, sir?"

"I've been there," Slade answered guardedly.

"Then the equivalent of thirty Frisian talers per touch," the attendant explained with a smile. "The length varies. This man and two others were touched at the same time." He gestured at Blaney. The crewman was quiescent again after his bout of "exercise". "The others have left—not dissatisfied, I'm sure. But this man's mind permitted a greater level of interaction with the sorm, and consequently even greater—pleasure—for the client."

The local man must have correctly interpreted Slade's grimace, for he shook his head at the tanker and added gently, "No, Captain Slade. The client can sever the connection at will." The attendant arched his neck back slightly as if he were baring his throat to a razor.

"No!" said the tanker. "No, I've seen that, you don't have to show me again." Then he said, "You know my name, friend?"

The local man's body relaxed. There may have been a hint of relief in his expression. "We aren't peasants here on Toler, Captain Slade," he said with dignity. "Our culture doesn't lend itself to crystal and metal, but we have a very satisfactory data bank. The Port Commandant entered information on our visitors, and the information was made available to potential users. You are, of course, a noteworthy man."

In a sharper tone of voice, the attendant went on, "You don't have to stand here and feed your fears, Captain. You can walk away. There's no sin in being afraid."

"I'm not afraid," said Slade harshly. "I just lie down here?" He sat, swinging his legs onto the nearest couch, even as the attendant nodded agreement.

The sheet rustled beneath Slade's neck. The big man relaxed all his muscles. He had been operated on without anesthetic. This pain would be nothing.

But the pain had nothing to do with his fear, either. Hairs prickled as something brushed past them, but even so Slade did not feel any touch on his skin proper. Then a sense of euphoria swept away every other feeling. He was still aware of his former fears, but his mind held them up to his detached appraisal and his laughter.

Slade slipped deeper into an outside awareness with the ease of a diver entering a blood-warm lagoon.

The attendant had been quite truthful about Toler's data bank, but the statement was a joke as well. The sorm's joke, in a way, because the sorm colony connected all those humans who were in fact that data bank.

The tree had developed its properties as a means of ensuring pollination and good planting locations on a dry and windswept world. Some of the runners by which the sorm colonies spread learned—and the term could not be understood to imply intellection—to contact the nervous systems of small burrowing animals. This gave the adapted sorms a degree of mobility unmatched by any other plants on the world. Moreover, as a colony added symbiotes, it gained a level of consciousness which no single animal mind could equal.

The adapted colonies spread and flourished. Tendril-dragging animals scampered from anther to distant pistil. When the symbiosis became more complete, animals could carry out tasks without being in immediate contact with the sorm. They would return after they had scrambled over barriers to plant nuts or whatever other task had been set them. It was less the attitude of a junkie seeking another fix than it was the thankful longing of a laborer returning home after a hard day. The result was a true and flawless partnership for the individual animals and for the sorm species as a whole.

The human settlement of Toler provided an increase of potential knowledge and reasoning power of a magnitude which humans had taken several million years to develop. That the amalgam outstripped in its way any single human was inevitable. And that the amalgam none the less resembled a human society was perhaps also inevitable. After contact, the Toler colony needed further human

contacts to survive; and in any case, the amalgam
built from the instincts and memories of its ani-
mate partners.

The sorm's problem was that its symbiotes could
not reproduce themselves. Male symbiotes lost the
capacity to ejaculate and, after a few days or weeks
of linkage, no longer even produced sperm. By the
time the symbiosis was complete enough for the
sorm to guide its partner in the complex operation,
the animal was sterile.

Ovulation was not affected, perhaps because its
cyclic nature recovered more quickly from suppres-
sion of hormones which the sorm's touch entailed.
Prostitutes—female members of the colony in
estrus—provided an indigenous birthrate when
the sparse interstellar traffic cooperated. Recruits
directly from that traffic made up the rest of the
colony's requirement.

Slade's body trembled. His muscles massaged
themselves and squeezed the blood in his veins
back to feed his heart's slow pumping. Slade was
unaware of that movement save as a datum re-
ported through the eyes of the smiling attendant.

The Toler colony never stripped a visiting ship.
It was common on any port for one or two of the
crew to go missing: jailed or floating in a ditch or
simply jumping ship to await a better berth on a
future vessel. On Toler, the minds that stayed behind in blissful comfort were those with a particular sharpness of focus which fused best with the
structure of the sorm. They were not always the
minds that would have rated highest in human
tests of intelligence, though that was often a
concomitant.

And all but the core of Slade's being rejoiced to

know that his was one of the minds that would be permitted to merge with the colony.

The feeling was not simply that of drug euphoria or the instant before orgasm, though it encompassed those things. There was also an enormous sense of physical well-being and the triumphant riding-down of an opponent. There was no dream quality to Slade's perceptions. They had the clarity of cells in a diamond lens. The tanker was barred from the control of his own body only by his multiplicity of viewpoints as a part of the sorm colony. The physical Don Slade was a needle among thousands of needles, safe and discrete but unnecessary for the moment.

"I am," insisted Slade's being. "*I am.*"

And of course he was, healthy still and happier than every man who had not been to Toler, had not merged with the sorm. But Slade's mind was drawing away, plunging toward the roiling sea of Tethys.

Slade hit the surface and tendrils of the sorm recoiled from the droplets of the harsh gray salt. A shudder wracked the tanker's body. His arms drove him upward, clutching madly for the spray-drenched air.

Slade had fallen off the couch. The big man hyperventilated. His arms swam several flailing strokes before consciousness reasserted itself. "Blood and Martyrs," he wheezed as he stared at the impassive attendant. "Blood and Martyrs!"

Blaney was trembling again on the next couch. There were tiny speckles of blood on the sheet on which Slade had lain. Through the hole in the sheet gently quested the sorm tendril. Its tip was not a single tube as Slade had expected. It was a brush of tiny filaments, now drawn to a ghostly point and slick with fluids from Slade's neck.

Slade rocked to his feet. His limbs worked. He had his sense of balance. Don Slade had a body and soul once more. He gave the attendant an open-handed slap that rocked the smaller man against the wall without stunning him as it should have. Slade's hand throbbed beneath its calluses.

The tanker strode through the door and the lobby, then back into the street. The greeter's expression had the same drugged calm as the attendant's when Slade recovered from the couch.

There was some activity around the ship when Slade returned. The tanker had seen no sign of food-shops, now that he thought about it. Hunger must have driven back at least some of the outlaws. At the entry hatch stood one of the crewmen with a ration packet in his hand.

"Get me Levine," Slade said. They were his first words since his whispered prayer in the sorm parlor. "It he's not on board, raise him through his implant."

"Implant?" the crewman repeated as if he had never heard of a bio-electrical commo link implanted in the user's mastoid. Maybe he hadn't. This ship was crewed by trash as ignorant as most if its passenger list.

"Via!" the tanker snarled. He strode aboard with his boots clanging on the deck and short shrift for the man who had half-blocked his way. "He's got *some* sort of radio with him, doesn't he?"

Captain Levine was scurrying down the corridor toward Slade already.

"Slade, praise heaven I've found you," the spacer called. "We have troubles!"

"Curst true we've got troubles," the tanker agreed. He looped Levine in an arm to turn the smaller man back to the bridge with him. "Sound recall, however you do that, and we've got to lift ship fast."

"That's what I'm trying to *tell* you!" Levine insisted. "We *can't* lift ship. I haven't got enough crew."

Slade took his arm away from the spacer. "Come on," he said quietly. "We may as well talk on the bridge anyway. Tell me about the problem."

"It's the sorm trees," Levine explained as he scurried along. "You know about them?"

Slade's brief nod was all the affirmation he trusted himself to make.

"Well, a lot of my boys went under and didn't come back," the captain explained. "They seem all right—" The pair of leaders entered the bridge where three nervous-looking spacers already waited. "But they won't rouse for shaking or cold water. The attendants just shrug and look away."

"Right," Slade said. He glanced around the four spacers. "You tried it? Tried the sorm?"

"I did," said one man slowly. "It didn't make anything to me. I mean, I just felt good. But my buddy's still there on the table." He waved generally toward the settlement beyond the bulkhead.

"This isn't a ship that—" Levine began. "Well, we need three people each in Navigation and Drive when we Transit. The controls aren't slaved to one master, each unit's separate and it has to be synched within parameters. Right now we've got a shift in Drive, but only me and Keltie in Navigation. And look, you don't run with a single shift very long. Shift and shift's bad enough."

"All right, sound recall anyway," the tanker said. "You've got a siren or something, don't you? I know where Blaney is, at least. I'll round up half a dozen mercs and see what I can do."

The big man paused in the hatchway on his way to the hold where the arms were stored. "And Levine?" he said. "Wait for me to come—no, you come along too. I wouldn't want to get back here and find the ship had left me in this hellhole. And believe me, the people who left me would live to regret it too."

And even without reading Slade's mind, no one who heard him could doubt the truth of that threat.

Slade had no difficulty finding the building in which the sorm had touched him. He might not have been able to give directions, however, to find it in the skewed checkerboard of identical walls. The building's door was now closed.

"Should I blast it?" demanded Blackledge. Slade had picked the first outlaws he met to accompany him and the captain. The other mercs carried pistols or submachineguns. The big tanker himself had chosen a 2 cm shoulder weapon this time.

"No," said Slade. He kicked at where he judged the latch would be, though nothing was visible from the outside. The panel exploded inward ahead of the tanker's boot-heel.

The greeter had disappeared, leaving the lobby empty. There was a small hole in the wall above the greeter's arm-chair, but the tendril was gone also. Slade had taken a certain pleasure in kicking the door down. Before he could smash into the sorm parlor the same way, however, the attendant opened the door from within. The local stepped back. "Your pleasure, sirs?" the man asked.

"Blaney," said Slade. He strode through the door with his gun in a patrol sling, muzzle forward. He did not expect that kind of trouble here, but he would have welcomed the excuse to open up. The crewman lay much as Slade had left him. "How do we bring him back?" Slade demanded. "*Fast*, and no cop. We're right on the edge here, you know it yourself."

The remainder of the group was filing into the parlor. They were nervous, even the three like Blackledge and Slade whose necks were scabbed from a tendril puncture. Their hands tightened on their guns as the attendant said, "The client can separate at will, Captain Slade. You know that. There is no other way to separate him that will not cause the individual's death."

"Cop!" said Blackledge. He slid a long knife from his boot. His left hand gripped Blaney's hair and drew the crewman's head off the couch. The tendril slid further through the cover sheet without relaxing its hold on the comatose human.

"Wait, *please*," said the attendant. The local man's voice held emphasis but no real concern. "If the trunk is injured or the root severed, the orphaned filaments will—"

Blackledge drew his blade across the tendril. The knife had a razor edge, and the steel was density-enhanced to retain that keenness. The cut ends of the root flipped up with a drop of sap on either of them.

Blaney spasmed on the couch like a pithed frog. His jaw was opening and clopping shut again to pass gulping sounds. That was not an attempt to scream, nor were his arms trying to wave help closer as they flailed. The brain itself has no pain receptors.

The thrashing stopped. Blaney lay still. His eyes were open and his body was as flaccid as if his skin were filled with hot wax. The crewman's face was growing freckled. Then the tips of the filaments waved through in a hundred places above the skin, gleaming with blood.

One of the outlaws screamed and emptied his submachinegun into the attendant's body. The cyan flashes lighted the close room and heated it in a gush of vaporized flesh. The local man slumped. His eyes were calm until they glazed. As the outlaws bolted from the sorm parlor, the tendril withdrew from the attendant's neck. It whisked itself back within the bolt-scarred stone.

Slade's finger was on the trigger as he stood, alone of living men, within the parlor. He did not fire.

The black-haired man was not even particularly angry as he walked back into the street. The sorm had its ways, just as Don Slade had his. The sorm had caused some difficulties just now by being the way it was, but the weather did that . . . and only fools got mad at the weather.

The trick in this case was going to cause some difficulties right back for the sorm. That was a lot more useful than losing your temper and going berserk.

The refrain trailed again through Slade's mind: "Down to the bottom of the sea!"

The wail of the ship's siren had gathered in most of the complement by the time Slade returned to the vessel. The bridge hatch was closed. Slade had to hammer on it and shout his name into a sound-plate before a crewman would admit him.

"Slade," said the harrassed-looking Captain Levine. "I think we'll be all right if we're left alone for a while. M'kuru here knows a little about navigation—" one of the four Drive crewmen nodded to Slade— "and I'm giving him a crash course that'll let us lift. After what happened in there, I'd say the quicker we all got off here, the better we were. Even with a short crew."

"No," said the tanker simply. "We're going to get your people back." A tic lifted a corner of his mouth. "Not Blaney, but the others. I've been into the system."

Slade touched the switch that winched down a ladder from the ceiling. The access port to the gangway along the top of the hull doubled as the bridge escape hatch when GAC 59 was in normal space. Levine watched with a puzzled look on his face as the big tanker slid the inner hatch back within the pressure hull. Slade activated the outer clamshell seal. "What do you plan to do?" the spacer called after Slade's disappearing legs.

When Slade did not reply, Levine scrambled up the ladder after him. The tanker was stretching his gun sling from carrying length to a shooting brace. "If we kill the trees," Levine said, "it's the same thing as Blackledge cutting the root. For God's sake, I don't want them killed that way!"

"I knocked open doors till I found a local who was still—attached," the tanker explained. On the catwalk, the two men were ten meters above the ground. They had a good field of view across the houses of Toler. "To explain it to the sorm. When it took one or two men from a crew, it didn't matter much. This time it took the same percentage, I guess, from our people, but too many of them were crew instead of mercs. Mind-set, I guess. And I couldn't get through to the sorm either; the fellow I talked to just stared and no more of our people were turned loose. Well, they weren't dumped out—I know they want to stay, but the colony *can* dump them, whatever that attendant said."

Slade sat carefully on the sun-heated catwalk. He locked his ankles and braced his elbows inside his knees. The gun was a cheap one without the electronic analog sight of the Slammers' shoulder weapons. A simple post and aperture would serve for this, however, so long as the alignment was accurate.

"But if you blow up trees," the spacer pleaded, "won't you—"

Slade fired and the air popped closed along the bolt's dazzling track. The nearest structure was the port control building. It had never been opened to the outsiders. The sorm in its courtyard started to branch about two meters above the ground. The scale-barked trunk at that point was about thirty centimeters in diameter before the bolt hit. The trunk was a cloud of blazing splinters a moment later.

The blond port official must not have been coupled to the tree when the powergun sawed it off. He was able to run out of the building shrieking as the stump smouldered and the tips of severed branches thrashed at random above the wall.

The Toler colony could afford to be larger than its conspecifics which depended on lower life forms to advance their needs. Each of the five hundred trees in the spaceport colony had deep-well irrigation and courtyard walls to break the force of the winds. Subsurface runners welded the colony together. The sorm trees were none the less discrete individuals whose life did not depend on that of the other members of the colony.

Whose life or death was individual.

Slade shifted his aim to a distant tree. The outlaws had probably not scattered too far from the ship in their quest for pleasure. The first bolt blew chunks from a wall coping. The second, after Slade corrected his aim, shattered another sorm. The courtyards were not built high enough to protect the trees from the gunman's brutal pruning.

Another hit. Another. Three shots in a row before the next tree sagged away from a half-severed trunk. Another hit. A miss, and Slade's hand slipped a fresh magazine from his coveralls to reload his weapon. The iridium barrel glowed, setting dust motes adance above the sight plane.

"You have to stop!" screamed the blond official from the ground. His face and teeth were white.

"Turn them loose," Slade called back. He locked the magazine home with the heel of his hand. "I'll give you time enough to stick a bloody root back in your skull. But if my people don't start coming back in the next five minutes, it's *gone*—every curst tree in this colony." He raised the powergun and clapped its fore-end for emphasis.

The Toler official blinked, struggling to form coherent thoughts. Then he began to shamble toward the building in which the nearest undamaged sorm still grew. To his back, Slade shouted,

"I don't care cop about what you do with other ships. But you leave my people alone!"

The tanker turned, panting with the release of tension. Captain Levine was staring at him.

The tanker's face bore a look of surprise. It stemmed less from his success than from the possessive he had just heard himself use to refer to the cut-throats below.

CHAPTER FIFTEEN

"Clear-sighted," suggested one current of Elysian thought. *"A response almost before he knew the problem."*

"A ruthless response," amended the other viewpoint. *"All those deaths accepted—caused—so long as they were not of his tiny caste."*

"Can anything human be responsible for all humans?" protested the first. *"Can we . . . ?"*

"Well, welcome to Stagira," said Don Slade to the scouting party he had assembled in Bay 4.

The only sounds beyond were the ping of cooling metal and the breeze hissing above the docking pit. "Via, we should never have come here," grumbled Reuben Blackledge. The outlaw's mouse-blond hair was beginning to grow out beneath its blue tips. "The whole colony's died off."

"They landed us, didn't they?" said another of the outlaws staring out of the hold. But the long corridors facing the heavily-armed party were empty, and even the glow-strips lighting them seemed pale from encrusting grime.

"That was on automatic codes," said Slade. The ship's crewmen were too valuable to risk in scouting, but Slade had been on the bridge during the landing. "The machines work, at least some of

111

them. If there aren't any humans to trade with, then we'll just have to pick up what we can, won't we?" To the microphone on his belt, Slade added, "Leaving the bay. You can secure in thirty seconds." To the score of mercenaries with him, "Come on, boys." The big tanker stepped off with his left foot.

The idea had been Slade's. In the confusion of the last hour on Toler, the others were stumbling back to the ship or aiding the sorm's victims to do so. The tanker had dragooned Levine and another navigator to help search the Port Office. It had been a grisly job for Slade and a far worse one for the spacers. They gagged at the thirty-odd corpses, some of them still twitching like frogs on a dissecting pan.

In the end, the search had paid off with a case of navigational microfiches which had probably accompanied the original settlers to Toler. There was electronic equipment which might have been nearly as old in storage. The colony had obviously shifted to symbiosis and biological data-storage very shortly after landing. It would have been almost impossible to decipher obsolete machine codes with the resources of GAC 59, however. There was no reason to assume that background radiation would not by now have degraded the stored data to random uselessness anyway.

By comparing the ancient microfiches with the vessel's own navigational data, Levine and his crew had found a nearby colony with a high technical rating which was no longer listed in current files. With luck, this one—Stagira—would be unfrequented but would have useful items that even GAC 59 alone could loot.

"I hadn't," Slade admitted aloud as he and his

men echoed down the broad corridor, "expected the hardware to be in such good shape and *nobody* around."

"Any sign of farms when we landed?" asked one of the men.

"No sign of nothing," said Blackledge, who had also been on the bridge. "Place is bare as a whore's bum."

"Didn't seem to be any native life at all," Slade agreed. "Hydroponics would've been simpler than surface farming, no lack of raw materials. That doesn't explain why they didn't build at all on the surface ... but there wasn't any lack of odd-ball notions when the first colonies cut loose from Earth, either."

"Here's a door!" called one of the men who had ranged furthest ahead.

"Then let's see what's behind it," Slade said in a calm voice. As he walked toward the portal and his clustering men, the tanker hitched up his equipment belt. The others carried shoulder weapons of one sort or the other. Slade wore only a holstered pistol—and, on his back, a satchel of plastic explosive. Fiddling with his belt gave him a surreptitious chance to wipe his sweaty palms on his coveralls.

"Shall I blow it in?" demanded one of the outlaws. Each man carried either a block of explosive like Slade or several blasting caps. The caps were touchy and bloody dangerous, but it was the men who carried the—quite inert—blocks of explosive who seemed most interested in shedding their burdens.

"Via, let's just try the touch plate," Slade said. When nobody else moved, he tapped the square in the center of the panel himself. There was no blast, no paralyzing shock as they had all managed to psych themselves into expecting. Instead, the door whispered sideways. It gave onto a scene in sybaritic contrast to the bleak corridor outside.

"Bingo," Slade called on his commo unit. Its signals would be drunk by the walls when he stepped inside, so the tanker wanted to tell those on the ship of the good fortune. "We've got our roughage and probably our protein besides. I'll scout around, see what we can raise, and report in a moment."

The air that puffed from the verdant interior was humid enough to condense noticeably in the corridor. The vegetation was varied. At least most of it was Earth-standard stock. There were no walls visible save the fifty centimeters between the corridor and the interior. The carefully-tended pathway felt like real sod beneath Slade's feet as he stepped inside.

"Just for the hell of it," the tanker said as the last of his men were following him into the artificial environment, "let's put something solid in the door's slideway. Pergot, your gun'll do. Just something to block it if it decides to close itself. Gives us room to set a charge."

The outlaw obeyed. He was unhappy about disarming himself, but he was unwilling to make an issue of the fact. The shoulder weapon's heavy iridium barrel should at worst only deform under the stresses that the closing mechanism could exert on it through the massive door.

As the men started to turn, secure in their retreat, the gun sank into the trackway's gray, nondescript lining. The door began to slide shut as quietly as it had opened.

Pergot lunged back, either to snatch up his disappearing weapon or to get into the corridor again. He accomplished neither. Or, at any rate, most of the outlaw did not reach the corridor. Pergot's left boot and right leg from mid-thigh lay inside the cavern when the door hissed to rest. Very possibly Pergot's head and hands were clear on the other side, so that only the half-meter of his torso had disappeared within the tonnes of door.

Something burst out of the undergrowth behind the party. The men were already tense with the horror before them. They spun, several of them screaming. The pig that had appeared now disintegrated in a squeal and cyan glare.

"Put'em up!" Slade shouted as he bulled forward. The pig was scattered gobbets. Wallace, who had jumped aside at the animal's appearance, was on the ground also. The garish tunic the outlaw wore was afire, and there were two cratered holes in the small of his back. A companion's submachinegun had raked him.

Slade smothered the fire with his own broad chest, then ripped the smoldering remnants free. "Poles for a stretcher—Kuntz, Reecee," he ordered, naming two of the men who wore heavy knives.

The SpraySeal from the tanker's medical pouch was closing off the wounds, but it could do nothing for the internal damage. Powergun bolts had limited penetration, but abdominal wounds like these would be bordered by cooked flesh as much as a centimeter deep. There was nothing Slade could do about that. He was not even sure the ship's medicomp was up to the task. The Slammers could have handled it; anybody who got back to a Battalion Aid Station with his brain alive was going to make it.

But right now, Friesland seemed about as close as the ship, with that massive door separating both from the scouting party.

Slade set a cone of Hansine against the base of Wallace's spine. The wounded man trembled slightly as the drug entered his system. It would disconnect his sensory apparatus until the dose was counteracted. That would not keep ruptured blood vessels from leaking, and it would not keep Wallace's belly from swelling as his intestines writhed around patches of dead muscle in their walls.

"What happened to Pergot's gun?" asked Black-ledge, now that there was leisure again for recollection. "That molding looked just like zinc sheet, but the gun slipped through it like water." After a pause, the outlaw added, "You know, the whole wall looks like it's covered with the same stuff. Howes, poke at it, why don't you? Maybe we can slip right through."

"Screw yourself, why don't you?" Howes snapped. He leveled his 2 cm weapon at the door, however.

"Hold up, dammit," Slade said as he stepped out of his coveralls. The tanker had worn standard battle-dress for the sake of its pockets and attachments. Most of the party was in looted finery of one sort or another. The tough fabric of the coveralls would make a much better bed for the stretcher.

Howes fired. The air sizzled in a blue-green flash. The door's sheathing acted as a reflex reflector, splashing the bolt back in the direction from which it had come.

The reversal was imperfect enough that the whole party caught some of the charge. Howes, the gunman, was at the center of the spreading cone, however. Foliage beyond the men hissed. Slade shouted at what felt like a bath of nettles over his bare calves and buttocks.

Howes dropped his gun. The skin of his hand was fiery, and the surface of his eyes had baked in the glare that seared away his brows. When the gunman began to scream, his cracked lips gemmed with blood.

"All right," Slade said. He immobilized Howes with one hand while his other fumbled the Spray-Seal from the kit again. The spray contained a surface analgesic that would take care of Howes' immediate pain, though the blindness was another matter. "We're going to move out," the tanker continued with both volume and authority. "We're going to find out who's behind all this. And then we're going to change it."

The tanker put the sealant back into the kit. His own buttocks and the similar burns of other pirates could wait for better supplies, though his harness chafed angrily as he moved.

"Marshal and Dobbs, first shift on the stretcher," Slade said. "Broadfoot, you guide Howes here. Let's move it, boys, we've got some convincing to do."

As the party moved off down the path, Slade scooped up the gun Howes had dropped.

They found the first building a hundred meters away, in a glade. Because it was windowless and completely unadorned, the leading outlaws drew up abruptly and raised their guns at an apparent fortification.

Stoudemeyer had been born on Telemark. "Hey!" he said in wonder, giving two syllables to the exclamation. He slung his submachinegun and pushed past the others to reach the door.

"Via, yeah," Stoudemeyer said as his hand caressed the door without touching the latch plate. "Captain, do you know what this is? It's a true to God bubble house! There's only five of them on Telemark, and I'd have said there wasn't another in the galaxy!"

"Well, what's it do, then?" Blackledge demanded. He gestured toward the man and building alike with a prodding motion of his gun muzzle.

"It does everything," Stoudemeyer said. He palmed the latch. "It does every curst thing you could imagine."

The others, even Slade, twitched a hair to the side as the door slid open. It was too reminiscent of the cavern's outer portal. The man from Telemark strode through without hesitation. "I tell you," he called over his shoulder, "being caught in here is like a bee drowning in honey. It don't hurt a bit. . . ." The door closed behind Stoudemeyer, then opened again before the babble of fear could even start. "The latch works fine from this side too," said Stoudemeyer, "but suit yourselves."

Blackledge was the first to follow Stoudemeyer. Slade was the last, and he decided not to order someone to stay back with Wallace. Never give orders you know will be ignored . . . and the tanker did not want to miss his own first look into this candy store, either.

The interior walls were a neutral gray when Slade first glimpsed them through the open door.

By the time he was inside, however, Stoudemeyer had activated a control orally. The house was running through a series of panoramas, three or four seconds apiece, in which the walls seemed to melt into the far distance. Then the whole scene would dissolve into a radically different one. Slade did not appreciate the level or realism until the third example, a knoll of sere grass beneath a sky of cloud and purple lightning. Hard-spitting raindrops began to lash the men from hidden outlets. Among the curses and shouts of anger, Stoudemeyer's voice cried, "Cancel climate! Cancel sound!"

The sparkling desert that followed—in a few seconds, for a few seconds—did so without the blast of heat that would otherwise have probably accompanied the blue-tinged sunlight.

"Tell it to find something and hold it, Stoudemeyer," Slade directed irritably. The tanker could not hear Stoudemeyer's response over the general rumble of so many men in a small building.

The background segued to a glade much like the outside. Via, it *was* the glade outside; there lay Wallace twitching under stimulus of the breeze that ruffled the grass beside him. It was as if the party had been covered by a glass bubble thick enough to block out all sound.

"What do you sit on?" an outlaw demanded.

Stoudemeyer shrugged. "Ask for a chair," he said.

"All right, give me a chair," said the other man. He stumbled forward and the fellow behind him jumped away. The floor between them rose into a sculptured chair mounted on a pedestal that seemed too thin to support itself and a seated man. Neither Slade nor anyone else doubted that the construct *would* hold; but prodding at it with a finger was as much of a trial as anyone would make for the moment.

The Telemark mercenary was basking in his sudden importance. "Swivel chair," he said, pointing at the floor in front of him. From the point indicated extended a seat with the liquid grace of an amoeba. The seat looked like the one earlier called to life; but when Stoudemeyer sat in this one, he was able to spin it in further display. "Everything," he repeated, "anything. All you have to do is ask."

Outlaws were moving apart as far as the four-meter diameter of the floor permitted them. They were experimenting with shapes. Some of the more imaginative were creating subtle forms from their home worlds. They could even mime wood grains and basketry.

"Food?" asked Slade. He could simply have checked for himself. He did not, however, care to push buttons—even verbal ones—at random when there were directions available.

Stoudemeyer waved expansively. "Ask," he said as if he himself were the provider.

"Bring me Tethian rock-cruncher in a pepper sauce," the tanker said firmly.

"I'm sorry," responded a voice. It seemed only millimeters from Slade's ear. "That is not in my inventory. You may describe the dish by reference to others; or, if you prefer, you may make another selection."

Stoudemeyer must have heard the house's response, or at least enough of it to extrapolate the remainder. He hopped out of his chair with the smug expression replaced by one of concern. "Hey,

I'm sorry, sir, I forgot. This place is probably as old as the ones back home. I mean—maybe eight hundred standard years. Can you believe it? That old and work like this still? He was a genius, a bloody genius."

"You mean try Earth food, not Tethys', because this place was built before the Settlement," Slade said to clarify what he had just been told. One point at a time.

"Right, or Telemark food," Stoudemeyer agreed. In test and demonstration, the man from Telemark said, "Bring me hassenpfeffer and a mug of, oh, any lager."

Slade could hear the voice saying from beside the other mercenary, "Yes sir, your food will be brought in forty—three—seconds."

"And this isn't half of it," Stoudemeyer confided to Slade. All around the room, outlaws were exploring this new capacity of the dwelling. Some of the men were demanding protein rations after a series of failures to come up with any other meal from the hidden menu. "The real thing about bubble houses is the dream-code feature." He kept his voice very low. "It's supposed to be as good as, as, you know—the sorm."

Stoudemeyer turned his head. He looked somewhat embarrassed. "I wouldn't really know, you know. On Telemark, you've got to own a province, practically, to even think of owning a bubble house. I mean, there's *five* that Kettlemann built before he disappeared. But everybody knows about them."

"Your dinner, sir," said the voice that was as cunningly projected as the rain had been some minutes earlier. The floor bulged like asphalt bubbling in the sun. The bulge rose on a stem like those that lifted chair seats. It halted with a hydraulic, not mechanical, smoothness at the height of Stoudemeyer's mid-chest. The bulge then irised open from the top to form a platter around a poultry-in-gravy dish which Slade presumed was hassenpfeffer. At any rate, the man from Telemark seemed satisfied as he took a thigh bone and began nibbling at the dark meat. "It's good," he said. "Try it."

Rather than attempt the meat right at that moment, Slade lifted the half-liter beer mug from the center of the tray. He expected the gravy to cling to the gray alloy of the container. The gravy did not, but the tray itself exuded a flexible tendril by which it retained the mug. Just, come to think, as the floor retained the tray. The tanker's pause was only mental. There was no obvious break in the slow progress of the mug to his lips. The lager, when he drank it, was cool and sharp and in no discernible way frightening.

"He was a genius," Stoudemeyer repeated around a mouthful of his pickled rabbit. "Certified Scientist Theodor Kettlemann. Started building bubble houses for the richest men on Telemark. I mean, nobody can figure *now* how this stuff works. And it still works." His gesture around the room spattered Slade with some of the tart gravy.

"Thing is," Stoudemeyer went on, "we had a planetary government then but not really, you know? And Kettlemann had some notions about genetics that didn't sit well with some people. He wouldn't work for anybody of Italian stock, for instance, even if they could trace their line right back to Landfall. And they were willing to pay his price. There was trouble about that. So when

Kettlemann disappeared, a lot of people thought he'd been snatched—or wasted—by somebody he wouldn't build a house for."

"And instead, he recolonized," Slade said. He looked at the tangle of furniture and men wrangling over food of various types. "Picked a barren world that wasn't of interest to anybody else but gave him raw materials. And peace. Via, though, this must have cost a *fortune* to set up, the transport and the processing equipment alone."

Stoudemeyer nodded. "Kettlemann might have had that," he said. "Around the time he disappeared, so did a lot of other people. Rich people with their families. There was a lot of talk about it, all the way from mass murder to secret bases that were going to wipe out all the wops when the time was right. The whole business didn't cause the Partition Wars, exactly. But it didn't help things one bit, either."

"Well," said Slade. "Maybe it's time to go find what passes for a government here. And get our butts off-planet. Doesn't look like there's a whole lot of this—" he released the mug which snapped back onto the tray of which it was part, "—that we could dismantle and carry with us. Though the protein and vegetation still is handy for our synthesizers."

As Slade turned to the door, he adjusted his slung weapon out of habit. What he saw in the wall caused him to pump the gun live and to kick the latch-plate with the toe of his boot. That was the quickest way of opening the door without interfering with the business of shouldering his weapon.

Wallace and the makeshift stretcher were disappearing into the ground.

The scene was not an artifact of the wall display. The drugged man had sunk a centimeter further by the time Slade could see him through the open door. "Contact, you bastards!" the tanker roared to the startled remainder of the scouting party. None of them had noticed what was going on outside. "Everyone out!" As he spoke, Slade launched himself into the glade behind his gun muzzle.

The turf was beginning to close over Wallace in a neat seam. Slade fired twice into the ground, aiming a hand's breadth above the peak of Wallace's head even as the seam covered that head. Point blank, the big powergun would shatter ceramic armor and burn a hole through eight millimeters of iridium.

The soil gouted upward, blasted by the vaporizing water trapped within each clod. Fifty centimeters down, the second bolt gouged bare a different layer. Not clay, as on a normal world, nor the bedrock overlain by manufactured soil as Slade had rather expected here. There was instead a dull gleam that covered itself as soil fell into the hole. Wallace lurched completely out of sight.

Slade did not fire again. He had seen what happened when that omnipresent alloy took a bolt from a powergun. Howes was enough of them to be blind and partly flayed from that nonsense.

Pirates were pouring out of the bubble house in panic. They lacked, in general, any notion of what was going on. Wallace's disappearance was not obvious except to one who had seen it in process; and that was Slade alone of the party. One man began to hose the undergrowth. A dozen others took up the activity. They flushed out a variety of birds and small animals as the succulent foliage burned.

"Hold your fire!" the tanker ordered. He had to shout three more times before he was at last obeyed. The volleying powerguns did not make enough physical racket to overwhelm a voice as strong as Slade's. The whole incident had a level of psychic noise that had to run its course, however.

Even as the last shot sizzled from a submachine-gun, Slade was saying, "Reecee, give me your knife." The party had no proper entrenching equipment, but the long fighting knife would serve.

Slade probed with the borrowed weapon, gingerly at first though he was sure there was no harm the blade could do to Wallace now. Other pirates crowded around. The hot barrels of their weapons added an angry tinge to the stink of ozone. The turf through which the blade cut appeared perfectly normal. The halves of a severed worm flexed to either side of the knife. Soil crumbled from a yellow insect larva the size of a man's thumb-joint.

With a curse and an order snarled to the men closest, Slade dug the blade through the sward in a vicious circle. Outlaws who were late in obeying the order now leaped aside to save their toes. The tanker used his broad left hand as a spade to fling up the turf the knife had cut. Then he slashed again, deeper. The soil was still rich-looking and crumbly. Roots no longer bound it in their web-work this far below the surface. Slade scattered two double handfuls, then cursed and began to scoop deeper with his helmet. The blunt edge and padded interior of the helmet made a bad shovel, but the loose soil did not fight his efforts.

The helmet thudded on metal like that which the shots had uncovered before. There was no sign of Wallace, his clothing, or the stretcher on which he had lain. Slade used his bare hands again to squeeze a patch of metal clear. The gray surface was now covered with iridescent ripples like those of oil on still water. The colors blurred and fused and sank to neutral gray again even as the men watched. The surface had its usual metallic sheen ... but Slade was no longer sure that it was metal at all.

Most of the men around Slade had no idea what was going on. Stoudemeyer had seen some and guessed more, perhaps much more. "There's a thing about Kettlemann that didn't make a lot of sense," said the man from Telemark. "He already had a reputation when he got into building bubble houses. But he wasn't an engineer. He was a geneticist."

Slade stood up, swearing very softly. He wiped dirt from the blade on his own thigh before he handed the knife back to Reecee. The party watched the tanker apprehensively, though they had not all realized that Wallace was missing.

"All right," Slade said. "We break up into groups of three. Every group has a radio. Reecee, Stoudemeyer, you're with me. We'll lead Howes. We're going to cover as much of this place as we have to to find who's in charge. Or at least where it's being run from. Report anything funny, and we'll all check in every quarter hour."

As Slade separated and numbered the remaining groups, he could feel Stoudemeyer staring at him somberly. The man from Telemark did not believe that the search would uncover what they needed to find to escape.

Slade could not very well object to his subordinate's pessimism. Not when the two of them were completely of the same opinion.

Four hours of searching disappointed Slade's hopes if not his expectations. The cavern was large but not endless. The parties sent in opposite directions around the wall had met on the other side of the circle. They had not found a door besides the one by which they had all entered, nor was there anything else that looked promising.

The groups had located thirty-seven bubble houses. There might have been some duplication before Slade directed groups to turn up a clod at the doorway of each house they found. Even so, it was probable that the cursory search had failed to find all the unobtrusive structures.

It was even possible that there was a headquarters building somewhere, a planetary capital—but by now, Slade and Stoudemeyer were not alone in doubting that.

The team Slade led personally sat around a table in the seventh bubble house they had found. The houses had been identical; though of course identical in their infinite variety. Howes had recovered enough to eat with the rest of them. He was still blind. His face had swollen like a pumpkin, but contact analgesics remained adequate for pain.

Slade gestured with a chicken drumstick. "The system works fine," he noted aloud. "Not just mechanically, but the life forms, vegetation, animals up to the size of pigs. At least to the size of pigs," he corrected himself.

"Only no people but us," Stoudemeyer said.

"Blood, we know why *that* is," said Reecee angrily. "Same curst thing killed them as killed

Wallace after we'd lugged him all that way. Your Kettlemann just *thought* this planet was empty, Stoudemeyer. Something got him and something's going to get us if we don't get the hell out."

"You know, I thought about Wallace," said the man from Telemark. He put down his fork in order to give full attention to what he was hoping to explain. "I think he was dead. It's this food, you see?"

"Go on," prompted the tanker. His expression was non-committal.

"Well, it's not magic, you know," Stoudemeyer explained. He raised his fork again as an example. "There's a synthesizer, but it starts with advanced constituents—proteins and carbohydrates, not rock dust and water. On Telemark they're fed by plankton, the bubble houses are, mostly. But here, where the whole place is controlled—not just the house— the system acts as, well. . . ." Every eye was focused on the lump of meat on the fork. "As a clean-up system too."

Reecee gagged. He lurched away from the table.

"I think you've got something very close," Slade said. His mouth had dried up, but he continued to chew away at the morsel already taken. You could not let—ultimate sources—get to you, or you'd never be able to eat fish from a sea in which men drown. "Only Wallace wasn't dead. I heard him mumbling as the soil zipped itself over his face. And Team Two said Pergot was still there at the door, what was left of him. The system doesn't recycle carrion. This was set up for very rich people, remember. It crops fresh meat as required."

"No, that's crazy—" began Stoudemeyer. His

chair seat extended itself upward like tube-stock being drawn from a billet. As the man's knees lifted toward his chest, his whole body dropped. The chair pedestal was being reabsorbed by the floor, even as the seat enfolded the man who had been sitting on it.

Sliding from his own chair and reaching around the table should have been two motions for the tanker. He accomplished his goal of grasping Stoudemeyer's hand with a fluid grace that would have done credit to a gymnast in free-fall. Slade's whole body, legs and back and muscle-knotted shoulders, reacted together as he pulled Stoudemeyer from the gray maw that was engulfing him. The victim was off-balance and unable to extricate himself in the seconds available to him. For the moment, however, his body was held by little more than gravity. Slade's brutal snatch-lift dislocated the smaller man's shoulder, but it popped him from the tube like the cork from sparkling wine.

"Outside fast!" the tanker roared. His left hand slapped the latch plate. Momentum and the continuing pull of Slade's arm cracked the whip with Stoudemeyer. The man from Telemark snapped through the opening, wheezing with fear and gratitude.

As Slade turned back, Reecee caromed off his chest. Their legs tangled as Reecee fell. It was probably too late for Howes already, even if Slade had not been tripped.

The blinded man's screams reverberated as what had been his chair closed over him. The action must have been triggered when Stoudemeyer shot free. The mechanism was more similar to a tar pit than to a mouse-trap; but it was quick enough to take Howes, fuddled by pain and drugs.

Reecee scrambled to his feet to run again. Slade caught the outlaw by the shoulder with one hand—there was no time to talk—and retrieved Reecee's fighting knife with the other. Should've brought a blade of his own, Via. . . .

Stoudemeyer's chair had reformed. Howes' chair and the man himself were a bubble on the floor, a giant copy of the shape from which the house extruded furniture and food. This bubble was shrinking. Howes' whimpering had been shut off instantly when the metal closed over him. Slade struck at the seam joining the bubble to the floor proper.

The atomic shells of the knife's point and edges had been shrunk in a magnetic forging process more rigorous than that which contains the plasma in a fusion plant. The result would stay needle-sharp as it was rammed through steel plate or ceramic body armor. It was not sharp enough to penetrate the fluid surface that had just swallowed the blind man, however. The blade skidded and rang. Slade shouted a curse and struck again. When the knife slipped away this time, it took a thumb-nail-sized circuit from the toe of Slade's right boot. The bubble was almost flat by now.

Howes was a pompous ass, a fool before he blinded himself and a useless burden since. Slade caught up the shoulder weapon slung on his own chair. He ran outside. His nostrils stung with suppressed tears.

"What are we going to do?" Reecee blubbered. "It can take us out here just as easy, can't it? What are we going to do?"

"We're all right if we keep moving," Slade said.

"But why's it taking *people*?" Stoudemeyer asked. He spoke in a normal voice, but the words were more an apostrophe to his own doubts than a question to his companions. "There's plenty of animals out here, the pigs and the rabbits. They must be here as food stocks. Why does it take us instead?"

"You're not going to sleep, Captain?" Reecee demanded. He was a big man also, but only blind panic could have driven him to bait Slade. The tanker stood with the knife naked in his hand. "You're such a hero that you're going to walk around laughing while the bloody *dirt* buries the rest of us like it did Wallace?"

"Don't guess it does take people," Slade said. He let out a shuddering breath. His hands were shaking, but there was no sign of his fear and adrenalin as he spoke. "I think your Professor Kettlemann just programmed the system with a narrower definition of human than you or I might've used. Different, that's sure a cop. Got any wog blood in you, Stoudemeyer? Bet your home-grown genius wouldn't approve. *May he burn in Hell!*"

"But what do we *do*?" Reecee repeated.

"We fucking *think* of something!" Slade roared back. As the outlaw stepped back, shocked as if by a slap in the face, Slade flung the knife.

It buried itself to the cross-guard in the sod between Reecee's boots.

It was usually easy to forget they were trapped in a chamber rather than a walled enclosure. The shock waves were a brutal reminder. The blast shuddered on and on until the noise that could not escape had damped itself to silence. Leaves had been stripped from the nearest trees. The ears of the scouting party continued to ring long after the cavern itself had ceased to do so.

The door by which the party had entered was still closed and still unmarked.

Slade set down the detonator. He began methodically brushing leaf-mold from his bare knees. When they were clean, he strode toward the door where other members of the group were already gathered and arguing. Slade's pack, with the shoulder weapon across it, lay by the tree which had sheltered him.

"Didn't do a *bloody* thing!" snarled one of the outlaws. He slammed the butt of his weapon against the dull metal. None of the men were too angry to remember what shooting into the door had brought Howes.

"We've got plenty more explosives," said Blackledge. "We'll put them all against this door and that'll do it."

"No," said Slade. "Not uncontained. Even if we did punch a hole, it'd seal before we could use it. We need to get the system itself. If we set our charge in one of these houses—" he waved beyond the trees, in the general direction of the nearest bubble house— "close it up with a time fuze, we might be able to kill the whole thing." The tanker took off his helmet and fanned himself with it.

"*Cop*," said Blackledge. His tone cleared a broad aisle between him and the tanker two meters away. "We don't need a house blown up, we need a *door* gone. This didn't work, fine. We got ten times that much left. We'll set it all off together, right here." The blue-haired outlaw's submachinegun already pointed squarely at Slade's midriff.

"Ten times nothing is still nothing," the tanker said tensely. He rapped the door with the knuckles of his left hand, holding the helmet.

"I tell you something else that's bloody nothing!" Blackledge shouted. He waggled his gun in needless emphasis. "The way you've been bloody running things! *That's* nothing!"

Slade fired. His bolt clipped the rim of the helmet with which he had hidden the pistol. Enough of the energy got through to handle the job, however.

The outlaw's submachinegun blew up. Slade had fired at it rather than at the man for better reasons than misplaced mercy. Even a brain shot might not have kept Blackledge's trigger finger from one last spasm. The flash of the magazine exploding was a blue-green so intense that it was almost white. Flaming droplets of plastic and metal sprayed the men.

Blackledge lurched sideways and fell as if a truck had hit him. His right hand and right side from shoulder to knee were charred black except where bone poked out. Blackledge did not scream because shock had not yet let the pain through. The only sound he made was the clicking in his throat as he tried to draw a breath.

Slade did not reach for his medikit, but he extended his pistol for careful aim. There was enough cruelty in the universe without letting someone suffer needlessly. Even Blackledge, even someone as useless as Blackledge. . . .

The tanker lowered his weapon again without firing the second shot. The rest of the scouting party relaxed unconsciously. None of them had thought to gainsay Slade. Even the pair of outlaws who had also been with Aylmer could see that a quick end was the best that Blackledge could hope for even if they managed to get him back to the ship.

"Petrie," said Slade, after the pause had allowed him to get his breathing if not his pulse back under control, "strip off your coveralls. Mine went off with Wallace, and we need another stretcher now."

Slade bent over the wounded man. The pistol's barrel was still too hot for the holster. Slade transferred the weapon to his left hand while his right took another cone of pain blocker from the limited medical supplies. Without the blocker, Blackledge would die of shock; and he might die too soon.

"Taylor, Hwang," the tanker went on as he straightened again, "you'll carry him. Be as easy as you can, but we may not have much time. Rest of you, gather your gear and let's get moving. We need one of those bubble houses to get out of this place."

In the confusion of movement and released tension, Stoudemeyer stepped closer to Slade. In a low voice the man from Telemark asked, "Do you really think there's a way, ah—Captain?"

"Lord help me," Slade muttered back, "I think there is."

"But what do I ask for?" called Taylor through the open door.

"Ask for any curst thing you want!" Slade shouted back. "Ask for raw beef. And keep asking, like I bloody told you!"

Beside the kneeling tanker, Reuben Blackledge began to mumble the words to a song. It sounded as if it were in Latin, a hymn from deep in the outlaw's consciousness. The coveralls lumped misshapenly over the wounded man's body.

In the bubble house, Taylor was saying, "Raw beef. More raw beef. More raw beef." The house's response was inaudible to the rest of the party outside. Except for Slade, the outlaws' hands were clenched on the guns he had ordered them not to use.

"The system has to be centralized," Stoudemeyer said nervously. "It may not replenish itself here, just because Taylor's—"

Taylor screamed. He leaped with his boots pedaling like those of a man who hears a rattlesnake beneath him. The real stimulus was a negative one, the feeling of the floor beginning to drop away beneath his feet. Taylor was out the door even as the third platter of synthesized beef was beginning to unfold in front of where he had stood.

Another mercenary shouted and jumped sideways as the ground began to shift under him. Slade jerked the igniter wire. He prayed that the time pencil's stated thirty-second delay was fairly close to its reality. "All right, dammit," he said as he jumped to his feet, "let's get back a ways. *Don't separate!*"

When he watched the process from the beginning, Slade could see the wink of metal as tendrils parted the soil. Blackledge twitched his left arm. It was the only movement of which the drugged man was capable. His chanting trailed off into a one-sided argument of some sort as the grass closed over his face, then his swollen body.

"Twenty-four," Slade whispered, "twenty-five, twenty—"

Forty kilos of high explosive went off, literally in the bowels of Professor Kettlemann's closed system.

It was hard to determine the epicenter of the blast. The ground seemed to hump up about ten meters from the point it had fed itself Blackledge and his wrapping of explosive. The bulge hammered the cavern's interior as if the ground were the hard-struck membrane of an enormous drum. Light had been omnipresent in the high ceiling. Now the light died in a logarithmically expanding wave from the point above the blast. It was a reversed vision of an incandescent bulb going out, when the filament retains an orange glow for instants after it no longer illuminates its surroundings.

Slade picked himself up carefully. Somebody cried out at the darkness. Several of the team were switching on the light-wands they brought and had promptly forgotten in the lighted cavern. Streaks flickered through the fuzzy yellow glows. It was not rain but grit, oxidized metal raining from the ceiling.

The tanker wiped and lowered his upturned face hastily. "Let's move!" he shouted to the men of his party. "Bloody thing may regenerate, or it may come down on our heads like a drop forge. Curst if I want to be around either way."

The door that had crushed Pergot was crumbled open like a heap of smelter slag. It buried whatever was left of the dead outlaw. Flies buzzed away from the pig carcass as the men stumbled past behind their light-wands. The corridor beyond was still illuminated. Slade wondered vaguely where it led, whether to more self-contained habitats or to something quite different. He had no real interest in finding out.

Several of the group cheered as they bolted into the corridor. Birds fluttered past them, called to the light.

Be damned to replenishing stores, thought Don Slade. What GAC 59 needed now was *out*.

CHAPTER SIXTEEN

"Ruthless even to his own men!" shuddered the mind of Elysium.

"The only salvation of his men," it replied. *"Not cruel, and ruthless only at need. Men use men. But mankind uses men for the species to survive. For our species to survive. . . ."*

As if in answer, the first current of opinion recalled an image from the castaway's mind. It was his last look at Blackledge's face. The dark, dilated pupils met Slade's as the ground sagged down and the fuze hissed on the wounded man's chest. *"Ruthless. . . ."*

"Captain Levine didn't want to lift ship so suddenly," Don Slade said to the Elysian faces before him, "Some of the guys who hadn't been in the scout party sort of wanted to look around for themselves, too. Nobody had planned to go looking for us if we hadn't come back, though, any more than we'd thought they would."

The big man paused and cleared his throat. It wouldn't do to put his foot in his mouth now. These were nice folks, gentle folks, and the last thing he wanted to do was to give them an accurate glimpse of life in the universe from which he came. "Some of the people who'd been with me, though, they were pretty strong about getting off

Stagira before something came through the hull to eat them. Used words like 'kill everybody on the bridge if the ship didn't lift ASAP'. Just panic, of course, but I wouldn't say they were joking right at that moment, either.

"While we were trying to get out of that cave, Levine and his navigators were thinking about their problem—crewing. Now, if we'd been able to touch down at some of the busier ports, there'd have been plenty of folks on the beach that we could have struck a deal with. But we were worried about competition, and besides ... there was a problem about the manifesting of the cargo from Desireé. The bigger places with their red tape might have kept us a year in Customs Quarantine."

Well, it would have been about a year before the courts got through their rigamarole and everybody aboard GAC 59 was executed with due ceremony.

"But there was a place called Windward, where the colony modified autochthones to handle very complex tasks. Even starship crew jobs. So when the men of the scout party pushed matters, Levine already had a course plotted to Windward. . . ."

"So, assuming your cargo meets the manifest," said Senior Patriarch Bledsoe, "we have a deal." He offered his hand.

Captain Levine shook, but as he did so he said sourly to the Windward official, "The thrusters are in the original packing, Patriarch. There shouldn't be any problem with them. I'm a good deal more concerned about whether your crewman is going to function as well as the ten-tonne unit we're trading for him."

"For *it*, good sir," said the Windward official.

Bledsoe's smile was wholly on his lips, not in his tone. "Human pronouns are as out of place for the Treks as they would be for so many, oh, thrust units. You'll see."

The local man had a fringe of white hair and a cherubic expression. He had driven a bargain, however, that obviously reflected the trouble the outlaws would have in selling their cargo on any world which did not wink at piracy. Bledsoe walked to the window. Don Slade already stood there, watching port activity. The two men were nearly of a size, but the tanker had a physical hardness which the other lacked. Muscles meant very little in modern, civilized warfare, however. Slade did not remember having seen a more heavily-defended spaceport on any world which was not in the midst of open warfare.

"We certainly expect you to test our merchandise as closely as we test yours, gentlemen," Bledsoe said. "There's a necessary programming period, of course, to interface the Trek with your system. About three days, I would judge, though there may be idiosyncrasies. After that, you can expect to have one of your control stations occupied at all times by a flawless, sleepless living machine. We'll modify your synthesizers to turn out a protein supplement that won't cause allergic reactions in a Trek; that won't be a problem. You'll find your purchase well worth the expense, I assure you."

"I don't wholly understand," said Slade. "How does what would be a six month cram-course for a human with top of the line hypnocubes turn out to be three days for a, a Trek?" He turned away from the bustle of planetary and intra-system traffic outside to pin the local man with his eyes.

Bledsoe shrugged. "There are advantages to being inhuman, Mister Slade," he said. "To being unintelligent in human terms. Your Trek will act within the parameters which it deduces from the equipment it operates and the task to which it is set. As I said, three days is generally enough time for the programming to be completed."

"Well, what I'd like," snapped Captain Levine, "is to have a look at one of these things. What are they, rocks with arms?"

"We'll have your unit delivered at once," the local man said with a narrowing of his eyes. "But surely you must have seen Treks working outside?"

Bledsoe motioned Levine over. Slade made room at the window with a grim smile on his face. The tanker had a notion as to what was about to happen. "There," said the local man. "Driving that truck."

"Good heavens, Patriarch!" Levine blurted. "Surely that's a human being?"

Like much of the labor force visible, the figure in the truck's open cab was a humanoid of medium height. A closer look disclosed that its gray color was not clothing but rather the skin or natural covering—fur or fine scales—itself. The gray figures differed significantly from the occasional true humans in only one respect: the humans worked with the usual amount of waste motion and chattering. The others, the Treks, carried out their tasks without any such flaws.

"They are *not* human, Captain Levine!" the Senior Patriarch said sharply. "And you will *not* be given another warning about your language. We aren't hard to get along with, here on Windward; but if you persist in blasphemy, you'll find we have rules and ways to enforce them." Bledsoe nodded toward one of the visible barbettes. Its twin powerguns had tracked the ship all the way to landing. Now the squat tubes were trained on the engine room, ready to gut their target at the first sign of trouble. Presumably the defenses were crewed by "flawless, sleepless, living machines" also.

Levine had lapsed into shocked silence. The tanker spoke to fill the embarrassing gap. "I suppose," he said mildly, "that you have, ah, normal recreation facilities for the crew while our purchase is being programmed?" Slade almost said "programming itself", but he caught himself short of another possible blunder.

"Normal and abnormal," said the local man. His expression relapsed into a knowing smile. "We can put some activities off-limits to your personnel if you like. All the establishments are, so to speak, managed by Treks. If you don't care, though, the sky's the limit—liquor, drugs; boys, women, or combinations; honest games—anything. We on Windward believe men have a right and a duty to take pleasure, though of course we support your right as commander—" He glanced from Slade to Levine and back again. Their relationship had not been made clear to Bledsoe. "—to control your crew for the good of the vessel."

Slade nodded. "Wide open should be just fine," he said. "So long as you don't have sorm trees."

"Pardon?"

"Don't worry about it," tanker said. "Let's get a team to emptying our hold, and let's get our Trek started on learning the hardware." He grinned. "The other hardware."

*   *   *

"Here's the high-speed vector shift," said Riddle, the Midwatch navigator who was handling the training.

The Trek followed the human's pointing finger to the cylinder switch with click detents for band jumps. The gray-furred humanoid had been trying to follow the training simulation by using the rocker switch by which the three units were brought into synchrony. Amazingly, the Trek had been successful within safety parameters if not those of comfort. That was, after all, as much as one dared to hope from the regular navigation crew.

The exercise continued smoothly. The Trek used both three-fingered hands to make adjustments now that he no longer had to keep one glued to the rocker switch. Its motions had less of the manic intensity of a one-armed pianist, as a result.

"She's absolutely incredible," muttered Riddle.

Slade glanced sharply at the navigator, then back to the autochthone. "Any time you're in front of a local," the tanker said mildly, "you call Treks 'it'. I think the best thing that'd happen otherwise is we lift off short another navigator."

Though it was natural, the Lord knew, to think of the Treks as human, as people. Their thigh and upper arm bones were noticeably longer than those of the lower limbs. Their facial features were understated in the manner of primitive carvings in low relief. The fur was less obtrusive than it would have seemed, because it was so fine and clinging that even at arm's length it seemed more like clothing than it did some facet of alienness.

The Treks had no secondary sexual characteristics, however. Riddle might find the creature's lithe quickness to be feminine. Slade, however, was reminded of a gunman he had known, and whose sex was not an issue once you had seen him kill.

The conning room was designed around a three-sided pillar. The primary controls were arranged on the sides of the pillar. Behind each navigation console, the bulkhead was covered with banks of status read-outs whose information was echoed to the main screen when the central computer saw a need to do so. The Trek shot frequent glances over its shoulder.

Slade began to open a ration packet. It was sealed in a tough polymer with a metalized inner surface. The autochthone turned in soundless delight. It extended a hand palm-upward toward the tanker. The palm was not fur-covered. The Trek's skin was a smooth, rich sable.

"Food?" Slade asked. He broke off half the ration bar and offered it. The Trek reached past the offered portion and took the half still in its wrapper. It opened the polymer carefully and waggled it so that the inner surface reflected the ranks of gauges to the rear.

"You want a mirror?" Slade said in surprise. The autochthone nodded enthusiastically. "Via, we can do better than this. I'll see to it." Slade looked at Riddle and added. "Do you really have to watch all that stuff too?" He waved at the mass of dials and data windows.

The navigator shrugged. "Well, they're there, they've got some purpose. And the way things work on this trash-bucket, the more you know, the better. But Lord! She's so—" Riddle ran his hand over the Trek's shoulder and biceps. "Good isn't the word. And without being able to *speak*."

Slade pointed at the Trek's throat with one blunt forefinger. The tanker was careful not to touch the smooth fur. "When the light catches it the right way," he said, "you can see there's a scar there. I suspect it could speak about as well as it does everything else, except for that."

Riddle leaped from his chair in an outburst of rage. "The bastards did *that*?" he shouted. The Trek nodded without apparent emotion. It resumed the activities of the training program. Riddle had not needed the confirmation anyway. "Those, those—animals!" he went on. His hand touched the Trek's shoulder again. "*She's* not an animal, *they* are."

Slade lifted the navigator's hand and dropped it back at the man's side. The tanker was tall enough to look down on Riddle's bald spot when they were both standing. "*I'm* telling you to watch your tongue, friend," Slade said. "If you can't learn to, you'll spend the rest of this landfall tied down and sedated."

When he felt the smaller man relax somewhat, Slade continued. "Now, how much longer are you on duty here?"

"Ninety-three minutes," the navigator said sullenly. He did sit down again.

"Fine," said Slade. "As soon as you're off, I want you to get over to one of the knock shops on the Strip and have your ashes hauled. Girls are a bit pricey, but don't worry about that, the first one's on me." His eyes narrowed slightly as he watched the balding man. "Or a guy, Via, take your choice. But you've got an order, mister, and don't think I'm kidding."

The tanker slapped his thigh as he walked out of

the conning room. His hard palm cracked where the pistol holster would have been had he bothered to wear one.

Behind Slade, the navigator glowered at the autochthone's dancing arms.

"—what can the matter be?" Don Slade caroled as he walked across the port apron. A cab would have brought him directly to the main hatch, but the tanker felt good tonight, felt like walking. Area floods made the port and the vessels in it shimmer in amber light. "Seven old maids, locked in the lavat'ry."

"Slade, where've you been?" demanded a voice. Figures detached themselves from the hatch. Captain Levine had been speaking. "They've cheated us, there's something wrong with the Trek."

"They were there from Sunday to Saturd'y," Slade continued. That was playfulness, however, not real disregard of the problem. Windward had stim cones, real Cajumel blendings, and some of the whores had carried professionalism almost to a level of enthusiasm.

The big man put his arms around his pair of greeters, Levine and Riddle. The latter's bald spot gleamed like polished copper. "Let's go see what the problem is," the tanker said.

"The problem is the curst thing's dying before we even shift atmosphere," said Captain Levine as the trio stumbled up the ramp. Slade kept hold of his two companions' waistbands as if they were coolies and he a rickshaw. "I suppose we ought to be glad it didn't happen in the middle of a Transit sequence, but dear heaven! the cost, a whole *thruster*, and all wasted!"

"Lot of people got wasted when we got the thrusters, too," Slade noted equably. "But we wanted them pretty bad. Want not, waste not, d'ye suppose, Captain?"

The Trek lay on the shelf of the vessel's medicomp. The creature might as well have been laid on the broiler in the gallery for all the use the primitive piece of hardware would do. The medicomp could not be reprogrammed to handle non-humn life forms. Since GAC 59 lacked even the most basic parameters such as the Trek's normal heart rate and body temperature, a more flexible medicomp would not have helped anyway.

The Trek lay supine. Its body was so flaccid that the soles of its feet touched the shelf. The ankle joints obviously did not lock. The creature's eyes were covered with yellowish scum which matted the fur around the orbits as well. Fluid of some other description, possibly the Trek equivalent of blood, was leaking out of its nostrils and simple ears. The creature's breathing was rapid and louder than the stand-by hum of the equipment. It did not take experience as extensive as the tanker's to recognize imminent death.

Slade stepped to the communications unit on the wall beside the medicomp. He tapped a three-digit code into the key pad to access the ship-to-ship radio; ten digits more to enter Windward's commo net through the port transponder; and finally the six digits of the Port Warden. At no time did Slade pause to check the number or to fumble with the key pad. His eyes narrowed over chill anger as he waited for the connections to go through. There was no sign of the evening's entertainment when he snapped at the men across from him. "Why in *Hell* didn't you get help from the locals before now? Do you *like* to watch things die?"

Riddle grimaced and looked away. He had not, come to think, spoken since Slade's return.

Captain Levine said bluntly, "I wasn't about to bring them in till I found you. I can deal with these people if I've got somebody like you standing behind me. But not by myself, not when they're sure to deny liability."

"Warden's Office, Third Son Tuburg speaking," said the commo unit.

"This is freighter Golf-Alpha-Charlie Five Niner," Slade replied. "Berthed on Pad Four. The Trek we purchased yesterday is in dying condition. Seems disease or poison. We need medical help right away or we're going to lose hi—ah, it."

"Roger," said the speaker. Slade was not sure whether it was a good sign or a bad one that the Windward watch officer broke the connection at once.

"All right, what happened?" the tanker asked. He might as well improve his time by getting the background while they waited. The Trek breathed with the harshness of a file on stone.

"Riddle buzzed me about three hours ago," said Captain Levine. He gestured with his thumb. "He said the thing's performance had deteriorated and now it wasn't moving at all."

Slade looked at the navigator. "Why were you still on duty then, Riddle?" he asked without expression.

The balding man looked away. "Hutchins didn't show up for his watch," he said.

"Didn't you say Hutchins paid you to stand a double?" the Captain interjected.

"No matter," said Slade. No matter that he was going to deal with at just this moment. "What happened then?"

Levine risked a puzzled glance at his navigator. "Well," he went on, "when I got to the conning room it was about like you see it here. Not quite so much, well, leaking, but sick. Limp as a coil of rope. So we brought him down here—" he nodded vaguely at the medicomp— "and called you. You weren't wearing your belt unit."

Slade wavered between anger and laughing, then laughed. "My belt unit's lying on my bunk, along with a lot of other garbage I didn't want to fool with tonight. And as for what I was wearing, Captain—for most of the night, I wasn't wearing a curst thing. And neither were the ladies I was with."

"Well, ah," Levine said. "We needed to get hold of you, you see."

"What did it eat, Riddle?" Slade said sharply.

"I gave her some water!" the navigator replied angrily. "Nothing to eat since *you* fed her."

"Then maybe we're all right," the tanker said as if he did not understand the attack. "If it wasn't fed anything but carbohydrates, then maybe it was just some bug it picked up. We're not responsible for that, not till we lift off, at any rate." He smiled wryly. What was the warranty on humanoids purchased by pirates? Especially under the seller's guns.

Help arrived in a growl of fans on the pad. Levine trotted down the corridor. "This way!" he shouted ahead. Moments later, the Captain was back. Two clashing pairs of boots and the bare-soled whispering of a Trek followed him.

One of the Windward humans was young and dishevelled. Slade did not recognize the symbol on the man's white cap. The tanker suspected that the fellow was not, by local law, a doctor. He and the Trek who carried the chromed medical case pushed past Slade and Riddle to the dying autochthone.

The other human was Senior Patriarch Bledsoe himself. In earlier dealings, the Windward official had covered the steel edges of his personality with a layer of bonhommie. That had not hidden the truth or even camouflaged it; but it showed the same willingness to deal rationally as did Slade's own careful control.

The bonhommie was gone now. "You were warned about certain rules, Captain Levine," said the Senior Patriarch harshly. Bledsoe must have pulled his uniform on in a rush, but his appearance was as sharp as it had been during the cargo negotiations. "I don't assume you have violated those rules—" not really a lie, so transparent were the words— "but if you have, you and your vessel will be expelled at once from Windward."

"But I don't understand, ah, Port Warden," Levine blurted.

Slade understood. So did Navigator Riddle. The balding man was pressing his palms fiercely against one another while his eyes focused on their trembling.

The medic muttered something cryptic to the autochthone which had accompanied him. That Trek made a quick gesture with its hands—sign language. It bore the laryngeal scar also, even though the speech that would otherwise be possible would clearly help in its duties. Job requirements are not always rational requirements, and a creature which speaks may too easily be thought of as human.

The healthy Trek rolled its wheezing fellow belly-down on the shelf. The Trek's strain at the activity suggested that the autochthones had less short-term strength than even human females of the same size. Despite that, the medic did not help his assistant turn the injured creature. The local man was instead pulling on a pair of disposable gloves. He bent forward as his Trek assistant spread the other autochthone's buttocks.

Slade knew too little about Trek physiology to guess whether the opening displayed was a cloaca or something more specialized than that. The black skin of its lips was distended. The surrounding fur was matted, though there was no sign of fluids leaking as they did from the creature's ears and nose.

"Well?" demanded Senior Patriarch Bledsoe.

The medic reached into his kit. Instead of speaking, he gave his superior a curt nod. The medic's face was a queasy contrast to the metallicly-calm expression of his Trek assistant.

Bledsoe's tongue touched dry lips. "Captain Levine," he said, "your crew will be delivered to you as soon as humanly possible. Humanly! You will lift off within five minutes of the last arrival." The official's eyes were as merciless as the twin-barreled gun turret aimed at the ship from outside.

"Senior Patriarch," Slade interrupted, "we'll clean our own house. You can watch if you like."

The tanker did not look at Riddle. The navigator

stood in near catatonia by the bulkhead. Slade's words rang about him with deadly earnestness. Slade was going to beat the balding navigator within an inch of his life, because nothing short of that could be expected to satisfy the Windward authorities. "And we expect to pay a stiff penalty over and above the cost of a replacement Trek. But—"

"Are you mad?" Bledsoe demanded as if he and not the tanker were the man who had killed for a business. "Mister Slade, I will have them slag this ship down around me before I will consider placing another Trek into this *cesspool!*"

The gloved medic put an injector behind the dying Trek's ear. The creature convulsed mightily. The medic jumped back to avoid the flailing limbs. He dropped the empty injector on the shelf.

"Sir," said the tanker. His anger was obvious and as great as that of Bledsoe. "We won't leave because we *can't* leave that fast in our present state of crewing. If that means blasting us where we stand, then you might want to see how our powerplant's been rigged." That was a lie, but it would be the truth if Slade had half an hour's grace. "If you're willing to deal, though, we'll deal with you on any terms that give us a chance to survive."

The medic and his assistant were already leaving the cubicle. Riddle stared at the Trek. It ignored him. The other autochthone was dead, though its extremities continued to slap the shelf and walls. The injection had only speeded the process made inevitable when the Trek absorbed human proteins.

The Senior Patriarch swallowed, "All right," he said, staring fiercely back at the tanker. "I'll send aboard a navigational unit with a link to the central computer. They'll set and lock your controls onto the nearest inhabited world, that's Erlette. And if that isn't satisfactory, Mister Slade—then yes, we *will* see what you may have done to your powerplant. Good day!"

The Windward official turned and bounced Captain Levine out of his way. Bledsoe did not even seem to notice the contact as he strode back toward the hatch.

"Slade, Slade, Captain," Levine pleaded, "does he mean that Riddle—"

As if his name were a trigger, Riddle ran down the corridor. "You bastards!" he shouted. "You bastards! You know they're human! *You know they're human!*"

Levine and the tanker tried simultaneously to jump after the navigator. The instant's delay they caused each other permitted the balding man to reach the hatch before they could catch him.

Bledsoe had continued to walk toward the vehicle that had brought him to the ramp. The medic and his assistant were already seated and waiting. So were two other Treks. One was the driver.

The other crewed the pillar-mounted tribarrel. The air cushion vehicle was not an ambulance but a gun-truck.

Riddle caught Bledsoe by the sleeve while the local official was still half-way from his vehicle. Bledsoe had ignored the navigator's previous taunts. Now he turned. Harsh light at an angle threw his face into a sequence of cold ridges and cold valleys.

Slade saw and understood the look in the Senior Patriarch's eyes. Captain Levine tried to squeeze past to run to his crewman. The tanker's arm encircled Levine's waist and immobilized the smaller man by lifting his feet from the deck. This was no time to interfere. It would be like trying to stop lava with a barrier of brushwood.

"You're human!" Riddle screamed to the Trek at the automatic weapon. "You've got to free yourselves; *kill* the people who torture you! *Kill* them!"

The medic broke his stony reserve. He leaped from the truck seat with a cry of rage. Bledsoe turned also. He was trying only to restrain the other Windward human, but Riddle reacted as if the motion were a challenge. Riddle's fist clubbed the older, heavier man on the side of the neck. Bledsoe stumbled to his knees with a grunt.

The Trek gunner fired a long burst into Riddle's body. The hot-griddle hiss of the shots was obscured by the shattering disintegration of the navigator's chest. Then both ceased, discharge and impact. What remained of Riddle slumped to the ground. Its left hand was extended as if in entreaty.

The iridium muzzles of the tribarrel glowed, and there was a glowing track in the ramp's face where a bolt had struck because the thorax at which it was aimed had vaporized. Ozone and decomposition products from the expended cartridges warred with the animal odors of burned flesh and voided wastes.

Slade released Captain Levine.

The gun's cyan flickering had frozen the medic in a half crouch from which he slowly relaxed. Senior Patriarch Bledsoe got to his feet with the clumsiness of a reanimated corpse. The right side of his face and uniform were freckled by the navigator's explosive death. "Five minutes after we deliver your last *man*, Captain Levine," said Bledsoe.

He swung himself aboard the truck. As the vehicle whistled off toward the Operations Building, the dimly-flowing muzzles of the tribarrel continued to track Slade and Levine in the hatchway.

CHAPTER SEVENTEEN

"He would really have blown up his ship," thought Elysium. "He would have killed everyone for kilometers around. And they had a right to expel the vessel, the folk of Windward. Their culture was threatened."

"He saved the ship and saved his fellows," Elysium replied. There was, there could be, neither heat nor rancor in the exchange. It was more as if two currents met in the sea, swirling and mingling. "He saved lives that would have been lost had he bluffed and been called on it."

Then, with all the unity that so many minds could muster on any subject; "He does not bluff when he threatens. When he offers slaughter, he means nothing short of it. . . ."

"The Transit to Erlette was about as smooth as any I'd made," Slade was saying. "It was sure as smooth as anything I'd made in GAC 59. That didn't keep Captain Levine from being concerned, though. . . ."

"This is just asking for disaster, Captain Slade," said Levine. "We'll come out of Transit in an atmosphere! Or we'll wind up in, we'll never be able to figure out *where*, as tired as my people are going to be."

"They tell me," said Slade calmly, "that everything's spot-on with no problems. And they seem
pretty relaxed, too, even if they have been pulling
a rotating double."

"Oh, that's fine, surely," said the spacer. His
tones of angry sarcasm would not usually have
been directed against Slade. "Windward had a
ground unit the size of Friesland's, *certainly* it can
preset us across seventeen Transit seconds. What is
there on Erlette? Will we find the Transit crewmen
we need there? On a place nobody's ever heard
of?"

"You know," said the tanker, "I *did* hear of
Erlette. While I was with the Slammers. But I'm
hanged if I remember why. Must've been a briefing,
people we were operating with or against or some
curst thing. *Hanged* if I remember just what,
though."

A dozen of the bridge displays winked and
changed in a sudden, organized fashion that meant
nothing to Slade. The crewman with the throat
mike and earpiece turned to Levine. "Want I should
request landing clearance, Captain?"

"Yes, curse it, of course," Levine said. He twisted
and punched up a line of figures on his own console.
"Before something *worse* goes wrong." The Captain's
lips pursed. "Though you know, that's not bad.
Maybe the old girl's settling in and the misalign-
ments are cancelling out."

Slade left the bridge as the spacers shifted into
the critical minutiae of landing. He wore a puzzled expression. "Wonder if I saved anything with
my souvenirs in the hold?" the tanker mumbled to
himself. "Not even sure I'll be able to find the
right box, of course. . . ."

*   *   *

The air still rocked with the echo of the thrusters. The landing site was in the flood plain of a creek. The water's encroachment could presumably be controlled by the dam at the valley's head, but there was no need of that now. The shallow water sprayed to either side of the service vehicle crossing to reach the starship.

The outlaws were restive. Their partying on Windward had been recent enough that there was not the need to let off steam that a longer Transit would have bred. Further, the party on Windward had ended sharply—brutally, for those who had the bad judgment to try to resist the local authorities. The men who could not be chivvied back were carried aboard the ship. Seven of them were dead. Now the survivors looked over the latest landfall in sullen frustration. The disaster that swallowed their fellows on Mandalay had left GAC 59 too weak to protest the treatment its complement earned.

Slade and Levine waited at the forward hatch. Bourgiby and Rooks, the two surviving members of the Ship's Meeting, were with them. The port's visible defenses were of the bare-bones variety to be met with on rural worlds: two powerguns on opposite sides of the valley. They were probably 15 cm, probably old; certainly able to open the ship like a ration packet if they were functional at all. Erlette would have been a good target for the original fleet to raid—if there were anything here to loot. The planet appeared to have nothing to recommend it to GAC 59 alone, except that the inhabitants did not seem to intend to slag the vessel.

Just yet, at least.

The service vehicle was a small bus. It pulled up at the ramp. Partly-uniformed personnel began jumping out of the cab and rear door. A few of them wore coveralls, but most made do with a flash-breasted jacket over nondescript civilian clothes. "Well, I'll be hanged," said Rooks.

There was no need for him to amplify his statement. A female driver/co-driver team was normal enough. That some of the port officials greeting the new arrivals were female was no cause for surprise either. However, there were about a dozen people in the service vehicle, and every one of them was a woman.

The trio which strode briskly toward the ship's command group was led by a lithe brunette. She was as leggy as Slade, though a decimeter shorter in the torso. "Captain Levine?" she said to the tanker as she approached.

Slade stepped back, thumbing toward Levine. The woman's extended hand shifted smoothly toward the spacer, though her eyes retained a glint of awareness of the bigger man. "Captain Levine," she repeated as they shook hands. "I'm Delores Rodrigues. I'm Mayor here on Erlette. This is Deputy Brandt and Deputy Morales. I can't tell you how thankful we are. And I assure you, there's been no recurrence of the disease in fifteen years. It's perfectly safe."

"*What?*" said Rooks angrily.

Levine's smile took a sickly cant. Instinct wiped on his trousers the hand that had just touched the woman.

"Why yes," said Rodrigues, looking across the eyes of the startled men. Slade was trying to place the comment with what he had heard of Erlette, but that heading was still all blank. "The officials on Windward gave us to believe that you were coming as a sort of, well, relief mission. Didn't they tell you?"

"Blood and martyrs!" Rooks snarled. "*Warn* us, you mean, those bastards! What do you mean, disease?" The outlaw had backed a step up the ramp. Bourgiby, his fellow, was silent but as clearly concerned.

"Ah, Mayor Rodrigues," said Slade, "I'm not sure how much garbling there might have been in your message from Windward." Message capsules were radio transmitters slung into on-stage Transit by a ground unit. They had considerable margin for error. "But this is simply a freighter with a cargo of landing thrusters and a need for some specialized crew . . . that we hope you could help us with."

"Well, yes, but . . ." the Mayor said. She turned her head. The main hatches had been opened also, against orders but inevitably. Outlaws and probably some of the ship's crew were beginning to exit warily. Though their total number was not yet obvious, it was already clear that they were greatly more numerous than the complement of an ordinary freighter. "They said you had over two hundred men aboard. Males. And surely you have, don't you?" She waved toward the groups spreading from the cargo hatches.

"Well, yes, but we're not specialists," the tanker said. Slade had concealed his surprise when the others froze at mention of disease. Via, he'd been in hellholes in service. Though the Slammers' excellent Med Section was no longer behind him, the big veteran's subconscious could not really believe in danger from microbes. Unreasoning confidence armored him against the unproductive fear that wracked the others. "We're not, ah, medical specialists I mean," he added.

Deputy Morales was a short, plump woman. Now she laughed briefly. "Via, mister," she said, "we don't *need* doctors. Like Delores said, there hasn't been a sign of the disease since it killed just about all the men on Erlette fifteen years ago. What we need is a little more variety for our sperm bank."

Morales pointed—her hands were surprisingly delicate—toward a white stone building. It was also one-story, but it was more imposing than the others of the community. Beside the building was a cooling plant, breathing a plume of vapor into the humid air. "And maybe some variety for us, too. What do you say, mister?" She popped Levine in the ribs and gave him a simultaneous leer. Her expression seemed to rock the Captain as much as the physical contact.

Brandt, the third of the greeting team, was brunette like the leader, but smaller and with fox-sharp features. "We've summoned citizens who might want to participate in, ah, direct methods," she said. Her voice was prim. Brandt kept her eyes focused so that they did not make contact with the eyes of any of the four men. "That isn't by any means all the, ah, women on Erlette. In the time we've been alone, we've made certain adjustments, of course."

Morales gave a coarse snicker and prodded Levine again.

Blushing but undeterred, the prim woman continued. "You and your crew will find an adequacy of entertainment, however. In exchange, we will expect cooperation with our efforts to increase the permanent gene pool." She too pointed toward the sperm bank. "There is no risk, of course. But we are aware that some males import an emotional significance to what is only a mechanical act, the transfer of sperm."

"Ah, Mayor," Slade said. "Sirs—" That was wrong, wasn't it, hell and blast this situation. "There's still the problem of our navigators. Our lack of them. Is there any chance that you have qualified people that might be hired on a temp—"

Rodrigues touched Slade's forearm to halt him. "Mister . . . ?"

"Slade," the tanker said. "I'm—well, it's complicated."

"Mister Slade," the woman resumed, "there's a great deal about the future to be discussed. Right now, there are organizational details to be handled. This is—" she turned up her palms with a smile— "an embarrassment of riches for us, incredible riches. But I'll call on you later this evening, if you don't mind. We'll be alone at my home, and we can work out a number of things."

The prim brunette beside the Mayor made a moue.

The memory of Mayor Rodrigues' smile lingered long after the trio of women had driven away.

"You know, Captain Slade," said Snipes, the ship's tall, bearded Administrative Officer, "I really respect you."

Slade put down the laser pencil He had just completed soldering the final lead to a post on the non-functioning commo unit. Slade's palms were sweaty. It scared the bleeding cop out of him to work with electrical blasting caps. Even before they were inserted in the block of high explosive, they could shatter your hands or your eyes if something went wrong. And the one poor bastard Slade remembered, the fellow who had three caps in a front pocket of his trousers at the spaceport on Friesland . . . A maintenance crew had switched on a Transit generator for testing. The powerful field induced enough of a current in the leads to detonate the blasting caps.

The screen on the upper wall of the shop was fed by one of the external vision blocks. There was nothing in particular to see. Erlette's port and capital were quiet except for light vehicular traffic in the dusk.

"The way you run these, these soldiers," Snipes continued. He was a good-sized man, one of those who used the exercise machines more as a matter of religion than of muscle tone. "But without getting, well, hardened like most men in your position would be."

"Now, do you have some luggage that'll hold all this?" Slade asked. "A box might do if it had to, but I'd like something that looked like it was a change of clothing without anybody asked. And not military."

The crewman glanced at the assembly, phony electronics and ten very real kilos of plastic explosive. "Well," he said uncertainly, "there's my own leave bag. I guess you could borrow it."

"Might I?" said the tanker. "Fast?"

Snipes was back in less than a minute with the bag. It was a nice one, self-adjusting to hold its contents firmly but without crushing them. Slade began to pack it with care. First the gray, taped blocks of explosive, then the guts of the commo unit. All of them were connected by looped wires and the blasting caps buried in the mass of explosive.

"I can tell," said Snipes, "that you understand women, too." His mouth worked. "I swear, there was no decent woman ever born but my mother. Lord rest her soul."

"Oh, I don't know," said Slade. He was arranging the leads with great care. "I was set to be married once. Turned out she married my brother Tom . . . but the way I was then, I wouldn't say Marilee was indecent. Or even wrong."

"But it made you look at yourself, didn't it?" Snipes pressed. He reached out and touched the hand with which Slade was shifting the charge. "Made you realize there were things, that for you— for a real man like you—a woman couldn't do as well as a man."

"Tell the truth, Johnsie," the tanker said, "it was more the Slammers that did that." Slade folded over the top of the bag and watched it seal itself into the smallest six-sided prism that would hold its present contents. "In twenty years under Hammer, I met curst few women I'd trust to close my back in a firefight. For killing, I'll take a man any day."

He stood up. Snipes extended his arm to hold the fingers in contact, but the thought behind the Admin Officer's eyes was changing. "And that's fair, I guess," Slade went on, "because for screwing, I don't have a darned bit of use for men." He smiled. "Most other duties, I'm pretty well neutral."

"Well, why *are* you still on board, then?" Snipes demanded. "You could be out there, having a, having an *orgy* like the rest of them. Couldn't you? Even Webb. 'Come on Johnsie, it won't hurt. They'll be so *willing*.' It just makes me. . . ." He trailed off with a grimace.

Slade was studying the view screen, partly to avoid looking at his companion's face. "Well," the tanker said, "I checked some of the old briefing cubes in the hold luggage you found for me. Didn't like what I learned." He shrugged. "Most everybody else had gone off already, like you say. There wasn't any point in raising a fuss then. So I—" He smiled again, tense with pre-battle nerves. The apparatus was complete and he had nothing to occupy his mind but the future. "I called my date and told her I'd need a couple extra hours to clear up some business. Which was true."

Slade wiped his hands very carefully with a solvent towel from the dispenser on the bulkhead. The skin of his hands prickled for a moment as it was cleaned. The skin of his neck and biceps continued to prickle for reasons unconnected with the towel. "She ought to be—yeah. I think that might be Delores right now."

Slade shook himself to loosen his muscles. "Take care, trooper," he said. He wore a cape against the chill and beneath the cape a civilian suit of brilliant silk from T'ien. The only military touch was a heavy belt on which a commo unit balanced the weight of a slung wallet.

On the screen, Delores got out of the same small bus she had arrived in earlier. This time she was alone in the vehicle. The tall woman began walking toward the vision block over the bridge hatch, growing on the screen. The garment she wore covered but did not hide her breasts, even in the screen's blurred image.

"Hold the fort till I get back," the tanker called over his shoulder. As his boots echoed down the corridor, Snipes heard him add, "Won't say I'm not used to the work, but it's a curst strange context."

Mayor Rodrigues' house was a low dome sunk a meter deep in the soil. The skylights, now shuttered, would not open without noise. There was no door except for the one which the woman now opened onto a flight of steps.

"Ah, you don't have a, a roomate?" Slade asked huskily.

The tall brunette smiled. "Not tonight," she said. "Not unless you want one." Rodrigues stepped to the tanker. She swept his cape clear with her arms before she squeezed as much of her length against him as their position made possible. Slade shifted awkwardly at the woman's weight and strength. He returned the hungry kiss and felt his groin return it also, despite his tension.

"Come, dearest," Delores said. She broke away to lead Slade down the short flight of stairs. Her fingers felt warm and moist on his. "You don't know how long I've wanted this."

Slade paused to lock the door. A twist of the handle set bolts in both transom and threshold.

"Some things I don't like disturbed," he muttered, nervous and seemingly embarrassed. His luggage was in the bus outside. Slade had not wanted to call attention to the case by bringing it inside at once.

The room they stood in was the whole front half of the circular dwelling. There was a table and a variety of cushioned benches for seating. The floor was of rush mats, fresh and green-smelling. In the wall bisecting the interior were three doors. Two of them were ajar. Slade could see the corner of a low bed in the center room. The room to the left had a tiled interior, surely a bathroom though the fixtures were of unfamiliar style. The third door would lead to the kitchen, closed off for no reason other than its inappropriateness to the intended activity.

Probably.

Delores was in Slade's arms again. His left hand flicked the brooch holding his cape. The fabric slithered away from his shoulders. The tanker's belt gear pressed against the woman's thrusting belly. She backed off, panting, and reached for the belt hook.

Slade caught her fingers with one hand. "Just a second, darling," he muttered. His free hand tucked down the indigenous lace of her blouse so that he could kiss one broad, dark nipple. "Just a second," he repeated as he straightened. He walked quickly to the right-hand door. One hand reached into his slung wallet.

"The bathroom's the other way," Delores said. She did not sound concerned, only out of breath. She was reaching behind her for the blouse fasteners.

Slade opened the door, onto the empty kitchen as he had expected. "Oh, to hell with that anyway," he said as he strode back to the woman. It was not particularly necessary that his movements make sense; only that they be seen as non-threatening to a woman in the Mayor's present circumstances. "Here," the tanker said as Dolores nuzzled his throat, "let me help with the blouse."

She turned willingly. As willingly, she extended her hands behind her. She gave a throaty chuckle as Slade guided the hands to his groin, and she did not first realize when the tanker taped her wrists that the program had changed abruptly.

"Dearest?" the woman said in puzzlement as she turned back to Slade. "If you like this, we can, of course . . . anything. But I hoped first . . . ?"

"Here, love," Slade said. He lifted the tall woman onto a bench. She still did not object, though she was frowning. "Just for a moment," he added as he taped her ankle to one leg of the bench. It was solid wood, fifteen or twenty kilos; heavy enough to keep Rodrigues from jumping quickly to a hidden weapon or communications device.

The tanker was breathing hard. His body had told no more lies than his victim's body had. "Via," he said. "Via." He drew the pistol from his wallet and held the small weapon loose in his hand. "Don't pull against that," Slade went on with a nod toward the obvious strain of the woman against her wrists behind her. "It's freight tape. You can cut it, and alcohol'll release the adhesive clean. But you couldn't pull it apart with tractors. The loops are tight enough that it won't help you to tear your skin loose."

"But *why?*" Delores said. She did not struggle

for the moment, but her body was tensed for a last
hysterical burst before expected death convulsed
her. "Donald, almost anything. . . . If not me, then
somebody on Erlette will—want whatever you want.
Willingly."

Slade sat down on another bench, facing his
captive. "I was on Sphakteria," he said. "Were
you?"

Rodrigues shook her head without comprehen-
sion of either the words or what was happening to
her. Her blouse hung free of one of the breasts it
had not hidden very well to begin with.

"I was, the Slammers were," the tanker went
on. "Both sides pretty well financed. We got a
book from Central on a dozen or so merc units
operating against us."

Delores' eyes began to widen. She tensed still
further.

"You won't be hurt," Slade said sharply. In his
calmer voice of moments before, he continued, "But
you're right, there was a company of scouting specialists from Erlette. All women and ready to prove
they had more balls than any man they were going
to run into." Slade shrugged. "The background,
though. . . . All the men on Erlette had died, not a
few years before from a sex-linked plague, but
thirty-odd years back even then. And they'd been
killed by the women."

"Don, none of that's true!" The Mayor gasped.
"At least, I mean about the men here on—"

"*Can it,* honey," Slade said. "I'm not going to
hurt you, you hear?" He glared at the woman until
she subsided. "It was true ten, twelve years ago
when I heard it, and it's true now. Word was, no
men were allowed to live on Erlette since that—

incident. There was a sperm bank and normal reproduction to keep up the population at a viable level . . . but male offspring got deep-sixed at birth."

The tanker shrugged again. "That's your business," he said. "I don't interfere. But I didn't much like the notion that the same thing happened to visiting spacers—after they'd contributed to the gene pool directly and through the sperm bank."

"Donald," the Mayor whispered, "that's all the most vicious lies. You and your men aren't in any danger, I *swear* it."

Slade nodded. "Then there won't be any trouble," he said. "All I want is for all the—all *my* men—to be sent back to the ship unharmed. And we'll leave. Anybody in the Sperm Bank tonight?"

Delores' face hardened. "Why?"

"Because it's solider than this place," Slade said, "and because I figure it's too important—" The glint in the woman's eyes agreed with his assumption even before he finished stating it. "—for any of your, ah, friends to try and be heroes around it. They might risk you, but if somebody puts a batch of holes through that place, your whole society goes down the tubes. Right?"

"There's no one there," the woman said. Her pause had stretched dangerously long. "You're completely wrong, Mister Slade . . . but I suppose we can humor you if you want no more than you say. I'm sorry that things had to work out this way."

"Oh, lady," said the tanker wearily. "I couldn't agree with you more." He snicked the short, keen blade of his work knife out of its nest between the scales. "Only thing is, I'd like even less for things to work out the way you and your friends planned."

With a single motion Slade cut the tape holding Mayor Rodrigues' ankles to the bench. Cradling her in his left arm, and using her body to shield the pistol from possible watchers, Slade walked out of the house.

Traffic was sparse. Slade was still concerned that the lights of another vehicle would show that he was driving the bus. The alternative risk was to tape Delores to the driver's seat and free her hands to drive. Slade was not silly enough to do that. The pistol he carried was a deadly weapon, but the bus in hostile hands was yet more dangerous.

There were no incidents on the way. The Sperm Bank was quiet on their arrival, save for the whine of its cooling plant. "I hope," said Slade to the woman beside him, "that you've got the key to this place. I can drive into the door a couple times—" He patted the control column. The fans were spinning at idle while the bus waited in front of the squat, stone building. "But that's likely to cause coolant leaks in your refrigeration system."

"The door has a key-pad lock," Delores said sullenly. "We can get in." Whether she would have said the same without the threat was uncertain.

Slade worked the punched combination as directed while the bus continued to purr. There was no alarm as the door opened. By now, an alarm would have done as much good as harm anyway.

The tanker slipped his pistol back in the pouch in order to lift Mayor Rodrigues with his left hand and the borrowed luggage with his right. As expected, the initial room was a lobby with a desk and more padded benches against the walls. The corridor beyond led to a laboratory and a series of cubicles where, presumably, the sperm could be implanted. Most of the hardware was ceramic rather than of metal or synthetics.

The rear half of the building was a rank of refrigerated, multi-drawer files. The air held a sharp trace of ammonia. On a stanchion in the center of the room was a voice communications unit. "Can you talk to your friends on that?" Slade asked. He turned so that the woman he held could see the phone.

"Yes." The syllable was more guarded, now, than angry. The Mayor had had time to consider the risk of her community that a madman *here* posed.

Slade taped the woman's left ankle to the stanchion. Then he cut free her wrists. "I want you to start calling people," the tanker said as he stepped back. "And first, I want you to tell them exactly what you see here."

With the care the apparatus deserved, Slade opened the case and tilted it so that Delores could see clearly what was inside. The Mayor was no demolitions expert, but the threat was utterly clear from context. Her gasp was proof enough of that.

"And I want you to tell them," the tanker went on as he slid his own commo unit from his belt sheath and keyed it, "that if I let up on this switch—" he pointed to the key his left thumb depressed—"the signal triggers the bomb." His index finger tilted down toward the case. "Ten kilos of Cylobar. If that doesn't ring a bell, tell them its propagation rate is ten kays per second."

The tanker sat down against the wall. He moved carefully, so that his thumb did not slip and he did not lose eye contact with the horrified woman.

"When you've got their attention that way," Slade concluded, "then we'll move on to my instructions."

He smiled, and his face was more threatening than the way he gestured with the commo unit he held.

"Slade!" blurted Captain Levine as female guards ran him into the refrigeration room at gunpoint. "Dear heaven, I'd prayed they wouldn't have gotten you, you *know* about these—but why's she tied? The Mayor?"

Half a dozen more of GAC 59's crew stumbled down the corridor. They were logy with the treatment they had received, but their condition seemed to be acceptable. The pair of guards fanned to either side of the doorway. Deputy Brandt followed the spacers with a bell-snouted weapon of her own. She trained the gun on the center of Slade's chest.

Slade remained seated. The gun muzzle looked no more angry and threatening than did the Deputy's eyes.

The tanker nodded to her. "Levine," he said calmly, "you're going back to the ship right now. The mercs are being delivered there already." The tanker raised an eyebrow toward Brandt, who nodded curtly. "You'll program the ship to Transit from ground—"

"*I* can't set a course alone," Levine broke in. "And a ground Transit, the gravity well could kick us seconds, *minutes* off course."

"I'd rather be lost by five Transit minutes," said the tanker dryly, "than be lifting off on thrusters when the Deputy here decides we're out of range for my handset."

Brandt's gun trembled.

Levine looked warily from Slade to the weapon. Then he trotted back down the corridor, toward the vehicle that had brought him. One of the power room crew started to follow.

"Hold it," said Slade in a voice that made gun muzzles twitch.

The crewman turned to Slade. "But why do we got to stay here?" he whined.

"Because," said the tanker, "I know Captain Levine won't take off with no crew. And I'm not quite so certain that you all would be careful to wait for me to board."

More guards and another group of crewmen clattered into the building. Slade looked at Deputy Brandt, who had been surreptitiously eyeing the open case. "Take a good look," the tanker said calmly.

The sharp-featured woman glared at him. Her front teeth nibbled her lips. "I need to talk to Delores," she said abruptly. Brandt took a stride toward the bound Mayor.

"Hold it!" Slade repeated, even more sharply than before. The Deputy turned. She pointed her weapon. Everyone in the room tensed. "You can talk with her," Slade continued, "but you do it aloud so I can hear."

"All right, *mister*!" the Deputy rasped. "I was going to tell Delores there'd been a few adverse drug reactions. What do you think of *that*?"

"Cele—" said the woman strapped to the stanchion.

"I think you'd better have the bodies brought to the ship," replied the tanker in an even voice. "Nobody stays."

"Why?" Brandt demanded shrilly. "Bother you that we'd roll them in with sheep-cop and use them for fertilizer? That's all they're bloody good for! All they ever were."

Slade got up slowly. His face was placid, though his jaw muscles bunched momentarily. The tanker held his commo unit at his side as he walked toward Brandt. The Deputy took one step back. She locked her left hand on the fore-end of her pointed weapon. No one in the room seemed to breathe.

"That for real?" Slade asked gently. "Or is it a toy?" He stepped forward. The bell muzzle bumped his chest. Another step. The woman tried to brace herself, but the tanker's size and strength thrust her back.

"Cele!" screamed Mayor Rodrigues.

With a cry of fury, the Deputy slashed her gun down to point at the floor. Slade slapped her, knocking the woman down with his open hand and all his strength behind it.

One of the guards almost fired at the gun-shot crack and Brandt crumpling sideways. Discipline held. The finger lifted trembling from the trigger.

"Now," said Slade to the dazed Brandt, "I think you and your guns had best get out of here. I'll wait to hear from Captain Levine—" he nodded toward the phone— "that the ship's ready and the men are aboard. Understood?"

He looked around the room at the women and at the crewmen edging back from the violence.

No one in the building would meet Slade's eyes, but they all understood.

*   *   *

"Touch her," said Slade to the crewman who reached for Delores' lacy blouse, "and we'll lift short one man more." The tanker did not bother to draw the pistol from his wallet.

"Well, I don't see—" the crewman began as he snatched his hand away.

The phone on the stanchion purred its summons.

The Mayor jumped as her concentration on other things broke. Before she could recover, Slade had stepped to the instrument and switched it live. "Sperm Bank," he said. "Slade speaking." The tall woman strapped to the post was a warmth and odor.

"Slade, they want me to tell you that everybody's back at the ship," said Levine. "Except me, they wouldn't string a line, so I'm across the creek at this curst *phone*."

"Well, is it true?" the tanker demanded. "*Are* all the landmen back aboard?" Slade had great experience in projecting a facade of tank-like solidity. As with tanks, his interior was complex and had a way of displaying frustration at awkward times.

"Yes, yes," said Levine, "but—" and the words tumbled out through the background hiss—"Slade, there's eleven of them *dead*, corpses!"

"Do you know a way to bring the dead back to life, Captain Levine?" the tanker asked. He directed a bitter grimace at Delores Rodrigues. The captive woman had shrunk back when the phone spoke of the deaths her plan had caused.

"Of course not!" snapped Levine. "What do you mean?"

"I don't know a way either," Slade replied, "so let's not worry about that. Get back aboard, and be ready to Transit the instant the hatch closes behind me." The tanker waited a moment longer, but the phone popped with the sound of Levine switching off without further comment.

"Time to leave, boys," Slade said to the men and the woman who had stared at him throughout the conversation. "Let's see what kind of transport they've got for us." He waved the crewmen down the corridor ahead of him.

As the men obeyed, Slade reached down and poised his knife over the strap holding Delores to the stanchion.

"Don't run," he said to the woman softly. "It'll be your life if you do, and I'd sooner avoid that."

He cut across the band of tape and stood, looping his left arm through Delores' as if they accompanied one another formally. She stared down at the tanker's left hand and his thumb on the switch.

Slade was smiling as she met his eyes. Delores raised her chin proudly. "Let's go, then, Mister Slade," she said.

The building's interior had been so isolated that the drizzle outdoors was a surprise to Slade. The guards whose hooded ponchoes covered their guns were no surprise at all. The crewmen were already being loaded on a small bus like the one Slade had driven the night before.

Deputy Brandt stared at the tanker. Only her eyes moved in a face that shone white on one side, swollen red on the other.

"Wait," Slade said as his consort started to walk toward the bus. He shut the door of the Sperm Bank with a metallic crash. "Does it lock?" he asked and tried the door again before anyone could make a pointless reply to his question. The door was locked.

"Careful," Slade added, still holding Rodrigues as he dipped his pistol out of the wallet with his free hand.

"What—" called Deputy Brandt behind him. Slade had already fired.

The pistol was one he had chosen as being smaller and more concealable than an ordinary service weapon. It spat a light charge through a 5 mm bore. The sound it made was more unpleasant than threatening, like the squawk of a stepped-on kitten. Metal splashed from the key-pad of the lock. Three more shots, sparks in the raindrops, followed to crater the pad's surface into uselessness.

Slade turned. He held the pistol muzzle-up because he could not return it to the wallet until the barrel had cooled. "There," he said to Deputy Brandt. "You can cut through that easily enough ... but I don't think you're going to be inside the building before we're the Hell off your planet—unless you're willing to blast. Your choice, madam."

Brandt spat at the tanker's feet.

"All right, Mayor Rodrigues," Slade said to the woman at his side. "You'll be released at the ship. Right now, I'd as soon you rode with us. Just in case."

As the bus drove off, Slade could hear the harsh timbre of Deputy Brandt's voice. The guards around her were scurrying for hand tools with which they could break into the Bank—without risking its contents.

The driver brought her bus to a lurching halt well short of the ramp. Realizing that, she lifted the vehicle again in a blast of dust and gravel, hopping twenty meters closer.

"Now *move!*" Slade snarled to the crewmen as the bus door tonged open. There were a dozen women near the ship, but only one or two of them carried weapons openly. The men obeyed with alacrity handicapped by the narrow aisle.

"Feel like coming along yourself?" Slade added to Mayor Rodrigues in an undertone.

"Do you think you're that good, Mister Slade?" the Mayor answered. "You're not, you know." She swallowed angrily, as if she expected the big man to hit her.

"Guess we'll never know," Slade said mildly as he stepped to the door behind the other men. "You're probably making a good decision anyway."

The tanker did not look back as he pounded up the ramp to the bridge hatch. He held the commo unit high in his left hand. The women watched the crew scuttle aboard with only the interest an event brings, not a catastrophe. How many times had they used up and discarded the crew of a freighter? You could hate cultures, but that didn't help you any. . . . Evil wasn't the affair of a professional soldier.

By the Lord, though, it was the business of Don Slade.

The ramp was already lifting to close the hatch as the tanker threw himself aboard. "Go! Go! Go!" he bellowed down the corridor. The hatch sealed with a sigh and a shock that reflection said was Transit but clutching fear had identified as gunfire. GAC 59 was clear of Erlette; the Lord knew where, but clear.

There was chaos on the bridge. "Stations!" the tanker shouted as he bulled his way through smaller men. "First shift to Transit stations, everybody else the hell out of the operations area!" He had briefed them in the Sperm Bank. There was no time now for yammering indiscipline.

Crewmen scurried to their duty stations or out into the corridor again. That left Slade on the bridge with Levine, Snipes, and one of the Meeting members—Rooks. Slade wondered if Rooks' partner, Bourgiby, had been an overdose fatality on Erlette. The tanker seated himself on the analog tub which had become his usual spot. He looked at the commo unit which he still held. Sighing, he replaced it in its belt sheath.

"You should've taken your finger off just before we lifted," Levine said savagely.

"Wouldn't have changed a thing," said Slade. He rubbed his eyes. He had gotten no sleep at all for over thirty hours. "I'd cut the power lead to this thing," he said, tapping the unit without looking down, "so they wouldn't get a blip if my thumb slipped. That'd tell them it was a fake."

"A fake?" Rooks repeated. "You didn't really have a bomb like you said?"

Slade stood up angrily. "Look," he said, "I'm a tank officer, not a technician. Sure, I suppose you could rig a bomb and a command detonator out of even the gear available on this tub. But *I* couldn't, not in a couple hours. Via! I put something together that looked real to me. And I prayed to the Lord that our friends down there—" he gestured toward a bulkhead. Only context could indicate that he meant the Erlette authorities— "couldn't prove it wasn't real except by daring me to fire it." Slade smiled past his restless irritation. "Things could've gotten interesting if they'd pushed."

"I was just about to stick it in," said Rooks. His voice built by stages from reflection to anger. "She patted me on the back of the neck and I thought 'The bitch ought to trim her nails.' And then I couldn't feel anything where she nicked me. Then my whole body. Couple hours ago I come around, my neck hurts and my butt hurts where they'd jabbed me again. And they load forty of us in a truck like cordwood, still half zonked and bare-ass naked. I wish you'd blown up every bloody one of the bitches!"

Levine and Snipes were nodding, perhaps for different reasons. Slade said, "It's not the people, it's their culture. And that's something their grandmothers locked them into. Ever been on Eutyche?"

Blank looks greeted the question. The tanker shrugged and continued. "They lock women up there. From birth. When she's sold into marriage, the father and brothers carry the girl to the husband under guard. Let your daughter run on the street and she'll be stoned to death by your neighbors before they burn your house down over you. It's not people there, and it's not people here on Erlette. It's just the way people live."

"Well, that may be, Captain Slade," said Levine. He was showing a little more backbone than his previous norm. "But it's a problem that has to be solved, this culture. And the only way I see to solve it was as Mister Rooks says. Blow them all up."

"There's some might say the same about other things; like this ship, hey?" Slade gibed. He rang his knuckles off a console for emphasis. "Isn't true, though. Not about Erlette, anyhow."

Slade struck a stance in the middle of the deck with his left fist raised. He extended the index finger. "They don't need men, because they've got the Sperm Bank." He extended the middle finger with the fist. "There's enough traffic here to keep the gene pool fluid and it seems to scratch any itches for something beyond lips and prosthetics that may arise among the citizens."

Slade's ring finger flipped up also. "So male infants go for the chop. Nobody could hide their baby boy through puberty . . . and even then, it'd just be something to hunt for officials who get into that sort of thing. You've got a society maintained by people like Deputy Brandt."

"So blow it bloody up!" snapped Rooks.

Slade smiled. "No," he said, "blow up the bloody Sperm Bank." He folded his fingers back into a fist. "Then they've got to coddle every male they've got, infants or immigrants. Or else their whole world goes down the tubes when the population drops below a viable level. Like a lot of places did where there was too small a settlement to begin with. Like Stagira, I suspect. That's all it would take."

"Then it *is* too bad your bomb wasn't real," Snipes said. It was hard to tell if his sourness resulted from the fact that a gynocratic society had not been smashed, or if the tone belonged to his interaction with Slade earlier.

The tanker laughed as he seated himself again on the analog device. "Via," he said, "the bomb was real enough. It was the controls I had to fake."

The other three men stiffened. "The Cylobar was

just as real as what we blew clear of Stagira with,"
Slade explained. "So were the blasting caps. Just
how real, I guess they learned on Erlette when we
jumped and the Transit fields generated a current in the leads."

Slade's lips smiled like a dog worrying flesh.
"And I only hope Deputy Brandt and her crew had
gotten into the building by that time."

CHAPTER EIGHTEEN

"He smashed the culture for spite," thought Elysium. *"Not because he believed the replacement would be better."*

"It will be better," the other current noted. Extrapolations flickering through the group consciousness supported that view.

"But all that mattered to him was bringing down the structure around the ears of those who had threatened him," pressed the flow that was too rigorous to be hostile, too chilling not to be negative.

"What he did," closed the other current, *"benefitted individuals and Mankind. If he acted from instinct rather than belief, so much the better for him . . . and for his universe, which is our universe as well. . . ."*

"When it's somebody else's specialty," Don Slade was saying, "and they've pulled it out every time despite the disaster they're predicting, then it's easy to discount what they say the next time. It happens—I'm told it happens—in military settings, too."

Those who *knew* as well as heard Slade were flashed a glass-edged vision: *the doorway of a command post, three men in gray uniforms pistol-shot on the ground and the neck of the fourth being broken by Slade's bloody hands.*

184

"They always think you can hold it if you've held before," Slade muttered. "They tell me."

The big man cleared his throat. "So it shouldn't have been a shock when we popped out of Transit only a kay above the ground the next time . . ."

The buzzer went off. All the instrument consoles were bathed in red lights. Such warnings were unnecessary, because only the dead could doubt there was an emergency when the starship flipped on its back in a gravity well.

Slade was on the bridge as usual during maneuvering. He was not strapped in. GAC 59 had no facilities to immobilize as many men as the ship now carried. Besides, the hot LZs on which the tanker was trained had no time for such frills.

Slade's legs shot up because his arms hugged the curve of the analog tub instinctively. Then Levine righted the ship in a corkscrew motion through a massive forward thrust. As a result, GAC 59 was moving at over a hundred kph when it plowed through the trees and into a field. Things began happening in a hurry. Slade probably lost his grip before the display unit shredded its clamps and flew into a console. By then the question was academic, even to Slade himself.

The sirens of the emergency vehicles merged in Slade's mind with the screams. Some of the screams were his own. . . .

"Because," Slade said, and the speakers amplified his voice so that it could be heard by all the hundred and three other survivors, "the authorities here think they're being exceptionally nice in not standing us against a wall and shooting us every one."

The tanker nodded toward the double doors of the hall. Many of the mercenaries turned to look also, though they all knew what they would see there. The detachment of Rusatan police wore neat, white uniforms. Some of them seemed unfamiliar with the submachineguns they had been issued for this detail. Those were the only guns in the room, however, and they were gripped the tighter when the local men felt the mercenaries looking at them.

"So," Slade continued from the dais, "staying here on Rusata isn't an option. Unless you figure to stay the way the folks will who were too late for the medics."

Men looked at one another, at themselves. The Rusatans had given the crash victims excellent medical treatment, but reconstruction had stopped with grafts of synthetic skin. Prosthetics, the locals had noted bluntly, were the business of the mercenaries themselves. The salvage value of GAC 59 would not cover the cost of necessary treatment— and the necessary shipment of the survivors off a world their presence would disrupt.

"It's not *fair*!" muttered Captain Levine. He sat beside Slade on the dais. "She was *my* ship. I ought at least to have had all she brought for scrap."

"That wasn't an option either, my friend," said the tanker in a low, dangerous voice. Slade cut on the amplifier again and continued, "So we have the choice of leaving on either of the ships in port right now. That's a human tramp out of Barmaki; and an Alayan ship."

"Those're the ones that look like bloody light-wands?" somebody demanded from the audience.

"The Alayans have exoskeletons, yes," Slade replied. He raised his voice so that it would ride over the disgust. "They have eight limbs, and they speak to humans through vocalizers. They also—" his voice went up a further notch; he rose to focus attention—"have extremely well-found ships, although they don't operate on the same principles that ours do. Captain Levine is going to talk to you now about the other choice."

Slade sat down. Levine glanced at the gathered men, then looked at his boots again. "It won't—" he began. Slade reached across the spacer and flicked the mike on his epaulette to 'ON'. "I've been over the ship," Levine resumed. "They want us bad, so they're making a price to Rusata. Doesn't do cop for us . . ."

He looked up. In a stronger voice, Levine continued. "It won't get us there. Not one more landing, not two or I'm the Messiah. They want us because they're worse-crewed than we were, and their captain thinks he can make Barmaki with me and what's left of my people." Levine nodded. Three or four of the audience nodded back, the remnant of GAC 59's crew.

"But they can't," Levine said. He stood up as Slade had done, but without the tanker's deliberation. Levine's hands washed each other unnoticed. "I don't know how they got here. One of their generators has kicked out three times, and it's heaven's own providence they weren't actually *in* Transit when it happened. Their captain hoped I could help fix it. You *can't* fix a generator except to pull out the boards and replace them. They're trying to use jumpers to the other generators, heaven blast me if I lie!''

Captain Levine paused, then sat down abruptly. In a lowered voice he closed, "I—I don't want the bugs either. But we'll all die if we ship with the Barmacids. I'm sure of it."

"The Alayans offer passage for as far along their route as the individual wants," Slade said over the worried murmur. "They won't alter their course, but they'll disembark passengers at any point. So long as the ground authorities are willing. They say that eighty to ninety percent of the worlds they touch are human, and—"

"And that's cop!" roared someone from the audience.

"All right, maybe it is!" Slade shouted back with the support of the amplifier. "But we know they *do* land on human worlds or they wouldn't be here, would they?"

Breathing hard, but in a more reasonable voice, the tanker went on. "People, this is no time to wedge our heads. We can take passage to someplace livable with the Alayans—or we can jump straight to Hell with the Barmacids. If anybody's that determined to die, there's people right here can probably oblige him." Slade waved again at the police.

The tanker had risen to a half crouch during his burst of anger. Now he settled himself again in his chair as the audience buzzed. "Oh," Slade added, "there's one other thing. Some of you may have the notion that going off in a human ship might leave the way open to—opportunities. Other than settling someplace." He nodded toward the police detachment, this time to explain why he had chosen a euphemism instead of saying piracy. "No guns leave here with us. Everything aboard GAC 59 except your asses and mine became government property when we crashed. If you don't like the word salvaged, you can say confiscated. It won't bother the locals a scrap, and it's how things are."

The buzzing lowered despondently.

"Now," Slade concluded, "you were each issued a ballot and a stylus when they marched you in. There's a box for your votes right here." He pointed to the foot of the dais. "We all go the way the majority decides. You mark A for Alayans, B for Barmacids. You drop it in the box. And if you want to live, you mark an A."

Levine shut off his microphone. As the hall rustled with men marking ballots, the spacer whispered, "I wonder what they'd vote if they knew the Alayan ship drives people crazy?"

Slade shut off his mike as well. "A chance of going crazy's better than near certainty of being lost in Transit," he whispered back. "So they'd for sure vote the same way they're going to now."

The first of the castaways were shuffling toward the box, clutching their ballots.

"Just as sure as I'm doing the counting," Don Slade concluded in a voice that did not move his lips.

The screams were attenuated by the hundred meters of corridor between Slade and their source. They were still easily loud enough to identify. The tanker was off his mattress and running for the sound even before his conscious mind was aware of the occurrence it had dreaded.

The Alayan starship was an assemblage of globes

joined by tubes. The ship appeared to have as
much and as little geometric certainty as a spider's
web. That is, the basic form was certain, but the
location of any single element within the whole
might well have been random.

There was no way the ship itself could land or
take off in a gravity well. Two of the globes carried
lighters for ferrying cargo and passengers to the
vessel in orbit. It had concerned Slade to realize
that the lighters were of human manufacture though
none of the vessel's other apparatus was. The situation suggested absurdly that the Alayans had not
touched down on planets before their scattered vessels encountered humans some centuries before.

The survivors of GAC 59 were in three connected
globes. The decks and fittings within were of plastic with evident mold marks. The globes themselves,
like the tubular corridors which joined them,
seemed chitinously natural.

Now men were running toward Slade down the
corridor as if the screams were whips behind them.
The fugitives were an incident of passage to the
big tanker, an impediment through which he tram-
pled as he would have a sleet storm.

There were no artificial weapons in the human
sections of the ship. The Alayans had segregated
even the slight personal effects the Rusatans had
let the survivors take on board. Men played ball
with wadded sheets and played checkers with scraps
of fabric on a board scribed on the deck with
fingernails. It was boring as Hell, but it should
have been safe.

Stoudemeyer leaped from his victim, Captain
Levine. Levine was the third, judging from the
wrack in the blood-splattered room. The pearly

glow from the ceiling glistened on Stoudemeyer's face. The man from Telemark now looked a bestial caricature of a man. Someone had clawed out Stoudemeyer's left eye so that it hung down his cheek by the nerve. Most of the blood on his face and bare chest had come from the throats of his victims, however—like Levine, now in spraying convulsions beneath his killer.

Slade snatched the blanket from an abandoned bunk. "Easy now, sol—" he began.

Stoudemeyer grinned wider and launched himself at the tanker.

The blanket had been extended for a makeshift net. Slade was wholly confident in his strength. He planned to wrap the madman in the fabric and hold him without further injury until more help dribbled back to view the excitement. Stoudemeyer's furious attack was no surprise, but the madman's strength was. Despite a conscious awareness of hysterical strength, Don Slade had met very few men who could overpower him under any circumstances.

As the short, pudgy Stoudemeyer proceeded to do.

The madman's clawed hands swept the blanket down. Slade caught Stoudemeyer's wrists and held him, but the blanket tangled both their legs. They staggered sideways and fell as a pair, Stoudemeyer on top. His face was marked with streaks and bubbles of blood. He glared at Slade with his good eye while the other bobbled on his cheek.

Slade shouted. He thrust upward against Stoudemeyer's wrists with all his strength. The madman giggled and continued to force his claws down toward his victim. Stoudemeyer's bloody gape was lowering toward Slade's throat inexorably.

Black with snarling madness himself, the tanker bit at Stoudemeyer's scalp. It was the only part of the shorter man Slade could reach with his teeth. They gouged hair and blood vessels aside before they skidded on bone. It was a useless attempt; but to Slade it was better than shouting for help that would not come.

Something bathed him in cold light.

Slade had been wounded before. He had even been left for dead on a field with hundreds of bomb fragments in his body. His flesh had chilled then and his mind had withdrawn to a single hot spark throbbing like an overloaded transformer.

He had never before been ice all over, though with full command of his senses. Slade could feel the tickling strands of Stoudemeyer's hair against the roof of his mouth. He could also feel the edge of the madman's incisors, against the pulse of the tanker's throat and just short of slashing through it.

The members that lifted Stoudemeyer gently away were blue and they were not hands. Slade could no longer control his field of vision. In and out of it drifted several Alayans. There were flickers of light at the violet end of the human range. It could have been cross-talk among the aliens . . . or synapses stuttering in Slade's own brain.

Sucker-tipped tendrils lifted the tanker upright. Something swabbed at the peak of his breastbone. The touch was cold momentarily as all things were cold. Then natural warmth and control flooded back through Slade's body.

"We regret," purred the vocalizer of one of the

three Alayans, "that we struck you also, Mr. Slade." The Alayan waggled the device he held in one of his upper limbs. The object looked like petrified sea-foam, but it was not difficult to connect it with the stunning chill that had ended the fight. "We could not be sure in the haste of the moment which of you was the attacker."

"Umm," Slade said. He spat to clear his mouth, then rubbed his lips. "Yeah."

The other two Alayans had lifted Stoudemeyer. The madman was still in a state of supple uncontrol as the Alayan device had left him. The Alayans were carrying Stoudemeyer toward the opening through which they had entered the passenger section. That passage was normally closed to humans.

"Wait a—" Slade began. Humans were entering the compartment again. Late-comers tried to push aside the earlier returnees who tended to conglomerate at the ends of the corridor instead of coming fully within the spattered compartment.

In a lower voice, the tanker continued. "Look, we've got to talk. I need to know—" his tongue paused between two questions, settled on the short-term one—"where you're taking him."

"Come," said the Alayan's vocalizer as he touched it. There was a flash of violet light from one of the six stalked projections—surely not heads—atop the alien's carapace. It might have been meant for a nod. "We will explain that to you. And now that you have more knowledge, we will explain again what you can expect to happen on the voyage."

The Alayan moved toward the exit after his companions and Stoudemeyer. His four lower limbs

made delicate, twinkling motions so that his tall
body seemed to roll rather than walk.

Slade wondered morosely as he followed whether
the Alayan had made a lucky guess at the unspo-
ken question, or whether they could read human
minds.

The corridor blurred in both directions as soon
as the door to the passenger chamber spasmed
closed. There was no apparent beginning or end to
the tube, and there was no sign of Stoudemeyer or
the aliens who had carried him off.

"You've dumped him into—" Slade waved a hand
at the glowing blue wall of the corridor. "Dumped
him outside. Didn't you?"

"Assuredly not, Mister Slade," said the soft, mechanical voice. "He will be cared for, be repaired
physically, as ably as possible. We will keep him
sedated, or co—"

"You're going to use him to drive the ship," the
tanker broke in again. Levine had told him the
scuttlebutt about the Alayan drive, suggestions that
the Alayans themselves had not denied in discussions before Slade made the survivors' decision for
them. A warping of real space very different from
the human technique of entering a separate Transit
universe. A warping of space achieved through the
warping of a human mind, the rumors went. . . .

"No, Mister Slade," replied the dancing fingers
on the vocalizer, "we *have* used him to drive the
ship. We cannot use his mind again, because it no
longer has a basis in objective reality. That is
always the case, I am afraid. You were aware of
the situation when you accepted our offer of
transport."

Slade ignored the last part of the statement. It was true; he simply did not care to dwell on it. "They always go—go berserk like Stoudemeyer just did?"

Light of no discernible hue played over one of the Alayan's—faces; a shrug of sorts. "Rarely that. We apologize. Generally catatonia, sometimes other forms of aberration. We did not expect this—" Warmth spread across the human's skin that implied the speaker had gestured in the infra-red. "—but one cannot be certain what the ash will look like when one burns a log."

"And you can't—do this—travel—yourselves," Slade asked through a grimace that reflected his difficulty in finding words. Slade no longer believed he was simply in a tube connected to the passenger compartment, though he had no better explanation of where the Alayan might have taken him.

"Any sentient mind will serve the purpose," said the Alayan. "Any mind with a grasp of reality and the ability to change reality through—fantasy, if you will. We direct the fantasies so that they become real . . . and the vessel moves in objective reality through the—pressure of the subject's mind. Unfortunately, that mind moves as well, in a psychic dimension from which it cannot be retrieved. We could use ourselves as subjects, but we do not do so while we have minds aboard which are not ours. That is the main value for which we trade."

The listening human realized that there would have been no hostility or even emotion in the words whether or not they were the construct of a vocalizer. The Alayans did not hate their passengers; nor did they treat humans cruelly, the way humans were often wont to do to their own species. It was a simple operation, like *triage*: separating victims into those who would survive and those who would not. Nothing in the process implied a desire that some not survive . . . a wish for Kile Stoudemeyer to bite through his fellows' throats and to spend the rest of his life in total sedation.

But better that than similar destruction of an Alayan mind. The choice, after all, was the Alayans'.

"I knew," Slade said, aloud but more to himself than to the exoskeletal creature before him, "that people—some of us—might go nuts because of your drive. I mean, Transit hits some people like that, the sensation's different for everybody . . . and it makes some people snap. I didn't figure that it wasn't *may* go nuts, it was like firing a gun and watching the empty case spit out. I think we'd better, ah, disembark at the next landfall. Unless—I mean, how many stops can you make on the—" Slade did not pause, but his lips stuck momentarily in a rictus as he finished, "—present fuel?"

"Everyone who wishes to leave and is permitted to do so by the planetary authorities," said the Alayan, "may of course disembark on Terzia. There will have to be a second—impetus—to reach that world, Mister Slade. More than that to reach any other planet which could be suitable for your purpose, for your leaving the ship."

Slade hammered his fist into the corridor wall. The wall absorbed the blow with a massive resilience like that of deep sod. The hazy light seemed to fluctuate.

"You may do as you see fit, Mister Slade," the alien went on. His faces flickered, occasionally in the visible spectrum, "but I would suggest that

you not discuss the situation in detail with your
fellows until you have landed. It would cause
distress, and it would probably lead to violence
and injuries more serious than any the need of
propulsion will cause."

"Who goes next?" the tanker demanded as he
stared at his hand.

"The choice is generally random," the vocalizer
said. "Not you, of course. Though if there is someone you would like to choose for the next segment?
Or however far you choose to prolong the associa-
tion after you have had time to reflect."

"Anyone?" Slade said. He turned and looked at
the alien: the courteous, slim-bodied creature who
was discussing his human cargo like lambs in a
pen. "Shouldn't be hard to find somebody dead
worthless in this lot, you'd think. . . ."

Not hard at all. Some of the outlaws were men
Don Slade had been on the verge of killing a time
or two himself. There were others, a few, whom
the tanker still did not know by name. They were
without personalities—to Slade. Without any of
the factors that would have made them people
instead of objects.

And there were those whom the crash of GAC 59
had disabled: paraplegics for whom no therapy
could do no more than maintain life, limbless torsos
who would be shambling wrecks even with better
prosthetics than they were ever likely to afford.

No problem for Don Slade. No problem for Captain Slade, who had hosed innocents with cyan
fire during more operations than he cared to
remember.

"All right," the tanker whispered to his clenched
fist. "Take me." He turned his back on the Alayan.

In the hollow distance, there was no sign of the door by which they had entered the corridor.

"You mean, Mister Slade—" began the mechanical voice. Its tone could not be hesitant, but the words' pacing was.

"I mean use me in your drive, curse it!" Slade shouted as he spun around. "I—"

He paused. The anger melted away from the fear it had been intended to cloak. Then the fear surrendered itself to the honesty of desperation. "There's none of them worth the powder to blow them away," the tanker whispered. "And I've sent men to die, the *Lord* knows. . . . But these're mine, like it or don't. And it's all too much like deciding who to butcher so that the rest of the lifeboat gets another meal. I'm not going to do that."

"Your principles do you credit, Mister Slade," said the Alayan, "but as the leader—"

"I don't have any bloody principles!" Slade said. "I'm just not going to axe one of *my* men for no better reason than to save my ass. Besides—" more calmly, now; almost diffident— "I don't see. . . . I mean, some of those fellows aren't bolted together real tight. Me, though . . . well, you'll see."

The Alayan's exoskeleton dulled for a moment to an almost perfect matte finish. Then the sheen that Slade had equated with health, but which probably indicated something else, returned. "All right, Mister Slade," the alien said. One of his tendrils played over an object on the belt around his midsection. The corridor began to fall in on itself. A door formed in the end of it as there had been when the pair entered. "You will not feel anything. There will be no pain. I cannot tell you exactly when it will happen, though it will not be soon."

Slade nodded. He stepped to the door. It was already opening onto the globe in which Slade had been sleeping when Stoudemeyer went berserk in the adjacent compartment.

"And Mister Slade," continued the voice which the tanker did not turn to face, "this passage will open for you if you wish to reconsider your decision."

"I won't," said Slade as he rejoined the wondering humans who called him their leader.

CHAPTER NINETEEN

Slade whuffled in his sleep. The blanket covered him for its feel rather than for need of warmth in the controlled climate of the passenger globe. Slade's hands tugged the fabric closer and his body shifted slightly. There was nothing to awaken the men snoring in darkness to either side of the tanker.

There was nothing to indicate to them that Don Slade was in Hell.

Slade was not sure how he had gotten there this time, though there was nothing unfamiliar about his surroundings. It was night, and thirty degrees of the horizon bubbled and writhed with the inverted orange funnel of a fire-storm. Somebody had been caught without nuclear dampers. A fusion bomb had gone off and had found fuel enough in the target area to multiply blast effect a thousandfold with winds of living flame.

But where was his tank? Where in *hell* was his tank, Hell was his tank . . . ?"

There was nothing nearby but mud and shattered trees. Powerguns slashed the distance with blue-green bolts. Occasionally they were answered or amplified by flares of high explosives that preceded their shock waves by many seconds. The mid-level overcast reflected the spire of the fire-storm into a soft, ghastly ambiance. It lighted the figure picking its way toward Slade across the mud and shell-holes.

Reflex moved the tanker's hand toward the pistol which should have been in his belt. The pistol was not there, however; and his hand was either missing or not responding to control. Slade could not be sure. Vision was no longer quite the accustomed process either.

"Sing out!" called Don Slade in warning. It was what he would have done if he were armed, if he could have slipped to cover behind a stump. What was *wrong* with his—

"What's the matter, Don?" called the oncoming figure. The voice was a pleasant tenor that cut through the hissing wind. "There's nothing more to fear, is there?"

"Via," said the tanker. "*Via*! Major Steuben!"

"Oh, call me Joachim, Don," said the other figure. "You did when we were alive, after all. And anyway, we're all equal here."

"Joachim," the big man begged. "Where are we?"

There could be no doubt that it really was Joachim Steuben. The uniform that rustled like a whore's undergarments; the boyishly-smooth face and the curly black hair, signs of wealth spent lavishly when they could no longer truly be signs of youth. The pistol in a cutaway holster high on Joachim's right hip, an ornamented bangle for a mincing queen—until he chose to kill. Joachim Steuben, slim and dainty as a white mouse . . . and the unit he commanded on the jobs for which no one else quite had the stomach, the White Mice. The Greeks, after all, had called their Furies the Kindly-Minded Ones.

Major Steuben commanded the White Mice until he died.

"Why Don," the trim figure said. "We're where people like you and I go when we die. We're in Hell." Steuben giggled, a sound that Slade remembered too well to mistake it for humor. "We're where everybody goes."

Something passed overhead with a freight-train rush, an artillery salvo aimed twenty kilometers down-range. The ground trembled to its passage.

"Joachim," Slade said. "I think we ought to get out of here." His legs would not move, he could not *see* his legs. "I think I'm going to need your help. I don't—"

"I thought loyalty was the answer," said Joachim. He spoke conversationally. The dead major was ignoring Slade's words as one may ignore another's words at a party, where there will be plenty of time for the other to make his point later . . . and none of it makes any difference anyway. "Be perfectly loyal to a man, answer his needs even when his words don't admit those needs." Joachim gestured with a dainty hand. "Do you know what loyalty brings you, Donnie?"

"Joachim, I didn't—" Slade began. He respected Major Steuben, but he feared Steuben as well. Joachim was like a tank under the control of someone else; not necessarily hostile, but unstoppably lethal if it was chosen to be.

"Loyalty," Steuben continued in his smooth lilt and harsh smile, "brings you a shot in the back."

"I didn't shoot you, Joachim!" the tanker said.

"I know who killed me, Don," said the smiling figure. "And I know that nothing matters." Joachim reached out with his right hand, his gun hand, and made as if to stroke Slade's cheek. The smooth palm did not or did not quite touch the tanker. "Do you fancy me now, Donnie?" the slim man said.

Slade tried to lick his lips. "I don't think so, Joachim," he said.

Joachim giggled. "It's as good as any offer you'll get here, my friend," he said. "And as bad, of course. I'm not real, you know."

The slim figure turned. The back of the silk uniform rustled. The cloth was tattered and charred around the crater which a cyan bolt had left in killing the Major. "Nothing is real for you any more, Donnie," Joachim called as he walked back through the wasteland. The sky warmed the brightwork of his pistol's frame. "Nothing ever will be real," said the lilting voice as the wind swallowed it at last.

"I'm going home, Joachim," Slade called. "Home is real. Joachim Steuben! *I'm* real!"

Across the horizon from the fire-storm, a calliope began to rave at the sky.

"What's the matter, brother?" asked a voice behind Slade. "Don't feel like such a big man now, is that it?"

Don turned his attention with the care of a man who needs a further moment to think. Via, do *I* look that old? Aloud he said, "Hello, Tom. I didn't expect to find you here."

"But it's just the place for Mad Dog Slade, isn't it, brother?" said Tom. He gestured at the shattered forest, at the shot-split night. "So it's the place for me, too, now that we're the same. Now that we're dead."

They were fraternal twins, not identical; but they

shared some features, and they had the same deep, powerful chests. Tom Slade was stocky where his brother was simply big; and the years since they separated had not been kind to the man who had stayed on Tethys. The orange haze hid the change in hair color, from fair to white; but the individual strands were coarser, now, and they were strewn at wider intervals across Tom's scalp than they had been twenty years before. Tom's face was wrinkled. At the moment, the wrinkling was exaggerated by the bitter grimace into which Tom had screwed his mouth.

"No," Don said slowly. "I don't think it's the place for me, Tom. Or either of us. Let's see if we can't find a way out, shall we?"

"Why?" snarled Tom. He moved closer with his hands spread at his sides, as if to grapple with his bigger brother. A blade had entered beneath Tom's ribs on the left side. The edge had been sharp enough to be drawn up diagonally through bone and the organs of the thorax. Tom's shirt flopped away from the gash. The bloody stain on the fabric seemed glisteningly fresh. "So you could kill me yourself, Don? I know you've always wanted to, dear brother. Well, you're too late. I'm *dead*." Tom's left hand deliberately spread the lips of his wound. "And you're dead too."

The tanker tried to reach out for his brother's dripping hand, but he still had no control over his own limbs. "Tom," he said softly. "I maybe wasn't what you wanted in a brother, but I never hated you. And . . . Via, Tom, if I'd wanted you dead, you wouldn't have had to wait around for it. Come on, help me and we'll get the hell out of here."

"We can't get out!" the shorter man shouted. "We can't! Don't you understand that?"

"No, I don't understand," Don said simply. "Look, I *have* been these places—" he would have gestured to the waste around them— "that's no more than the truth. And I'm not interested in standing around in another one, buck naked or whatever the *hell* I am. Now *help* me, curse it!"

The other figure slumped back from the tanker. "I can't even help myself," Tom said. "Any more than I could help my jealousy of you when we were alive. And I'd tell you I was sorry, Don, but it doesn't really matter now. Nothing—" and the figure turned, walking away from Don Slade as distant sirens howled—"ever mattered. I see that now. . . ."

"Tom!" the tanker called. "*Tom!*"

"Shouldn't bother you that he doesn't listen to you," said another voice. "After all, you never listened to anybody else, did you?"

The speakers always approached from behind; but Don Slade noticed that however he turned, the glare of the fire-storm was on his left side. "Hello, Father," he said. "I guess I could have figured that you'd be here."

Councilor Slade looked much the same as he had when Don last saw him on Tethys. That was not surprising. Though the Councilor had lived eighteen years after Don left home as a recruit for Hammer's Slammers, he had always seemed aged.

As with the son who had succeeded him, time and duties had taken a harsh toll from Councilor Slade. His hair was gone, save for a fringe, and his eyebrows were starkly white as they pinched together in the angry expression Don remembered so well.

"Then I'm sure I've given you some pleasure," the Councilor snapped in reply. "Cherish it, brat. You'll find no other pleasure ever again."

"I guess I am glad to see you," the tanker said. "I've regretted the way we parted often enough. I don't mean I'd have ever come back to Tethys if you were—" the swallow would not come—"still alive. But I wanted a chance to apologize for my part in the way things worked out. It wasn't all my fault, but I'm sorry for the part that was."

"You're a liar!" the Councilor screamed. He clenched his fist and shook it. His frailty would have made the gesture ridiculous were it not for the fury that glinted from the close-set eyes.

Three shells burst squarely overhead. They were so high that the pops of the charges were several seconds behind the red sparkle. Don cringed, equating the mild warning for the rain of fire and fragment the pops presaged. Aloud he said, "Do people tell lies here, Father? I don't feel like it myself." Then, "Why did Tom say he was jealous of me? He's the one who had it all."

"Did he?" Councilor Slade said with a gibing laugh. "You're the one who had Marilee, though, aren't you?"

"I knew the lady," Don admitted. He was surprised to learn that an anger hotter than mere frustration was still possible for him in his present guise. "And she brought me down about as hard as I care to remember. I don't say I didn't deserve it, but . . . she *married* Tom, he *knew* he'd won that one!"

"He knew much better than that, boy," said

Councilor Slade. "But you've lost here forever, now."

There was a deadly hush across the wasteland. "Go on, brat!" Councilor Slade cackled. "Call me a liar! Call me a liar!"

And the bomblets from the firecracker rounds overhead began to burst across the landscape like the white heart of a furnace.

The scintillant blur was too bright and total for there to be any other sound or shape in Slade's universe. He should have felt the shrapnel gouging him apart, but the circumstances that prevented him from taking cover also seemed to shield him from the agony of dissolution. Slade rode on the white tide, buoyed up by the blasts whose crackling merged into a roar which in turn became cotton-flock silent.

And toward him through the fluffy silence walked Marilee in high boots and a flame-colored body suit.

"Oh, Via, girl," Slade whispered. "Oh my Lord. Are you dead too, Marilee?"

The wasteland was gone. The light that bathed the cloud-top ambiance was a soft white instead of the hellish orange of the previous scene. Marilee smiled. She looked older; but dear Lord, they all were older, it had been twenty years. "No, Don," the tall woman said. "I'm not dead, any more than you are."

She stretched out a long-fingered hand. Slade reached instinctively to meet her, and he *did* have an arm that moved, a body he could see—

But their hands did not quite touch. As the big man took a step forward to fold Marilee into his arms, she raised a finger in warning and shook her head.

Slade froze. "You're not real," he said in a flat voice.

"I'm very real," Marilee said, "but what you see now isn't my physical body, Don." Her grin flashed in a way that tore him with the recollection. "For that matter, you're not really *seeing* anything ... but I suppose you'd figured that out."

"More or less," Slade said. "What I'd mainly figured was I wanted to get out of this bloody place." He shrugged the shoulders he could now see and feel again. "That place, I mean. But I'd rather be on Tethys than here, too, so long as ... well, you're still on Tethys, Marilee?"

"The part of me that isn't in your mind, yes," the woman said. "We could use you there. But there's a problem."

"Shoot," said the tanker. He could not solve all problems, but he knew that he could solve most of them if he had the time to mumble the details over in his brain.

Marilee lounged back onto haze that seemed to have no more solid reality than any other part of the surroundings. "You see, Don," she said, "your mind is driving an Alayan ship to a planet called Terzia. And at the same time, your mind is creating a false reality for itself. You'll be incurably insane when the ship reaches Terzia. You won't be able to recognize reality."

Slade's tongue touched one corner of his mouth, then the other. "I won't be able to recognize you?" he asked.

"Your reality will be within your mind," the

woman said. She was smiling again. "As this is."
Her spread fingers gestured. "As I am."

"Then I'll make a reality in which I'm sane,"
said Slade. He stepped forward. His voice rose as
he added, "By the Lord, I *will!*"

Marilee's image receded from Slade without los-
ing its infinite clarity. Her smile was broader.
"That's right, Don," she called as she disappeared.
"Remember that we need you on Tethys. . . ."

Slade grunted and swung to his feet. The men
sleeping near him did not notice. The three Alayans
who had entered the globe sprang to alertness like
semaphore arms working. All the Alayans carried
the frothy apparatus with which Stoudemeyer and
Slade had earlier been subdued. The flickers of
radiant cross-talk were strikingly obvious since
the globe had been darkened for the passengers to
sleep.

"Hey, stay calm," the tanker said. He raised his
hands close to his shoulders, palms forward. It
was a gesture of submission, but it was a pretty
fair posture to strike from also. Slade knew he was
not crazy, but he did not intend to be frozen into
permanent silence before he could explain that to
the Alayans.

"We apologize for disturbing you, Mister Slade,"
said the middle of the three aliens, "but we are
now in orbit around Terzia. Would you please come
with us so that we can make arrangements with
the planetary authorities?"

Other humans were awakening in the compartment. The lights began to come up smoothly,
though it was some hours before they would have

done so in the normal cycle. There was a buzz of conversation. Somebody cheered.

"Listen, that's fine," said Slade with a false smile. "But there's no problem, you see? I'm all right. Why don't you just drop those things for the moment?" He twirled his index finger toward the glove-like stunners without lowering his hands from their position of defense. "I'm fine, believe me."

The Alayans did not need to turn to look at one another because of their multiple faces. The chamber danced with coded light for a moment. Then the alien in the center dropped his device on the floor. His vocalizer said as his companions followed his lead, "Of course, Mister Slade. If you'll just step this way."

The tanker was not surprised to find himself in a corridor without termini, facing a single Alayan instead of the trio with which he had left the globe. "Now, I know what you're thinking," Slade said hastily, "but it didn't work that way with me. I'm still sane."

"I will not argue definitions with you, Mister Slade," said the Alayan. "If you mean that you perceive the same reality that you did—earlier . . . the reality that I perceive—then I think you are wrong."

Slade gestured, tossing distinctions into the air. "Look," he said, "it doesn't matter. The main thing is that you know I'm not dangerous. Right?"

A scintillant pattern played across all of the Alayan's faces. Slade did not understand what had happened until the vocalizer spoke. With its mechanical lack of humor, it said, "We know that you are not dangerous, Mad Dog Slade?"

The tanker began to laugh. The tension of the past forty hours, while he waited to be driven mad, released itself in guffaws that doubled Slade over. "Via, Via," he wheezed when he could get his breath. "Somebody's been talking to you, haven't they? Well."

Calmer, but with a smile still cramping his cheeks, Slade went on. "Still, you know what I mean. I swear to goodness if it weren't for some of the things about your ship, I'd travel around with you just to get to know you people better."

The big man sobered fully. He added, "After I'd taken care of some things back home. I hear they need me there."

His face was as placid as a gun barrel.

CHAPTER TWENTY

"He led those who trusted him into Hell," noted the dispassionate mind of Elysium. *"He decided for them, so that some died and some went mad without any knowledge of what they were being sent into."*

"He led them," responded the other current. *"He decided for men who had chosen him to decide. When it came to a clear choice, he was willing to sacrifice himself for those he led."*

"I thought it was simple enough," Slade said to the Elysians facing him. "We'd disembark at the first world we hit, Terzia it was going to be. Now that we knew, *I* knew, I've got to admit—what sailing with the Alayans meant. And the tenders brought everybody down to the surface of the planet without argument.

"But the trouble started when I formed everybody up between the tenders and the Citadel to hear the new plans . . ."

"This might be worth it for booze and women," muttered Bourgiby as he mopped sweat from his neck, "but so far I've seen damn none of them around."

The landed castaways were watched over by native males whose powerguns were certainly not of native manufacture. The guards were not overtly threatening, but neither were they friendly. No one could say for sure whether the locals spoke any human dialect.

Slade stepped forward so that the men he had formed in double ranks could see him. The guards were watching closely. They did not interfere. Neither did the trio of Alayans who had come down in the tenders with their human cargo. "Ten-*shun!*" the tanker roared. He hoped that past habit would silence and focus the group on him, though few of them would have been from outfits noted for obedience to their officers.

"Excuse me," said a voice. "You will be allowed to speak, but first I have an announcement to make for the Terzia."

Slade turned. His mouth had been open already to unload grim truths on the castaways. The speaker was surprising enough that it was a moment before the big man remembered to reply.

The Spanglish phrasing had been human-standard, so far as there was such a standard, but the speaker was a male Terzian, an autochthone. He was a little stockier than most of his fellows; and his skin, while swarthy, lacked the olive tinge underlying the others'.

Besides his human trousers, the autochthone wore a commo helmet with a directional amplifier. Even if Slade had wanted to contest the local's right to speak, human lungs would have been hopelessly outclassed. The amp boomed out, "The Terzia, who rules this world absolutely, offers greetings and condolences to you who have been landed here. She offers honest employment to all who care to remain. Our exports here on Terzia are minerals and forest products. There are collector's positions open in both fields. A man who applies himself will be able to save the price of passage off-planet within a year."

The groan from the mercenaries needed no amplification to be heard.

Rooks broke from the ragged line. "Hey, what is this?" he called as much to his fellows as to Slade. "I thought the deal was—" he turned toward the trio of Alayans who were waiting near the human ranks—"we had passage as far as we wanted to go. And this sure as bleeding *hell* isn't where I want to go!"

The Alayan's vocalizer had a volume setting that permitted it to thunder over the chorus of support for Rooks. "That is correct, sir," boomed the machine voice. "You are welcome to travel with us as far as you choose." There was a brief pause. "Our eighth landfall following this one will be Desmo."

The tone of the pandemonium changed. There were cheers and a number of whistles. The ranks had already dissolved. Now there was a movement toward the Alayans. Men were demanding details of time and circumstances from the coolly-erect aliens.

Desmo was headquarters for a score of relatively small mercenary units. The planet acted also as a recruiting center for several of the larger ones. The world was by no means loosely gripped by the Military Tribunate which ran it. Still, Desmo's entertainment was varied and was geared toward the needs of young men in a dangerous line of work.

It struck Slade that he had never seen more than three Alayans at a time. Part of the tanker's mind held that thought and wrestled with it, while the reflexive part of him roared, "Hold up, curse you! If you get on that ship, it'll drive you nuts!"

Not all the assembly could hear the words, but Slade's bellow gave up less than the aliens might have hoped to their machinery.

"Yeah, that's what I said," the tanker went on grimly. He had their attention again. Slade stood arms akimbo, angry at the men for being fooled and angry at the way the Alayans and the Terzian authorities had combined to that end. "Their ship moves by snapping people right out of their skulls. Just like Stoudemeyer. That something you want to see happen to you?"

The mercenaries seethed like the water of a stone-lashed pool. The sun hammered them in this jungle-lapped clearing. Their skins were pale from the voyage and near-confinement on Rusata. Neither the Alayans nor the ground authorities had as yet provided protective gear. The series of assaults by the sun and various figures of power left the men enervated and afraid.

In the bright sun and the confusion, it was hard to tell how much the Alayans had been talking among themselves. Now the vocalizer of the central alien called, "Mister Slade?"

The loud question split the mercenaries between those looking at the Alayan and those looking at Slade himself. "Are you speculating?" the Alayan continued in the brief hush. "Or do you mean the voyage has affected your own mind?"

"You know what I've been through!" the tanker shouted. "I won't have you doing that to these others, do you hear me?"

Somebody in the crowd laughed. Slade took two strides toward the sound. He caught himself as mercenaries scattered or even braced themselves, secured by the armed guards.

"*Listen*, you people!" Slade said. The grip he kept on his temper showed in the tremble of his voice. "I've led you the best I know how—"

He was interrupted by the amplified voice of the Terzian official. "For those of you who will be transients on our world," the autochthone was saying, "follow me to the free entertainment center in which you may stay while cargo is being transferred to and from your vessel."

There *were* females on Terzia after all. An even dozen of them issued from a door in the tall spire which seemed the only building in the region.

Over the bellows of enthusiasm, the autochthone continued. "Those of you who intend to stay, fall in at those trucks." He pointed toward a pair of scabrous-looking stake-bed vehicles. "They will carry you immediately to the labor barracks."

The Terzian turned. The rush of the human audience to follow him was so immediate that the men forced their way past Slade in their haste.

The tanker bunched his shoulders momentarily. Then he simply got out of the way. The females had slipped into the building again. The male autochthone led the surviving mercenaries toward the same entrance as if they were the children of Hamelin—or the rats. At the very door, one man paused and looked back. Snipes, the Admin Officer. Then he sneered at Slade and disappeared with the others. The portal clicked shut behind him.

Slade closed his eyes. His lips pursed and flattened in a sort of exercise to work the feeling back into them. It was not anger that weighed on him, but the crushing sense of failure. The sun felt good, like the clean sun of Tethys burning away fatigue on a gravel strand. After a minute's stillness, Slade opened his eyes and stepped toward the empty trucks.

"Where will you go now, Mister Slade?" asked the voice behind him.

The big man turned. The Alayan was alone. His limbs held no weapon, only the vocalizer on which his tendrils expertly worked. The Alayan's six tiny heads goggled without human expression.

"I'm going to the labor barracks, I suppose," said Slade. "I thought about some other things I might do—" he looked up and down the spindly alien, wondering again whether the chitin would have cut as the exoskeleton splintered in Slade's grip—"but I need to get home. They tell me."

The alien mimed a human nod with his central pair of heads. "You can travel with us, you know," the vocalizer said.

Slade smiled. "I might," he said. "Would you use me for the fuel instead of the men? Now that we know it doesn't bother me?"

"You know we cannot," said the flat voice. "You are functional, Mister Slade—obviously functional. But our need is for reality, not function. We will get you to your homeworld at least as quickly as any other system of freighter connections is likely to do."

"Figured," said Slade. "Well, I'm not going to watch that, my friend."

He turned and stared up the glistening flank of the spire behind them. "You kept your bargain, and you didn't lie. Can't blame you for not wanting to lose your fuel supply, and I can't blame the folks here for discouraging immigrants." He shrugged. "Our sort of immigrants. But I'll work my passage out in a mine or any *curst* place before I watch you burn up my men!"

The Alayan nodded again. "I understand, Mister Slade," he said through his vocalizer.

Despite the emotions wracking him, Slade was quite convinced that the alien *did* understand.

"But please remember," the Alayan continued, "that—men—are lost during any long voyage. Because of our precautions, no one has been shot while gambling or been driven mad by adulterated stimulants. Most of your men will disembark on Desmo, Mister Slade, in better health than they will have a year later."

"What'll you do then?" Slade said harshly. "Send yourselves to Hell? Or rot for want of fuel?"

The Alayan's faces danced with a radiance only hinted in the sunlight. "We transport intelligent life forms among the stars faster and more cheaply than any rival," the vocalizer said. "We never lie about the terms, though we do not emphasize them either. We will find a cargo on Desmo, Mister Slade. And we will find fuel."

The Alayan walked back toward one of the tenders. He moved with the fragile dignity of an aged man. Lord preserve those men who would sail again with the creatures ... but Don Slade had done all that he could himself.

Do you have to feel you have failed because outlaws won't take your word that a situation is dangerous? Cop!

A door snicked open at the base of the tower. Slade could not be certain whether it was the one through which his men had entered or a different one. The Citadel was huge. Its smooth surface and relatively small diameter to height tended to conceal its real bulk, however.

A woman stepped toward Slade. She was flanked by two guards. The guards were male autochthones, but the woman had to be human: the first human Slade had seen on this planet, besides the men with whom he had landed.

The woman was beautiful, beyond any questions of need or abstinence. The dress she wore was rich and clinging, and her dark, honey hair fell across her shoulders beneath a fillet of green crystal. A part of the tanker's mind was surprised that the woman's beauty and importance were not riding in a vehicle, even for the hundred meters or so which separated her from Slade. In fact, she did not even wear shoes. Her toes flexed liquidly against the sward as she walked.

"Dear Lord have mercy!" the tanker muttered. He had been seventeen the last time he felt as he did now.

"Captain Donald Slade?" the woman called. Her voice had the alto clarity of birdsong at evening.

"I once was that, yes," Slade said. He was suddenly aware of how sweat-stiffened and prickly were the clothes he wore. "You represent the

Terzia? I'm here to sign on as a miner, I guess."

"I think we can do better than that, Captain," said the woman. She was close enough to extend a hand to grip Slade's warmly. She smiled. "I *am* the Terzia."

CHAPTER TWENTY-ONE

Don Slade slept in a comfortable room. If he wished, he could have opened it into a porch by cranking the roof and west wall into recesses. There was no need for that. This night on Elysium, Slade was tired enough to sleep on a heap of cinders.

No resident of the planet above the age of six was asleep.

The mental netting that linked the folk of Elysium was as real and as resilient as a spider's web, but it did not change the fact that humans evolved as social *individuals*. It was as individuals that they talked now in family groupings before they joined again in the decision that the society would make— as an individual.

Onander filled a mug that he had thrown and fired himself in youth. He handed it to his daughter. Nan already sipped from a similar mug at the astringent blend of coffee, cacao, and milk.

"Well, we certainly can't keep him here," said Onander. By watching himself fill the third mug, he did not have to catch the eyes of either woman.

"No, dear," said Nan in a tone which was further from agreement with her husband than the words themselves were. "That wouldn't be at all fair to him, would it?" In a slightly different voice she added, "The Terzia acts in such *human* ways on occasion. It's a little hard to believe, sometimes."

The surface of Risa's drink began to tremble until the girl set the mug down with a thump. The blush on her cheekbones clashed with the coppery tinge of her hair. "He's not something we have to be afraid of, you know," Risa said. "He's alone. And he's been acting quite nicely. Well? Hasn't he?"

"Well, he's certainly been acting," said her father. His tone was sharpened by the rasp of Risa's demand.

"Now, dear, that isn't fair," said his wife before Risa could respond. That would raise the emotional temperature still further. "Everyone tries to be pleasant to strangers. That's all Don's doing. But of course, Risa—" She looked calmly over to her daughter—"he is very dangerous. And we couldn't allow him to stay, even if he wanted to."

"Well, what *is* the mural in the Hall?" the girl demanded, more in frustration now than anger. "What sort of men—and women!—fought the mutants? Weren't they like him? *Our* ancestors. Why should we be afraid of Don?"

"Oh, Risa," Onander said softly. He reached out a hand. His daughter took it willingly, greedily. "The battle was no myth; but the mural is a warning, not a trophy. Those were our ancestors, yes. Some of our genes. . . . And we *all* of us, despite the unity we've begun to achieve; all of us could be back in that Hell of violence and slaughter, very easily."

"But the mutants aren't here, Father," Risa said. "They're still on the colony ship or they've died out. Or maybe they landed somewhere after all, have their own world—but they aren't on Elysium."

Onander turned his daughter's hand palm-upward. He cupped his own much larger hand above it on the table. "The mutants were half the war, my dearest. When our ancestors built the matter transmitter, they left the mutants behind. But they couldn't leave themselves behind."

He paused, looking from the paired hands to the eyes of his daughter. "Don Slade is a credit to the race in many ways," Onander continued softly. "And no, if it hadn't been for souls like his among our ancestors, we would never have survived to settle Elysium, to make it what we have for the past millennium. But there are things in us which if awakened would drop us back into chaos as suddenly as our ancestors escaped it. And you know that also, my Risa."

"He wouldn't be happy, dearest," Nan said sadly. It was hard to tell whether the sadness was on her daughter's behalf or for more personal reasons. "Not even for a little while, now that he's so focused on getting back to Tethys. He really does believe it will be home to him after twenty years, you know."

"Yes," Risa said with a sharp movement of her head, a nod or a peck. She slipped her hand from beneath her father's. When Risa drank from her mug, it was with loud gulping noises.

"I think," said Onander heavily, "that it's about time to make a decision." Nan met his eyes and nodded; Risa nodded to her mug of bitter drink.

The trio fell silent around the handsome kitchen table. The alcohol lamp burbled softly beneath the pot of drinks. Occasionally a local equivalent of insects would be batted away by the repulsion field guarding the open window.

Physically, the family was of three separate entities . . . but their minds were merging, and all over Elysium minds were merging to decide the fate of a sleeping castaway.

"Captain Slade?" the voice whispered. "Don?"

Hours of tension and a heavy meal had drugged Slade as thoroughly as a deliberate anesthetic. The reflexes were still there, however, even if they had to fight to the surface through meters of cotton batting. "Roger," the tanker said, groping for the equipment belt that should have been close to his head.

Risa touched Slade's hand with one of hers. He felt the edge of the bed give under her slight weight. "I came to tell you," the girl said, "that they—that we are going to send you to Tethys."

"That's—" Slade said. "Well, I don't know how I'll ever be able to thank you. But if Elysium ever— has need for what I have or what I am, it's yours."

Slade had been momentarily blind when he rolled out of sleep. Now the tanker's eyesight was returning with a rush. The door of his room was closed. Starlight through the window above the bed showed that Risa wore a pastel garment, high-necked and frothy. The garment covered a great deal more of the girl's skin than had the suit she wore in the air car, but it covered that skin with little more than the shadow it threw.

"Girl" was the wrong word. Dear Lord, but there could be no doubt but that Risa was a woman.

"You won't be able to remember us, though," Risa said as she sat primly. "We—we're peaceful here on Elysium, and they think that if word got around...."

"Sure," the tanker said. He shifted so that he was upright with his back against the window ledge. His legs were tucked beneath him and covered with the sheet. "I, well.... There's some places like yours where I figure they wouldn't let a stranger go at all. For the reason stated. I'll admit I half thought...."

Slade's voice trailed off. The woman beside him had been in his mind, however. She knew that the thought had been multiple, not partial. *A door closing and the hiss of lethal gas from vents. Burly men holding Slade on either side and the prick of an injection. A greeting, and as Slade turned, a blast of gunfire.* The tanker had known too many situations in which an individual did not fit the circumstances. It was never something he had liked: Slade preferred to think of his enemies as gunmen facing him. But he had heard the stories, sure he had.

Lord have mercy on the soul of Joachim Steuben; and on the soul of Donald Slade, who was headed the same way in the Lord's good time.

"Ah," Slade added, "I wouldn't have anybody think I was in the habit of shafting people who'd done me favors. I don't blame you folks for wiping my memory, but—it wasn't something I'd have talked about anyway."

"There will be some things that will remain," Risa said. She twisted slightly toward the man. Her knee bumped Slade's. When he edged away, she twisted further. "You'll remember meals, probably, though not where you ate them. You'll even remember faces. A memento of . . . us here on Elysium."

The tanker was frowning in concentration. Aloud he said, "The kindness you've done me will be that, Risa. That will stay, I'm sure. I don't forget help I've been given, or who gave it."

"Don, I'm not a child," she said. Her left hand touched the sheet over Slade's thighs, then slipped with a butterfly's delicacy to the man's bare torso.

Slade touched Risa's hand loosely enough for affection but not so loosely that the hand could fumble the way it seemed to want to do. "I know that," the tanker lied. Then he went on fiercely. "And *you* know that I'm not an adult, not like anybody here would recognize. I never will be. *You* know that!"

"Don, that doesn't matter," Risa said. She tugged her hand, away now and not downward. It came free at once.

"Sure it matters, Risa," the tanker replied. "It would matter to you if you saw a friend getting into something that was going to do a lot more harm than good. Wouldn't it?"

Risa sat bolt upright again. "I think that's my decision, isn't it?" she said in a voice harder than any she had used before to Slade. Her garment blurred away from her bosom like shock waves from bullets.

"No, Risa, it's not," Slade said gently. "Not unless I'm—do you have dogs, here? Domestic animals of some sort, anyway. Not unless I'm an animal. If I'm a human being, then it does matter. *That's* your decision, Risa. Am I a human being, to you?"

The girl burst into tears.

Slade wrapped her to his chest, safely now and a little sorry of that fact, but. . . .

"I didn't mean," Risa gurgled. "I just didn't want you to, to leave and—"

"I'm not going to forget," Slade whispered to the soft, curly hair. "Anything that leaves me mind enough to remember meals is going to let me remember you saving my life. And . . . you being you. You being here makes it a better universe, Risa. And I'll know that too."

Risa straightened, sniffled, and stood up. "I—" she began. Then she said, "You've been good for us here on Elysium, Don. It doesn't usually happen, but I think . . . it might be that if you went traveling again, after you've settled your business on Tethys, that you could find your way here again. I'd be a little older then, of course."

Risa turned and walked out of the room. She closed the door softly behind her.

Blood and Martyrs, Slade thought. Sixteen going on forty. . . . And here he was, forty himself and that a miracle the way he'd lived. He had been going to lay back on Tethys, he'd told himself that. But Tom with his chest split open and Marilee calling for help, well. . . . Marilee knew the sort of help you got from Hammer's Slammers. She knew what to expect from Don Slade when she told him there was trouble.

And if they were no more than fancies in a madman's skull, Tom and Marilee and the others— then they were Don Slade's fancies. Maybe there would be a chance to settle down afterwards, if he lived to be forty-one.

Blood and Martyrs. Slade was smiling as he drifted off to sleep again.

In a room not far from Slade's, Nan and Onander held one another. The man was weeping softly.

CHAPTER TWENTY-TWO

Dawn awakened him with her rosy fingers.

The air was brisk enough to be comfortable, and it had enough of a salt tang to remind Slade of home. He stretched in bed—and found himself lying on gravel instead of a mattress.

"Where in the *Hell* am I?" the big man grunted. But the real Hell of it was, he knew the answer before he voiced the question. What he did not know was *how* he had come to lie behind a space-port warehouse on Tethys.

"Via," Slade said in wonderment. He was wearing boots and a two-piece work-suit of neutral gray, not livery. There was a hand-scrip in one pocket. It held about a month's pay for a laborer in both Tethian currency and in crystalline Frisian talers. There were identity cards as well, three of them in three different names ... and one of them the card Don Slade would have carried had he stayed on Tethys and succeeded to the Slade Councilorship.

The last thing Slade remembered clearly was boarding a lifeboat on Terzia. That boat sure as blazes had not landed him here ... but the only other thing in his mind was a girl's face, elfin cute and smiling beneath a tumble of red curls.

The tanker remembered what the phantoms of

his mind had told him aboard the Alayan ship, also. He scraped a small hole in the gravel and hid within it the card in his own name and one of the others as well. He kept only the one calling him Donald Holt. Into the same small hiding place he dropped the seal ring from his hand. The ring was unremarkable till its weight indicated that it was of projectile-grade osmium. It would look precisely the same in a bath of molten steel. It was the only thing Slade had kept with him from the day he lifted from Tethys as a Slammers recruit.

He filled in the hole with a gentle motion of his boot sole and noted the number of paces from it to the corner of the warehouse as he walked away.

Somebody had wished him well; the nondescript clothing and the false identities were proof of that. The memory of the red-haired girl followed Slade, but he could not really get a grip on the thought. "I sold my clock, I sold my reel ..." the tanker sang to himself. But this Johnnie had come back from soldiering. . . .

A train of low-boys were emptying at the front of the warehouse. The foreman of the crew glanced at Slade sharply. The big man was not one of the warehouse team, however, and therefore not worth worrying about. Slade noted that the foreman and the truck drivers all seemed to be in red-piped clothing suggesting Dyson livery. The low-ranking cargo-handlers wore plain gray.

"To buy my love a sword of steel ..." the castaway murmured as he smiled. He wiped his palms on his thighs.

It was still home. The sky to the west was the right pale gray with its hint of violet. The air had the odors of childhood, though they were over-

printed here by ozone from landing thrusters. Slade
had never spent much time at the Port when he
was growing up, though it existed as an enclave in
the family estates. A neutral enclave, administered
by a board appointed by the Council as a whole.
Now everyone with rank seemed to claim alle-
giance to the Dysons. Welladay. . . .

It was a city, now, the spaceport. There had
been houses for the permanent staff and their
families, a few hundred households at the time
Slade had left. From the look of the barracks—
some of the buildings very new, still under construction—there were many times that number
present now.

Of greater concern were the shanties spreading
beyond the formal buildings. Some of them seemed
to be rigged out for entertainment of one sort or
the other. Certainly they did not house workers.
Men and women lounged among the shanties now,
while the bustle of business continued on the field.

There were three huge starships down and a
number of intra-system ferries and tenders. One
of the latter had landed recently enough that
steam was venting from its hull as the thrusters
cooled. The cargo bay was still closed, but a handful of passengers had disembarked. Humans were
always fringe cargo, save for the occasional new
settlement—and, more often, the transport of a
mercenary regiment.

Nothing like that here. Most of the passengers
were entering a large air car in Krueger colors.
They seemed to be a honeymoon couple and their
servants, returned now with subdued expressions.
Slade had never thought that the uncertainties of

a long journey were a good way to begin married life; but then, he had never been married.

There was one man apart from the Krueger party. He was talking to the driver of a utility van outside the port office as Slade approached. Though the man's back was to the tanker, Slade could hear him saying, ". . . to Slade House?"

"Much in the way of luggage, then?" the driver asked.

"Pardon me, master," said Don Slade as he stepped almost between the two men, "but I couldn't help—*Blood and Martyrs*!"

"Came to look for you, my man," said Danny Pritchard with a slow, tight grin.

The driver was blinking from one ex-soldier to the other. Pritchard touched Slade's jaw to silence him and said to the driver, "A standard cubicmeter case is all. In the office. And an extra—"

"Thirty libra," Slade said, cued without either partner's conscious awareness of the question.

"—if you fetch it to the truck yourself."

The driver shrugged. He took the scribbled claim check and sauntered into the building.

"Been back long?" Pritchard asked as the two men sized each other up.

Danny looked a little more gray than Slade had remembered him. Fit, though, the Lord knew. Slade's exercises had not included walking. He was sure that even the kilometer he had just strolled through the Port village had raised blisters on his right sole and heel. "I don't think so," he said aloud. "Say, did you have anything to do with that?"

"With how you left Terzia, you mean?" Pritchard asked.

"No, I—oh, never mind," the tanker replied. "There's other things to worry about now, I guess."

His friend frowned and nodded his head. "Look," said Pritchard, "how much do you know about what's going on here the last while? Anything?"

"Is my brother dead?" Slade asked.

Pritchard nodded.

"Yeah," Slade muttered, aloud but to the part of his mind which believed in Hell. "Well," he continued, "I guess I'm not color-blind." He nodded toward a Port official in full Dyson livery, calling orders to a gang of laborers. "I suppose there's some things to straighten out back at the House, too."

"Don, I don't know how bad it is," said Danny Pritchard. "But it seemed like I ought to take a look. With the Colonel's blessing."

"I'm not asking anybody in to fight my fights," Slade said sharply.

"And I'm not offering to," Pritchard snapped back. "I'd have thought you'd seen enough with the Slammers to know that blowing people away's a curst poor way to settle things anyway—unless you figure to get them all. How many people do you think you and I can kill, Don?"

"Via, I'm sorry," the big man said. He chuckled. Clasping his comrade on the shoulder very lightly, he went on. "You know the only thing I was ever fit for was line command. Got any bright ideas, staff mogul?"

"Yeah," said Pritchard. "Got the idea that you lie low for a couple days instead of barging right into things. The Council's going to meet at Slade House, you know?"

"Are they now?" said the tanker. He squeezed

the knuckles of his right hand between his lips. "Look," he went on, "have your driver drop me at one of the processing plants on the way. Number Six, that's the oldest one and it's close to the House. Nobody ever went hungry if he stopped by one of our plants when *I* was a kid."

"All righty!" called the driver as he wheeled out a plain, rectangular case. "Luggage it is."

Slade and Pritchard moved to either side to help shift the case to the end-bars to which it would be strapped. "You fellows figured out where you're going yet?"

Don Slade laughed. "In the short term, at least," he said. His muscles bunched as he slid the heavy case into position. "In the short term."

CHAPTER TWENTY-THREE

The steel door of the food-processing plant was not only unlocked but ajar. "Hello the house!" Slade called as he swung the door fully open. He waited outside for a further moment. The air car had already disappeared into the eastern sky. The sea sounded a dense background, loud without being obtrusive. The gasp of the pumps within the long, concrete building was by contrast relatively mild.

"Hello there," Slade called again as he stepped inside. He closed the door behind him.

There was a door to the right which would lead to living quarters for the crew during their month-long tours. Beside it was a bright alcove glassed off from the rest of the pump room, the foreman's office. The multiple vision blocks within flashed their images to one another with no human to watch them. Tubing and crates moving beneath the tubing on conveyors covered the long, left-hand wall. There was a slideway leading from the office to the bright splotch which was the open, seaward end of the building.

As Slade watched, a blur grew against the brightness. It accelerated toward him. When the blur slowed to a brutally-sudden stop, it took on shape: a slide bucket holding a hard-looking man in faded Slade coveralls. The rocket gun he rested on his right thigh happened to be aimed squarely at the intruder's chest.

"And just what might *your* business be, buddy?" the man asked Slade. He was not young, but his voice quivered as little as did the gun he held.

"My name's, Don Holt," Slade said with only a moment's hesitation to remember it. "I was hoping you might have some work for me." The fact that the foreman was leaving the office empty to check the lines implied the crew was short, but Slade would have said the same thing in any case.

The man in Slade livery snorted. "I'm the foreman, my name's Pretorius," he said. "And I guess that means you're looking for a meal. Well, I guess we can find you that, sure." He swung his legs out of the bucket and stepped toward Slade. His weapon was now aimed at the roof.

The tanker frowned. "Guess I could use some food, sure," he said. "But I haven't forgot how to catch that for myself, either. I said, I'm looking for work."

"Are you?" said Pretorius without inflexion. "You'd be from around here, then?"

"Been a while, though," said Slade in elliptical agreement. "When I was a kid, I thought all mercenaries got rich. I spent the past twenty years proving I was wrong and a curst fool." He smiled in near humor, then touched his left earlobe. It was a half centimeter shorter than the right one which had not been fried by a powergun.

Pretorius dipped his gun momentarily, like the neck of a bird bending to drink. He arrested the motion before it was an actual threat, but there was no particular warmth in his voice as he said,

"Is that a fact? Then I'd think you'd have found work at the Port, boyo. And just maybe you did, hey? And they sent you here to see what you could learn."

"Could be I got an offer," Slade said. "Could be I didn't like the color of suit they were going to have me wear, too. Look, if I'm unwelcome here, I'll just walk on out. My daddy ran a catcher boat from South Three until a knife-jaw got him. I guess I can find some kin down that way if a strong back don't interest you." He turned away from Pretorius and the gun.

"Blazes, man," the foreman called. "Don't leave me short-handed as I am."

Slade looked back at the foreman. Pretorius was holding out his weapon by the balance. "Here," the older man went on. "You know how to use one of these?"

Slade frowned. "Guess I can learn," he said.

Powerguns would have been useless against the sub-surface life forms that were the bane of processing plants. Instead the crews used short-barreled rocket guns like this one. They fired low-velocity missiles which were unaffected by the media through which they lanced toward their targets. The bursting charge was much bulkier than a powergun wafer liberating comparable energy; but the charges went off in their targets, not on the surface of the sea.

"Come on, then," the foreman said. He pointed to the second slide-bucket. "We've got a ten-meter wriggler giving fits on section two. Isn't big enough to take a nip out of the line, but it keeps tripping the alarm. Come on—you want to learn, I'll teach you."

*   *   *

"And what have we got here?" asked the leader
of the men who strolled toward Danny Pritchard
as the air car took off again.

Pritchard looked them up and down with a lack
of expression which was itself significant. All but
one of the four men wore belt knives. The leader
instead toyed with a nunchaku, a pair of short
flails chained together at the slim ends. None of
them wore guns, which had been for decades
proscribed on the Council Islands of Tethys save for
certain jobs and locations. That scarcely made
Danny safe at this moment.

The men were among those who had been loung-
ing against the shading wall of the courtyard when
Pritchard arrived. There were a score of others in
various liveries present, but no one seemed to pay
any attention to what was going on. The leader of
the men moving in on the visitor wore Slade Blue
defaced with a crimson stripe down either leg. The
other three were Dyson retainers in full scarlet.

"Friend of the family," Danny Pritchard called
cheerfully. He sidled away from his luggage so
that it did not block him if he had to jump back
suddenly. Hidden at the small of the ex-soldier's
back was a glass-barreled powergun. He would
use it if he had to—but the illegal weapon's single
charge would still leave three opponents. "I'm here
to visit the Widow Slade, at her request. You're of
the House?"

The man with the nunchaku flipped his weapon
out toward Pritchard's trunk. The lid clacked as
the further baton touched it. "Can't have any contraband coming in here," the man said. "Think
we'll check it right here."

"What the *hell's* going on here?" demanded a voice shrill with tension.

Men who had been covertly watching as the visitor was baited now glanced up in open surprise. The four men who had approached Pritchard now fanned away as if Hammer's man could be safely ignored if they were willing to leave him alone. Not the smartest possible assumption; but they were not pros, only bullies, and not the cleverest bullies Danny Pritchard had met in his career either.

The man who had shouted from the House doorway was young and thin. Pritchard had seen a cube of Marilee—as she was—Dorcas. The youth's features were a near double for those of the woman twenty years before.

It was an open question how Teddy had expected to stop the trouble if his righteous indignation were not enough. The fat old man a step behind him and to the right had a notion of his own, however. The old man's gun-hand was hidden within his loose-fitting jacket.

"Checking for contraband, Master Teddy," said the man with the nunchaku. The weapon twitched in his hand like the tail of a cat which lay otherwise motionless.

"Durotige," said the old man behind Edward Slade, "get your butt out of here. Out of the yard. *Now*."

"You don't scare me, Blegan!" snarled Durotige.

"Good," said the old man, oblivious to his presumptive master. "Because you'll try something if I don't scare you, Durotige."

"Time'll come, old man," said Durotige. His words were bluster, however—as Blegan's had not been. The man in crimson over blue spun on his heel and marched toward the gate. Its hinges were rusty but they squealed open when Durotige tugged with the fear of death behind him. The trio who had supported him drifted away as well, though they pointedly did not walk toward the gate.

Edward Slade joined the visitor. The young man glanced angrily about the yard at the liverymen who had not intervened in the trouble. They were now insouciantly directed on their own affairs again. "Sir, I apologize for the boors you've met in my House," Teddy said. Someone chuckled from behind a car at the words. "Leave the trunk. I'll have Housemen bring it in."

"No problem," said Danny Pritchard as he swung the gear handle from one corner of the trunk. He began spinning the handle with an ease that belied the trunk's weight. Coon Blegan had grimaced when his master spoke of leaving the trunk. The old servant knew as Pritchard did himself that if left unguarded, the luggage would surely be ransacked.

Wheels lowered from the four corners, jacking the trunk up by smooth degrees. Powered units were simpler while they worked; but they stopped working when your traps were off-loaded into a swamp, or somebody turned a valve that flooded the cargo bay with nascent chlorine. Most mercs got along, as Pritchard did, with muscle-powered come-alongs for their hold baggage.

This time the trunk held clothing along with a submachinegun, three spare barrels, a thousand rounds of ammunition, and a suit of body armor. Pritchard had not been going to leave it in the courtyard if the only alternative had been to lift the full hundred and eighty kilos on his back.

The one-time officer extended the lever into a T-handled tow bar. "Shall we?" he suggested to the others.

But as Danny followed Blegan and young Slade, he swept his eyes around the courtyard. It was filled with men and equipment and arrogance. Pritchard had been a staff officer for a decade and Hammer's heir apparent for over a year. It was still easy to recall the days when he had been only a blower captain himself. The days in which Danny Pritchard's decisions involved no more than how to kill the most men in the shortest time.

CHAPTER TWENTY-FOUR

"And with one shot he kills it!" said Pretorius to the men who shared the dinner table with him and Slade. "Bam! Right into the gill chamber."

Chesson and Leaf, the other two members of the crew, smiled. The men maintained the filter lines; programmed the extrusion circuits depending on what the filters were bringing in; and more than occasionally disposed of the larger forms of sea-life when the rhythm and scent of the filters drew beasts to the station.

On Tethys, as almost universally on water oceans, the vegetation was mostly one-celled and the herbivores scarcely more complex. Virtually every life form big enough to be seen with the naked eye was carnivorous. Those carnivores ranged very much larger indeed, and not all of the Tethian varieties were toothless filter-feeders like the largest whales of Earth.

"Look," said Slade in more embarrassment than pride at the subject, "it was one shot after the beggar surfaced; but it was three before that had missed him under water. Don't know about you, Piet, but I was getting a mite nervous about a five-round clip and no reload."

"You'll get used to the angles, Soldier," Leaf said. He waved a rock-cruncher limb with a flag of

242

muscle dangling from the joint. "I remember when the shells didn't have guidance units and you had to allow for deflection as well as refraction."

"Via, but it's been a long time since I ate one of these," said Slade as he forked another mouthful of cruncher himself. He wanted to change the subject; and besides, what he was saying was no more than the truth. "My old man always said nobody eats like a Councilor except the men who fish for the Councilor."

"I tell you, Soldier," said Chesson morosely. He was the youngest of the four by a decade; an eel-like, sharp-faced man. "You're eating a curst sight better than anybody's sending to Slade House this month past."

Leaf and Pretorius looked askance at their fellow, but Chesson plowed on bitterly. "Nobody minds sending a prime catch to the master, do they? Always been proud to, we have. Master Thomas knew he'd never had a better crew than the boys at Station Six. Isn't that so?"

Chesson glared around the table. The others nodded. "But there's no bloody good to that now, is there? Master Teddy can't take care of himself, much less us, and the Mistress—well, she's got some choice as to where she wants to sell herself, and no curst other choice in the world. That's a fact."

"Dyson, I suppose?" Slade said as if he were still concentrating on his meal.

For a moment, the only sound was that of the equipment washing itself down in the pump room. The filter lines were flushed and closed down at night. There was no safe or practical way to police them after dark. Temporarily-increased production would not make up for the certain damage when adult orcs or knife-jaws decided to make a meal of the lines.

Pretorius said, "No, it's not just him." The foreman took a second helping of potatoes in white sauce. "It's the whole Council, all forty of them."

"Thirty-nine," Leaf corrected.

"Whatever," the foreman snapped. More soberly, he continued. "Took'em all together. Could easy enough have let Master Teddy take the Council seat when Master Thomas was killed. But no, set up a guardianship—the boy's nineteen! Via! I was captain of a catcher boat when I was nineteen. And then they hand the guardianship to Dyson, and every bloody thing to bloody Dyson."

"Bastard squeezes his people," said Chesson as he glared at his plate. "They say, blazes, what's it matter who sits on his butt in the House? You see them maybe twice in your life, so who cares what all they do to each other? But it's not true. If this was a Dyson plant—" he waved around the room and toward the packaging units beyond the wall— "there'd be a guard sitting with us to make sure we ate common rations. And none of the equipment out there'd have been replaced in thirty years."

Slade looked at the hard, weather-stained faces around the table. "Never heard much good about the Dysons myself," he said. He was trying to control the shudder of anger that swept him as he thought of the past. "But that strikes me as crazy. Bad business, let alone being a son of a bitch. I may not've run a Council House—" barely true— "but I don't guess it's a lot different from a company of mercs. You don't have to spring for every bit of hardware comes on the market. But if you run your plant down, buy junk or don't replace it, you aren't competing anymore."

Slade smiled, an expression as grim as anything anger had brought to the faces of the other three men. "Of course," the tanker concluded, "the business I was in you got your ass blown away too. I guess that's different from sea products."

"Might be a change Tethys'd be better off seeing," said Chesson. He gave a black look at the rocket guns racked by the door, ready in an emergency.

"Folks aren't bastards because that's profitable," said Pretorius, "though they may tell themselves that's why. They're bastards because they were born that way. And—" he looked around challengingly— "as long as I've lived, I don't know of anybody who was better off for being a bastard in the long run."

"Nor me," echoed Leaf. Even Chesson nodded agreement, though there was nothing in the younger man's face to suggest that he fully understood his foreman's point.

"So sure," Pretorius continued, "Dyson isn't a businessman the like of any Slade right back to the Settlement—and it isn't that the Slades couldn't show a hard hand when the need was."

Nods all around, Don Slade joining the others. His lips were stiff and his face still.

"But Dyson has the Council," said Pretorius, "and I suppose that means he has us in a few days or so. After all, who is there to stop him?"

"Who indeed?" muttered Don Slade as he clenched his great right hand.

*　　*　　*

"Well, Major Pritchard," said Marilee Slade, "Coon Blegan—you've met him, my son's ... companion—"

"Nothing wrong with the word bodyguard," said Danny Pritchard mildly. He had seated himself when the woman offered him a chair, but she continued to pace the Trophy Room. Even flat-footed, she was taller than he was anyway.

"The word implies that we need bodyguards," Marilee said. "That Tethys is no longer a civilized world." When Pritchard made no response but a smile, the woman continued. "At any rate, Coon says I should hire your Colonel Hammer to clear undesirable elements off Tethys. I suppose you agree with that?"

She was not really hostile toward *him*, Danny decided. She was just very frustrated in general. Very possibly Marilee had watched his arrival through the window now behind her, and her sub-conscious preferred to over-compensate for the em-barrassment she must feel.

Aloud Pritchard said, "Well, I might disagree on moral grounds if I thought it would work, ah, madam. But since I never *have* known it to work in circumstances like yours on Tethys, I'll pretend to be a practical man and disagree on practical terms instead."

The tall woman paused in mid-stride as her brain correlated the words her ears had heard a moment before. She looked at the man who lounged at ease, smiling at her. "Major—" she began in a tone more diffident than that of her angry assurance an instant previous.

"Please," said Danny Pritchard. "That was Alois' little joke, I'm sure, when he announced I was coming. Mister Pritchard. Or Danny, which I'd prefer. But I'm not a soldier anymore."

Marilee sat down with the abruptness of a gun returning to battery. She laughed as she looked out the window through which she could see nothing but sky from her present low angle. "Well," she said, "Danny, I suppose you'd better explain that. I hadn't expected to hear from a mercenary that force doesn't accomplish anything."

"Ex-mercenary," Pritchard corrected. The smile was back. "And force accomplishes a lot of things. They just aren't the ones you want here. Bring in the Slammers and we kick ass for as long as you pay us. Six months, a year. And we kick ass even if the other side brings in mercs of their own—which they'll do—but that's not a problem, not if you've got us." Unit pride lasted even after the unit's work became a matter of distaste. Pride beamed now from Danny Pritchard's face, and his hand caressed a tank that only his mind could see.

"So," the man went on. He got up without thinking about the action because he was focused on plans, on possibilities. "There's what? Three hundred thousand people on Tethys?"

Marilee's eyes narrowed. "On the Council Islands, about. There's a lot more in little holdings on the unclaimed islands, but I don't think anyone can be sure of numbers."

"So," Pritchard repeated. The word was his equivalent of the Enter key when his mind was computing possibilities. "You want to kill fifty kay? Fifty thousand people, let's remember they're people for the moment."

"I don't *want* to kill anybody!" the woman snapped. She swung abruptly to her feet again.

Her boots rapped on the inlaid floor over which her visitor's heels had glided unheard. "I don't even want to kill Bev Dyson. I grew up with him, after all, I . . . maybe he did kill my husband. But I don't want to know that for sure. And I don't want *him* killed."

"You see," said Danny Pritchard, as if he had not heard his companion expose a part of herself that she had not known existed, "if we go in quick and dirty, the only way that has a prayer of working is if we get them all. If we get everybody who opposes you, everybody related to them, everybody who called them master—everybody."

"They aren't all dangerous!" Marilee shouted. She turned to the wall of trophies and went on in nearly as loud a voice. "They aren't any of them dangerous, except maybe a few. What are you talking about?" She spun back to Pritchard.

The ex-soldier nodded in agreement. "They're not dangerous now, but they will be after the killing starts. Believe me—" he raised a hand to forestall another protest— "I've seen it often enough. Not all of them, but one in ten, one in a hundred. One in a thousand's enough when he blasts your car down over the ocean a year from now. You'll see. It changes people, the killing does. Once it starts, there's no way to stop it but all the way to the end. If you figure to still live here on Tethys."

"M—Danny!" the woman said. "I told you, I don't *want* killing. Why do you keep saying that?"

"What do you think the Slammers do, milady?" asked Danny Pritchard. His grin was wide as a demon's, as cruel as the muzzle of the guns he remembered using so well. "Work magic? We kill, and we're good at it, *bloody* good. You call the

Slammers in to solve your problems here and you'll be able to cover the Port with the corpses. I guarantee it. I've *done* it, milady. In my time."

He was still grinning. Marilee Slade gasped and turned away. The blast-scarred skull of a knife-jaw was on the wall behind her. The yellowing skull was two meters along the line of the teeth, a record even for the days of the Settlement when the creature had savaged a guard tower and three men. For a moment, the knife-jaw looked less ruthless than did the man who had seemed so mild until he began describing options.

"All right, Mister Pritchard," Marilee said to her clenched hands. "My son says we're better off letting the law take its course, even when that course is against us. I—I don't think I believe that. I *know* Tom's death wasn't, wasn't chance. But I didn't mean to bring in an army, either, even without what you just said. I suppose we'll let Bev have his way, then, and—hope for the best."

She shook herself. "I'm sorry," she said. "I didn't mean to be ungracious. Will you have refreshments? A stim cone?" She stepped toward the refrigerated cart resting against a sidewall.

"No, I'm fine," said Danny Pritchard. His face had loosened from its rictus. Now he sat again in the chair from which thought had propelled him. "You see," he continued mildly, "using the Slammers on your problem is like settling a tank on a nut to crack it. I . . . I'm not the sort to say, roll over and play dead to injustice. Even when injustice has the law behind it. You were hoping Don would come home. It's for him—and for me and for the Colonel, there's a lot of us who owe Don— it's for him I came here. We pay our debts. But what did *you* have in mind for him, for your— brother-in-law?"

Marilee continued to face her visitor. Her hand crept up unconsciously to caress the trophy skull above her. The cranium between the two eyesockets had been punched away by the shot which killed the creature. It had been a 10 cm bolt from a gun like those on the drones in the courtyard, anti-tank weapons really and the only medicine that could dependably put paid to the monsters which disputed the Settlement. Nothing like them threatened the Council Islands anymore. The beasts bred and hunted elsewhere, now, the progeny of the creatures which had survived. Natural selection had proved to the most savage natives of Tethys that Man was still more savage.

Marilee thought of herself and of her son. The awareness was not a happy one.

"I thought perhaps if they saw him," the tall woman said aloud. She was trying to find words to answer a question she had herself avoided asking. "I thought, they can ignore me, ignore Teddy. They could even ignore Tom because he was too *good*, too curst good to treat them the way his grandfather would have done. Maybe even his father."

Marilee took her hand from the skull and laced her fingers together. She bent them back against one another fiercely. "But they couldn't ignore Don, could they? And besides . . ." she added, her eyes drawn to the window but her mind drifting far beyond the present, "I never really wanted him to leave. Whatever I said."

"Well, knowing Don," said Danny Pritchard from his chair, "I'd expect him back just about any time now."

"He mustn't come now," the woman blurted. It's too late. The Council's committed. They'd *kill* him."

"*They* would?" said Danny Pritchard. "Those down in the yard?" The professional began to laugh. "They'll learn something about status in Hell if they try, milady. They will that."

CHAPTER TWENTY-FIVE

The slideway rose and fell like a tank racing over
broken ground. Danny Pritchard had only a plastic bucket and not the hundred-odd tons of tank
armor between him and danger, however.

The sea lifted and ebbed beneath him at no fixed
period; or rather, at a period set by as many vari-
ables as a sun-spot sequence, theoretically calcula-
ble but for human practice lost in uncertainty. The
water was a lucent gray-green, metallic. In it moved
blurs of other colors, jetsam sucked from the current to be filtered and compacted by type in the
tubes running back to the building on the shore.

The concentration of microlife and the leakage
of juices from the processing drew larger beasts
upstream. They could be seen playing as black
shadows about the tubing—two meters long, three
meters; one of them five meters at least, Danny
would swear. It looked as slippery as a flame and
as ravenous. No danger to the filter lines, perhaps;
but sure death to any landsman who slipped from
the bucket into the water.

Don Slade looked up, mildly startled as the bucket
slid to a halt at his guard station. The rails and the
catwalk supporting them stretched further out to
the posts manned by Chesson and Leaf. Each of
the men were responsible for five hundred meters

of line. Slade had been bending over the rail. He
held a rocket gun in his right hand as if it were a
giant pistol. In Slade's left, when he straightened
so that it could be seen, was a length of twelve-
centimeter tubing. He had been prodding it down
into the water.

"Hey, snake," Slade called cheerfully. "Come
watch me improve my technique." The tanker bent
over the rail again.

Pritchard walked carefully to the bigger man.
The filter lines, with the platforms and slideway
above them, did not attempt to remain rigid in the
sea. Strong as the lines were, the sea was stronger.
If the apparatus did not give and flow with the
moods of the water, the water would smash it
with the casual ease of a vandal with a shop
window. Knowing the necessity for flexibility did
not prevent the motion from making Danny Pritchard queasy. "All right, trooper," the Adjutant said
as he joined Slade at the rail. "What've you
got—Via!"

The thing that twisted up through the water had
a long nose-spike and ragged teeth the color of
blood. Like a trap slamming, it struck the tube
Slade used as a lure. The tube sprang upward. It
was almost wrenched from Slade's grip. At the
surface of the water, refraction bent the white tubing sharply. A meter below that hinge, the jaws
were grinding the tough plastic into drifting motes.

Slade fired. When the shell struck it the sea
fountained, reaching for the gun muzzle with lam-
bent clarity. Then the water boiled red as the charge
blew apart the carnivore's head. The nose-spike
and part of the upper jaw lifted from the explosion,
then splashed back into the water.

The creature's body began to drift, still writhing, beneath the filter line. Part of the cloud of blood preceding the carcass had been sucked into the line already with the plankton.

Slade pulled up his ragged-ended lure. "You see," he said, "I know where the end of the tube is." He tapped the plastic with the muzzle of his gun. "So I shoot for that, where I *feel* the tube is, and that teaches me how much to hold off when there's only what I can see the next time."

"They hit on this?" Danny asked, tapping the white plastic. He had expected the tube to have a soft, greasy feel, but it rang like steel beneath his fingernail. This was pressure tubing for repairs to the compaction segment.

"They do when I wire some meat onto it," the tanker said with a grin. "Hungry as some of those beggars act, they might anyway. Shows you what greed gets you.

"And—" his face cooled—"that brings us to the question of Bev Dyson, doesn't it? If they say anything as bad about him at the House as they do down here, then I regret nobody called me home before. I started a job near thirty years ago with a wrench, and it sounded like it's past time to finish it."

Pritchard stretched. He laced his fingers behind his back and lifted his arms as high as he could. With his eyes closed against the hugeness of the sea, the lift and fall of the platform was even soothing. "I'm the honored visitor touring the estate," he said while still bent forward. "Your sister-in-law loaned me a car." Pritchard straightened and looked at his big friend squarely. "Tough lady, but she needs help. What she doesn't need is you barging in and getting your ass blown away, snake."

"I said you were in charge, Danny," Slade said mildly. The big man scanned the sensor read-outs on his board. One of them was flickering orange, a beast rippling to and from a distant portion of filter line, nothing to be concerned about as yet. Slade's fingers pulled a rocket from a bandolier loop and slid it into the loading gate of the weapon. "Tell me what you think needs doing, and I'll see about getting it done."

"There's a Council meeting in two days," said Pritchard. "They're gathering in person at the House, the whole Council. Going to decide on the guardianship of your nephew Teddy."

"Council's in Dyson's pocket," Slade said without emotion. He nodded toward the station, though two of the men were actually downline of Slade's post. "What the crew here says is just what I saw myself. The Port's supposed to be neutral ground. Dyson put his own men in and my brother—" Slade's big hand squeezed fiercely on the alloy barrel of his gun—"let him do it, the. . . . Well. So now they're all afraid to burp for fear their cargo'll get looted or deep-sixed, inbound and out both. He's got the votes he needs, just like he did on that stupid business of me being the real heir. Cop!"

Danny looked at the bigger man sharply. "You could be, you know," Pritchard said. "Marilee swears that your brother told her that the night your father died. That your father had whispered it to him, just at the end."

"And *I* swear, my friend," replied Don Slade, "that it's cop even if it's true. Look, what do seven-

teen minutes one way or the other matter, for
running this, running *Tethys*—that's what we Slades
have done for six generations, Council be damned.
You think if I'd really wanted it, that I'd have let
a few minutes stand in the way? Blood and Martyrs,
snake, *you* know me better than that!"

Pritchard laughed. "Well, you were younger,
then," he said.

Slade grinned back. "Yeah, and meaner'n a knife-
jaw, my friend. Via, remember that bar on Em-
porion? The bouncer thought I was just blowing
air till my tank came through the wall!"

Both men laughed and linked arms. "Well," said
Pritchard, "let's say you rode in to the House on a
supply truck tomorrow. I've seen what you looked
like before you left Tethys: hair to your belt. I'm
willing to bet that without that and the beard,
maybe a little dye and editing, there's nobody you'll
see who's going to recognize you this long after.
Not if you got through the Port. Now, there's likely
to be a problem in the yard itself, but I think . . ."

Danny Pritchard continued to talk in a calm,
professional voice while the big man beside him
nodded. Overhead, fairy skimmers folded their gos-
samer wings and dived into the rich sea life around
the platform.

Slade simply noted their delicate motions. He
knew that he could handle moving targets without
any need to practice on these.

CHAPTER TWENTY-SIX

Fadel Buckalew, a Steward's Assistant, drove his provisions truck with a hard-handed determination. He managed to ground the steel skirts jarringly on the shingle a number of times, though without achieving more than a moderate speed. Slade had never claimed to be much of a driver himself, but at least the tanker did not regard air cushion vehicles with an angry hostility the way the young Houseman did.

"So," Buckalew said, "old Piet tells me you met the Mad Dog and that's why he's sending you to the House. That a fact?"

"Something close," said the tanker. He knew that Pretorius had never referred to his "Master Donald" as Mad Dog Slade. "Came in on the same ship as a visitor to the House, guy named Pritchard. In Transit I'd mentioned meeting a Captain Slade of Hammer's Regiment on his way back to Tethys himself. When Pritchard got to the House and heard how things were, he thought I ought to go tell the Mistress my story. The foreman thought so too."

The truck ground its left side against the rocks beneath the layer of creeping native vegetation. Though some of the nastier forms of sea life bred on Tethys' scattered islands, there was nothing native to the land which was significantly developed, even the plants. Terran vegetation had been imported, but it grew over the rocky soil only where encouraged: around the manors of the Councilors, and in small plots, among the dwellings of lesser folk.

The sea supplied roughage as it did protein through processing plants like the one Slade was leaving. When people grew vegetables, it was for the sake of luxury or whim, not need. The grass plots, though, served a need: that of Earth-evolved humans to see something green that was not synthetic nor the sea's metallic choice of dress for the moment.

"Well, it's none of my business," the Houseman said, "but if I was you, I'd go back to sucking seawater. Not that *I* would," he added hastily as he realized that he had just suggested a position of basic labor was not beneath him.

"But I mean," Buckalew went on, "you're safe back there—" He gestured. The truck slewed and grated. "But if you go up to the House, meddling with Council affairs, well . . . the Mistress may be glad to see you, I don't say she wouldn't be. But there's some wouldn't, and you'll meet them before you do her."

"Yeah," said Slade, "I was kind of hoping you might drop me around in back."

Slade was uncomfortable with the conversation and with his outfit. The Station Six crew had been adamant that nobody in coveralls would be allowed into Slade House now unless the Mistress led them in by the hand. Master Thomas had been a stickler for proprieties, Pretorius said. Chesson was young, but even he could remember the free and easy days when labor was nothing to be ashamed of and working for the Slades was all you needed to talk to the Councilor.

Don's father had not been a gun-toting brawler like his own progenitor, a throwback to the harsh days of the Settlement. Neither, however, had he stood on ceremony with those who served him. The tanker found it interesting that his brother had insisted on such punctillio, when according to that code—and his own belief—he had no right to be called Councilor at all.

Well, people did strange things, and tanks did strange things. Don Slade had learned to deal with some of the strangeness without bothering himself too much with causes.

Dealing with the problem meant, in this case, wearing the non-service clothes Danny Pritchard sent along for Slade to wear. The tunic was russet, with puffy sleeves gathered at the wrists. It was big enough for Slade's shoulders and would have held two of him at the waist. The slacks were doe-skin, again ample in the waist and thighs— but so tight when his calf muscles bulged that the tanker had considered slitting them up from the cuffs.

Slade wore the boots he had awakened with at the Port. They fit; and he might soon have need for footwork.

Buckalew had taken his time about answering his passenger's implied question. "Well, I tell you," the Houseman said with a sidelong glance which shifted the truck, "I'm sorry, and you not used to the House and all . . . but it'd be worth my teeth at the best if I got smart about where I pulled in. Especially with the load I'm carrying from your buddies in Six."

"What's in the load?" Slade asked in surprise.

"Nothing, that's what's in the bloody load!" the Houseman snapped. "Cans of process, that's what we've got. Via! I know and everybody at the House knows that they're bringing in crunchers and that they're taking heart fillets out of duopods—all the good stuff, just like always. But what do they send *me* back with? Process! Compressed protein. Compressed flotsam! One of these days a load of boys from the House is going to come see your buddies, and they're going to wish they'd changed their ways before."

"Well, I don't know," said the tanker without emphasis. "I'd say the crew at Six would be easier folks to talk to than to threaten. True of a lot of people, of course. Been reminding myself of that for going on twenty years."

"You see how it is," said Buckalew. He waved—Slade cringed and the truck rasped—toward the tall outline of the House on the horizon. "I'm in enough trouble, coming back with nothing but turtle cop. If I drop you at Service, they'll be sure I off-loaded anything worth eating there too. You see."

"They will," the tanker repeated. He flexed his fingers, one hand against the other. "Well, I guess I'll see pretty soon."

"Come on, Bucky," crackled the voice through the dash speaker. There was a rush of static or laughter. The voice then continued, "We know it's you, but come on up where we can watch."

The Houseman was shivering. The truck hovered at idle, millimeters off the ground. Its cab was pointed at the closed gate in the three-meter wall.

Buckalew touched the key of the microphone/speaker, a bolt-on set not integral with the vehicle. "Master Hensen," Buckalew said, "you know I'm not . . . could you maybe let me in by the gate this once? You know I don't. . . ."

Buckalew let his thumb slip from the key. The speaker roared, "Get your butt up here, goon, or we'll come and find you!"

"They make you jump the wall to get in?" Slade asked.

Vehicles built for use on Tethys normally had enough extra fan capacity to fly without depending on ground effect, the bubble of air trapped between the ground and the vehicle's skirts. Otherwise they could not be driven over Tethys' omnipresent seas without the likelihood of disastrous attack by the larger predators. The supply truck was heavily laden, however. The ride from Station Six had made it clear that the Assistant Steward did not have the greater skills needed to safely lift the truck from its cushion.

"Well . . ." muttered Buckalew.

"Via, man," Slade said, speaking the obvious. "You'll kill us both if you try that!"

Buckalew nodded miserably as he fed power to the fans. "I know," he said. "I've been buying my way off these runs till today." The truck took a tentative hop and yawed its left front into the gravel.

Slade closed the throttles. His hand gripped the knobs and slid them back as if the Houseman were not trying to fight the pressure. "Get out," Slade said. His voice was thick and irregular, like bubbles boiling through tar.

"Come *on*, Bucky, we're *waiting* for you," the speaker called.

"W-what?" Buckalew whimpered.

"Get *out*!" Slade repeated. "I'm taking this mother in!"

The tanker reached past Buckalew for the door, unlatched it, and thrust the Houseman out of the cab. Slade moved his own big body under the controls. The speaker started to make another demand. Slade's right forearm crumpled the box into hissing somnolence.

Throttles, attitude adjustments. The Houseman was backing away from the vehicle with a frightened look on his face. Slade dialed up the thrust. Fan pitch and nacelle attitude were not crucial safety factors when operating by ground effect, because the air cushion balanced irregularities and averaged the total power. On true lift, however, the fans required individual settings unless the load were perfectly balanced. This truckload of supplies assuredly was not balanced.

Slade boosted ten centimeters on instinct, over-corrected for a bump on the tail skirt, and lifted over the wall in a curve that was graceful but considerably faster than he had intended. Slade wasn't much of a driver, that was the Lord's simple truth, but he was the right man at the controls just now.

"All right, Bucky!" crowed the loud-hailer on the helmet of a man in crimson. There were dozens of men in the courtyard, backed cautiously against the walls and the line of parked air cars to watch the show. Most of the observers were clapping, though the sound of that and their hooting was lost in the rush of the fans at high load. Slade had neither the time nor the inclination to check the varied liveries below, but there was one man in Slade blue—with a slash of crimson down either leg.

The tanker was even with the upper windows of the House and the Council Hall. His truck was quivering in polarized reflection to either side. The man with the loud-hailer was against the House door, where an armored drone protected him to either side; a pity, but—

"Well, come *on*, Bucky," the loud-hailer called. "All you've got left's the easy part, right? Chop your throttle and I promise you'll come down!"

"Right, fella," Slade muttered as he cut power fifteen percent to the four front fans and cocked the left rear nacelle to the side. Adrenalin made the tanker's arms tremble, and his mind was icy with rage.

The truck slid down a column of thrust. Its rear end was slewing around a pivot point just forward of the cab. Slade could still not hear the hangers-on nor could he see the men among the parked air cars as the truck rotated down toward them with the majesty of Juggernaut's Carriage. The drooping left skirt caught first with a ping and a shudder. Then the whole laden back end crashed along the line of cars.

The lightly-built luxury vehicles disintegrated at the impact. The truck's skirts were steel, flexible only at the edges. They were meant for the sort of rough work on the shingle that Buckalew had been giving them an hour before.

At the end of the line of cars, Slade twitched up his throttles and hopped awkwardly aloft again. The crumpled back end of the truck brushed the corner of the House as it turned. He shouldn't have been greedy about the last car or two . . . but it was with less damage than Slade had expected that he thumped the truck down at last in the center of the courtyard. One of the fans was singing where its blades touched a twisted duct.

Slade shut off all power. He felt for the moment—only the moment, and he knew that—as if he too had been shut down after a successful operation.

There were blue and orange flickers in the shadows which the lowering sun cast across the courtyard. Electrical fires had started in several of the mangled vehicles. With his fans shut off, the tanker could hear the screams of the men pinched and battered when the cars slid from the metal-rending impact of the truck.

There were screams of rage as well, from those who did not have their injuries to occupy them. The Dyson minion with the loud-hailer had lost his helmet and was cowering against the door. A group of men were rushing toward the truck from the other side, however. Three of them wore knives and Dyson livery. The fourth was the one Danny had warned about, Durotige, though his nunchaku was hidden for the moment beneath the tail of his blue tunic. Durotige was a big man and hugely aroused at the moment.

"The Lord eat your *eyes*, Buckalew!" Durotige shouted through the dust which still cavorted around the truck. "Or I will!"

Slade opened the cab door before the other men could reach it. He stood on the entry step, gaining from it a height advantage he would not otherwise have had over the turncoat. "Buckalew's not here," Slade said. "You want to eat *my* eyes, friend?"

In Slade's right hand was a length of control rod, half a meter of chrome steel brought from the Station. It rang as he slapped it against his left palm.

The four men pulled up very abruptly. One of them made a motion toward his knife. He thought the better of it.

Durotige did not lose his mental balance for more than a second or two. "Sure, you're tough with that in your hands," the turncoat said. "But you're not man enough to fight me without it, are you?"

It was a dangerous gamble ... but the situation was dangerous any way you sliced it, and that was nothing new to Slade.

"Just you and me?" the tanker asked. He waved the rod in a glittering arc, taking in the men with Durotige and the others moving from cover now that the danger of the truck had passed. "And you don't pull a knife?"

"Hey, buddy," called someone in green and lemon yellow, "you're in enough trouble already. Don't get your head bashed besides."

A pair of Dyson retainers from the clot around Durotige moved in on the man who had spoken. He backed, but not quickly enough to keep the men in crimson from seizing him from either side. One of them snarled, "Butt *out*, fishbrain," and punched the speaker in the ribs.

"Just you and me," Durotige promised loudly. He spread his arms wide and waved his bare hands toward Slade. "And with nothing we don't carry right now—soon as you throw down that rod. Just what we stand in. Guess you've got a few years on me, but you look fit enough. Anyhow, it was your idea.'"

Slade smiled. He rolled the rod back and forth on his palm for a moment. Then he slipped it behind him, onto the seat as he stepped down from the truck. "You're on," Slade said, knowing that in this instant all four of them might pile on him to wash his life away in the dust with their knives and their numbers.

The House door was spilling out far more people than had been in the courtyard when the truck set down. Not liverymen alone, but Councilors, at least a dozen of them. The Council Members were notable for their studied avoidance of any form of dress that might be taken for livery. House colors were for retainers. Many Councilors affected ancient formal wear: stark blacks and whites, and starkly-uncomfortable cuts.

The shattered vehicles drew some of the attention, but that would keep. The two big men now moving from threats to action focused the eyes of both Councilors and retainers.

The Dyson men did not jump Slade with Durotige. They hopped away, well aware of the amount of area which the nunchaku commanded. One of the liverymen guffawed.

Durotige backed from Slade's advance also. He obviously wanted his victim to be too far from the rod to recover it when he learned how he had been tricked.

Just for a moment, Slade thought that his opponent really might intend to settle matters with his fists. Then Durotige reached back, under the flapping tail of his tunic, and slid out his linked flails with the air of a successful conjuror. "Just what we stand in," he repeated. The Dyson retainers cackled in glee at a safe distance, though they were closer to the action than were the other spectators.

"Why Durotige," Slade said. "You didn't *tell* me about the numbchucks."

Durotige blinked as he realized that his opponent knew his name. Before all the implications of that could penetrate, Slade threw himself into a broad imitation of a karate stance.

The tanker's views on personal combat were those he had heard from his grandfather thirty-odd years earlier. You don't hit a man with your bare hand unless you're naked and they've nailed your feet to the ground. No one in the crowd knew that, however, least of all Durotige. The turncoat grinned and moved in with his weapon flickering.

For the benefit of his audience, Durotige executed a series of passes back and forth between his straddled legs. The nunchaku shifted, spinning, from hand to hand in perfect rhythm. It was the sort of nonsense that could have cost Durotige his weapon . . . except that the men in crimson were ready to toss it back should a slip of the hand send it skittering loose.

Slade shouted, "Hai!" and stamped his right foot. It was simply an effort to end his opponent's posturing. The tanker carried his hands up, with the fingers extended as if they were capable of smashing bricks. He had sometimes vaguely wished that he did have the training for formal unarmed combat, but it had never been worth his time. There were sledge hammers for smashing bricks, and for more serious matters—

Durotige made his move. His right hand fed the

nunchaku behind his back and over his left shoulder where the left hand took it. Instead of executing another shimmering bit of jugglery, the turncoat lashed out in an overarm cut at Slade's skull. He held one wooden flail by the base. The slashing attack extended the paired flails the length of both and of Durotige's long left arm. It was virtually too fast for Slade to have dodged, had he wanted to.

Instead, the tanker blocked the whirring club with his right forearm.

The blow cracked like lightning close enough to touch. The outer flail rebounded as it was supposed to do. Because the link was not rigid, none of the shock was transmitted to the hand in which Durotige held his weapon.

The turncoat smiled in the certainty that he had shattered his opponent's arm. The sound had been wrong, but there was no time now for nuances, the blow *had* to have been effective. Durotige recovered and struck precisely the same swinging blow again.

The pain of Slade's radius splintered among the blood and soft tissues should have left the tanker open for the follow-up, despite its lack of finesse. Slade was grinning. Durotige noticed that only as the nunchaku cracked again on the right forearm which reflex should have protected at any cost after it was broken.

Slade's left hand caught Durotige's and clamped it firmly to the baton it held. The tanker's snatching motion had started as the nunchaku swung. The motion did not disintegrate in pain as expected when the second blow landed. The turncoat found himself held, face to face with his opponent. The flails dangled uselessly beside them.

Grinning like Hellgate, Don Slade swung his right forearm as if it were a club. Durotige caught the blow with his own free hand. The hand-bones crackled. All the strength went out of the turncoat's arm. The blow, only partially blocked, chunked against his skull. Durotige sagged forward with a bloody welt across his left temple.

Slade's grip would not let the turncoat fall. The tanker hit him again, still with the forearm and not a fist. Durotige's skull rang like an imploding vacuum-bottle. Slade thrust his opponent away to fall, the body liquid, the head staining the dust.

With a quick motion, Don Slade retrieved the nunchaku which had fallen with their owner. None of the onlookers had moved closer when the fight climaxed. The nearest faces, those of the Dyson men, gaped in amazement. To Slade's hormone-hopping glance, the men were little more than pale blurs on crimson blurs, the status they would retain until they moved toward him themselves.

The tanker gripped the base of a flail in either hand. He twisted the weapon against itself so that the three links of chain were taut. "Well?" said Slade. His voice echoed despite the size of the courtyard. "Who's next?"

Using torsion to do what no human muscles, not even his own, could do in a straight pull, Slade parted the flails and hurled them in opposite directions. One of them clacked above the door of the House.

"Bring that man to me," ordered a cold voice from the silence. Lights pinned Slade, though they were not really necessary in the present dusk.

Slade turned. Time had not robbed Beverly

Dyson's voice of its familiarity, nor of the swelling rage that it fed in Slade's belly.

Councilor Dyson and a trio of liverymen had come from the Council Hall. To see the fight from that angle, the quartet had to walk around the truck grounded in the middle of the yard. Two of the retainers now flared handlights at Slade from ten meters away. Sidescatter showed that the third liveryman gripped a case. Not even the most ignorant could imagine the case held an information system and not a gun. Dyson himself was behind the lights and shrouded by their glare. He was a slim figure, as cool as his voice.

Slade's right sleeve was torn from the blows it had taken and returned. He jerked the dangling fabric free with his left hand. The length of pressure tubing which covered the right forearm gleamed in the strong lights. There was a smear of blood near the wrist, but the nunchaku had not marked the rigid plastic. A single toothmark winked just above the line at which the tanker had cut the section from his lure.

"I said *bring him*," Beverly Dyson repeated in a voice with more life than before. Slade, who was expecting the next words to call a spray of gunfire, was amazed to hear the Councilor continue, "Don't worry, my good man. I have an offer for you."

"No," said Slade. He turned quickly, smoothly, a shark twisting against a fool who would grasp its tail.

The gunman might be ordered to fire or might not. It did not matter whether Slade faced the blast. The men who had accompanied Durotige were two paces closer, now. Their confidence had been in their master's promise of good treatment, not in their own numbers. Now they scuttled back so quickly that one stumbled on Durotige's outflung hand. The turncoat still lay in the dust. He was breathing stertorously. Blood oozed from his matted scalp, his nose, and his left ear.

"No," repeated a clear voice. Slade's own refusal had been the rumble of a beast. It had been intelligible only by its tone and the right fist clenched to grip the armoring tube.

A party of four was striding from the House. The lights now silhouetting Slade fell brightly across the newcomers. Marilee was half a step in front. Her face was as firm and clear as the denial she had just spoken. She was not the girl Slade had left on his brother's arm at the Port, but she was perfectly the woman from his dream of Hell.

The youth must be Teddy. He walked to one side, tight where his mother was whip-supple. Danny Pritchard was on the woman's other side, with Coon Blegan beside him. Blegan pushed away one of the crimson toughs who had not moved in time; but it was Danny Pritchard who carried the submachinegun.

He did not attempt to hide the weapon. Pritchard's index finger lay beside the trigger guard, not in it. To Slade's practiced eye, that was sure proof that no bluff was intended. There was one up the spout, and the safety was off.

Dyson's men might carry guns: despite the law, and as a symbol that their power was beyond the law. The Slammers used their guns to kill, with a frequency no one could keep track of, and with an effectiveness that Danny Pritchard himself would as soon have forgotten.

"This man came as a visitor to my House," said

Marilee in the same clear voice as before. She spoke toward Dyson but loudly enough that every one in the courtyard could hear her. "I won't have him harassed."

The woman stepped past the tanker to one side while Pritchard passed to the other. The principle, not the individual, was first in her mind.

And dear Lord, did *none* of Slade's closest acquaintances recognize him after twenty hard years?

"That man has a gun," said Councilor Dyson in genuine surprise.

Slade turned to watch the confrontation of which he was no longer a part. Dyson was pointing to Danny's weapon. The Councilor himself had not moved, but his three retainers were edging backward so that light played across their master as well as themselves.

"And his clothes aren't red," retorted Marilee. "What's the matter, Bev?"

"In the future, no trucks will land in this courtyard," said Teddy. His voice was high and on the edge of control, but it was a man's voice for all that. "It's dangerous. And anybody interfering with trucks unloading properly will be expelled from the Estate. Do you hear?"

"Put that away!" Dyson rasped to his liveryman, the one who had half opened the case holding his own gun. "And put those curst lights off!" the Councilor added as angrily to the other pair.

Dusk was darkness in the aftereffect of the glare. Dyson stepped forward, beyond his men but not so close to those facing him that he could be thought to be holding a normal conversation. "I don't know what you think you're about, Marilee," the Councilor said, "but it won't work in the Hall. Do you understand? There will be no guns in the Hall. None!"

"The Hall is the Council's business, Dyson," the woman replied. Her words cut through the twilight like lyre notes. "The House is mine. You and your rubbish are not to enter the House again. Good evening." Her heel and toe gouged the dust as she turned. "Gentlemen," she added cooly, "let us go inside."

The rank that Marilee had led to the confrontation returned as a file behind her to the House. Slade was the last man. He fought the impulse to throw back his shoulders as if better to absorb the shots that might still arrive.

Slade had found a good group of people back here.

CHAPTER TWENTY-SEVEN

The interior of Slade House had shrunk in the years he had been away. He would not have expected that. When Don Slade left Tethys, he had his full growth; but he had long been divorced from the life of the House in which he lived. The memories that lived when the earth spouted around him and the sky screamed hellfire were those of his childhood.

In memory the corridors were high and dimmed by mystery, not neglect. Rooms built to house the warriors of the Settlement now stored mementos of that harsh, vivid time. And through all the memories blazed the figure of Slade's grandfather, Devil Don, the Old Man; the craggy, powerful model for Slade's life.

The Old Man had surrendered the administrative duties of House and planet to his son as soon as the son could handle them. But while the duties had been his, the Old Man had performed them with the fierce skill he displayed whenever he forced himself into a business that he hated. In retirement, he fished and hunted across the seas of Tethys, brawling with men half his age. And he carried with him the grandson who bore his name, and whom he swore had been minted from the same die as himself.

The odd thing was that as Don grew older, he resembled his grandfather in no physical respect but his size ... and for all that, the Old Man was right, was dead right. To copy his grandfather, Don let his hair and beard grow—into a black mass as different from the Old Man's white, silken locks as could be imagined. Brother Thomas cut his own fair hair short, but only surgery could have kept every acquaintance from remarking that he looked just like the Old Man.

As the party turned up the helical staircase just within the entrance, Coon Blegan paused to speak to the doorkeeper. "If you had any guts," Blegan whispered—Slade could hear him, but Teddy and surely Marilee could not—"you might even be good for something."

"Up yours, old man," said the natty-looking doorkeeper. He gestured with his shock rod, real as well as symbolic power.

Slade reached from behind and plucked the shock rod away. It was a baton of thumb-thick plastic half a meter long. Electrodes winked at either end. The doorkeeper yelped and tried to snatch the instrument back. Slade's left arm blocked the servant with no more effort than a wall would have displayed.

The doorkeeper's kiosk was cast concrete like the rest of the House's construction. Slade held the baton at its balance with equal portions extending to the thumb-side and heel-side of his hand. He punched upward toward the corner of the kiosk doorway, where the integral post and lintel met. The two ends of the baton took the impact. The instrument crunched into halves.

The tanker handed the pieces back to the doorkeeper with a courteous nod. "Yours, I believe, sir," he said.

Coon Blegan watched with a look of surmise that Slade had not meant to arouse. Pritchard had paused partway up the stairs, just in sight. Waiting, his weapon was unobtrusively at his side.

Most of those drawn into the courtyard were still there. They were fulminating over the damage to their vehicles or gazing with secret delight at the wreckage of some rival's car. The few who trooped babbling back within the House passed the tableau without noticing it. Even Slade's arm could have been a handshake from the angle past his body.

The doorkeeper took his baton back with a look of amazement as silent as the deftness with which it had been stripped from him. Slade gestured to Blegan. The old retainer grinned and proceeded up the stairs. The tanker followed, without a look back at the open-mouthed doorkeeper.

This was the family staircase. The door from it to the second floor on which the guests were lodged was locked. Slade had spent very little time in the family apartments on the third floor in the last years of his youth on Tethys. The tanker subconsciously expected changes. There were none, none he recognized, save for the size.

The staircase debouched into a walled entryway with a door to the corridor serving the remainder of the floor and a separate door to the Trophy Room which engrossed the quarter of the floor facing the courtyard and the Council Hall beyond.

Teddy was holding the Trophy Room door for Danny Pritchard. From within the room, Marilee said, "Mister Pritchard, Danny. I appreciate your presence tonight and the risk you ran. You were invaluable."

Danny did not move forward. When Slade reached the top of the stairs, he could see that the woman stood not beside the doorway but within it to block passage. "But you'll understand that I want to speak alone to the 'man who met my—brother-in-law returning."

"Of course," Danny said with a neutral smile. "I'll feel better for a hot bath after all that." He turned. When his back was to the mother and son, he winked at Slade.

"I'll stay, though," Teddy was saying. The anteroom was crowded. Slade and Blegan were big men, Pritchard not a small one. All of them were trying to keep a courteous distance from the family quarrel brewing.

"No, Edward," Marilee said. The edge in her voice was slight, but it was still out of line with anything which was overtly going on. "You have your duties. I'm sure many of our guests will be demanding compensation for damaged vehicles."

"Yes, I'll take care of that," the youth said with a dismissing gesture, "but Mother—"

"Teddy!"

Teddy's head jerked back as the tone slapped him. "Yes, Mother," he said in a subdued voice. "I'll be down in the Audience Room if you need me."

He squeezed past the big men at the stair head without noticing them as individuals.

So softly that even Slade could barely hear him, Blegan whispered in the tanker's ear, "I'm a fat old man, friend. But I wouldn't want anything to happen to the Mistress." Then the retainer turned to follow Teddy down the stairs.

Pritchard was already gone, toward his own suite among the family rooms. "Come here, Mister Holt," said Marilee as she stepped aside.

The Trophy Room had been intended as a museum of human valor rather than of the dangerous sea life of Tethys. The result had made it both. Because the only light in the room at present was the red glow through the west window, the skulls merged with their own shadows. That did not matter to Slade. He could have drawn every piece from memory, have labeled it, positioned it on the wall of his mind. Slade was a child again, walking softly in front of romance.

The glow-strip under the big window was not bright, but its light shocked Slade out of his reverie. His hand was extended, almost touching one of a pair of screw holes. They were below the level at which most of the trophies were mounted. The holes had been filled, and in the ebbing twilight they should have been invisible.

"Yes, there used to be another one there," said Marilee with detachment. She seated herself in the chair from which she had switched on the light. "A larval arguş. My husband had it removed. He said it didn't fit with the others, only a larva."

"Yes," said Don Slade. "Not a—thing worthy of a hunter." He had squeezed shut his eyes, but that did not help. The pressure of the eyelids and muscles only forced the welling tears up faster.

"It wasn't exactly a hunting trophy," the woman said to Slade's back. "My brother-in-law—Captain Slade—was eating lunch with his grandfather on one of the islands in the Random Star. The arguş must have just hatched. It crawled out and stabbed the Old Man in the small of the back. He just happened to be there, you see, but the defensive spines are quite dangerous. They paralyzed him."

"Yes, the spines can be nasty," said Slade thickly to the wall.

It had been a meter long and gleaming with the pearly iridescence of the eggshell still dragging behind it. Its eyes were broad patches on the exoskeleton, the color of fresh bruises. The spines along the lower edge of its carapace squirmed like a thorn hedge in a windstorm. Most of them were dripping yellow with venom, but some already were smeared with the Old Man's blood . . .

"Don killed it with his hands," the woman was saying. "He pulled it off his grandfather and pounded it to death on the ground. For weeks after that, they thought he might lose both his arms from what the spines did to him. He was seven years old, then."

"Yes," Slade repeated, "the spines can be nasty."

He turned away very slowly. His face was under control again. The left shoulder of his tunic was damp where it had hunched to mop away the tear which had escaped. Not for a husk of lacquered chitin, and not for Slade's past youth. For the Old Man, who had mounted the larva with his own hands and, stiff himself with the aftereffects of the venom, had carried his delirious grandson into the Trophy Room to see it. "You wanted to question me, Mistress," said Don Slade.

"Sit down, Holt," the woman said with a brusque gesture. "I'm told that you've seen Captain Slade more recently than Mister Pritchard has."

Slade moved to the indicated bench. It was a

low one at a discreet two meters from the seated woman. "Yes, Mistress," he said. "He was on Desmo, landed there from an Alayan ship."

"The same Alayan ship that brought you and Mister Pritchard to Tethys?" the woman interjected.

Slade looked up sharply. The trophy wall had stunned him into a quiescent state which fit very well the persona of a laborer in private conference with one of the planet's great. The question brought the tanker to alertness again. He had not known that Danny had been carried by the Alayans. "Yes, Mistress," Slade said. "That is—they don't land, you know. Tenders carry you to orbit. I suppose it was the same ship. Ah, Captain Slade had business on Desmo, seeing to some of his men. But he told me he'd be home soon and—look me up.

"He was really looking forward to getting home," the tanker added softly. His left hand was absently working loose the tubing from his right arm. The sawn edges were sharp enough to have cut his skin near the elbow, and the battering given and received by the armor had despite its protection caused the tissues to swell.

"I suppose," said Marilee in a tone that supposed nothing, "that Captain Slade will have a family by this time. From what I recall of his youth, presumably he will have a harem. I don't suppose local strictures on marriage apply to off-planet mercenaries, even when there are such—strictures."

The tubing slid loose. Slade extended his right hand with thumb and little fingers touching so that they would not catch the front edges of the plastic. The air was thrilling on the film of sweat and sweat-thinned blood.

"There's mercs who settle, and mercs who move," Slade said with his head lowered. "The Slammers moved. Nobody could afford to keep them long enough for it to be the other way."

He turned the length of tubing, looking at it from one angle and then another to have some ostensible focus for his eyes. "You don't carry women along unless they're part of the unit. There aren't so many of them, and fewer still who'd be interested in a man. I didn't notice anybody traveling with Captain Slade."

The tanker risked a glance toward his hostess. She met his eyes abruptly, but it was not his face at which she had been staring.

Slade looked down again and cursed. He twisted his bloody right arm so that its underside was no longer in the light. Beneath the stains and slickness were still the scars the argus had left on a child. The skin had stretched and filled with muscle over the years, but the unpigmented keloids would remain till the grave. Slade licked his lips and said to the woman, "You wanted your brother-in-law to come home, Mistress."

"No!" said Marilee. She had been leaning forward. Now she thrust herself against the back of her chair. "I wanted him, and that may have been a mistake even then. But I don't want Don to come home now. It's too late. They'd only kill him."

"They're trash, Mistress," said the tanker. The emotion in his quiet voice was not anger. "You can't live, worrying about trash."

"My husband was a good man," said Marilee, "a *good* man—"

"I know that."

"—but he let Beverly Dyson build his organization for two years. All very careful, taking over the Port that was too much work for any of the other board members to bother about. Loans to some, help of other kinds and blackmail besides to some who needed more than money."

The woman swept to her feet again. She stood like a warrior queen. Her voice rolled out in challenge. "All very quiet, Mister—Holt—and none of the thugs, the gunmen, till all that had been taken care of. But the thugs are here, they killed Tom. And they'll kill anybody else who threatens Dyson's plans, I see that now."

"Look," said Slade as he stood also. Half his mind would have taken him nearer to the woman, but instead he walked back toward the trophy wall. They were part of what had forged him, those monsters; and beyond that, he felt a certain kinship with what they represented. "You knew that—Mistress," he said, "when you called your brother-in-law home. Nothing's changed, except your nerve's giving out. And it's not your nerve that matters when h-he gets home."

"That's not *true* about nothing changing!" the woman cried. She raised both hands. "It was a chance for the Council to back a strong leader against Bev Dyson. All right, not Teddy . . . and not me either, some of them because they're fools and some because they didn't see the skills for this—kind of business—in my background. Man or woman. But I thought somebody they *could* respect, and somebody who *could* organize them, lead them—Bev doesn't have any army, and all the Council together could muster enough men to, to get him away. I thought they'd all jump at the chance not to be bullied by Bev Dyson, but . . ."

Marilee sagged in on herself without completing the thought.

The flaring pectoral fins of the orc had been razor sharp when Don Slade first grew tall enough to touch them gingerly. That edge had long been worn round as awe was slowly replaced by ritual. Slade touched a fin now. A part of him visualized the creature alive, forty meters of it spiraling up toward the platform on which the Old Man waited with a rocket gun.

Memory of his grandfather was by no means out of place to current needs. "And Councilor Dorcas, your brother?" asked Slade as his hand caressed the deadly fin.

"The present Councilor is my nephew, I'm afraid," said the woman. She paced to the window. Through it now gleamed only the lights of those trying to deal with the wreckage in the courtyard. As generally on Tethys, the haze of clouds blocked any but the brightest stars.

"He's even younger than Teddy—isn't that amusing?" Marilee continued. "But well-advised, I gather. The vote to put the Slade Estate in guardianship was unanimous. I don't expect there to be much change tomorrow when the Council determines who the actual guardian should be.

"So you see," the tall woman continued as she faced her visitor again, "why I no longer believe that any possible rallying point would make—" she sniffed— "men out of the Councilors. Except perhaps for me to retain a mercenary regiment. I was almost willing to consider that course, until I talked to Mister Pritchard the other day. I will die before I bring that to Tethys. I will die."

"Yeah," said Don Slade to the window. "Well." Seconds after she thought he was finished, the tanker continued. "I suppose the Old Man's room's been cleaned out years since. I mean, Counc—"

"I know who the Old Man was," the woman said. "Even during Council sessions, there has been space to spare in this House since it ceased to be a barracks. My husband would never enter—his grandfather's room, Holt, but he never permitted anyone else to enter it either. Would you like to, to . . . ?"

"Yes, Mistress," said Slade. "Very much."

Slade stretched. The muscles that rippled across his arms and shoulders gave the lie to his dyed, razor-thinned hair.

"And—" nervous again, but soft as she paused— "you'll be staying tonight in the House?"

The tanker shrugged. He touched the orc again. "I'll get back to Number Six, Mistress. It'll cause less trouble. If you can arrange transportation when you get someone to let me into the Old Man's room? I doubt the truck I came in will run me back." Slade's smile was as bleak and distant as that of the orc.

"Of course," said Marilee. Her voice was normal, but it sounded thin in her own ears as her world shrank down to a point. "I suppose you can understand why Don can't appear now?"

The man did not speak. He stood before the trophies. He looked as massive and powerful and inert as a stalled ox.

"Perhaps," Marilee went on, "things might change. Soon. And it will be safe for Captain Slade to return to Tethys."

"Tethys won't be safe for *any* man, or a woman,"

said the tanker flatly, "until there's enough men—or women—to make it safe. I've heard what I needed to hear, Mistress."

Marilee turned and bent over the chair-arm controls. She gave quick orders to the Under-Steward on call. Then, in a clear voice, she said to the man behind her, "That will be all, then, Holt."

Only when the door closed solidly did Marilee open her eyes again. She felt as if the maelstrom had just swept past her last hope of survival.

CHAPTER TWENTY-EIGHT

The pumps were already sluicing the lines again in start-up mode, testing the system for leaks which had opened during the hours of darkness. Their *hoosh* announced Slade as he entered the crew area, then closed the door behind him.

"Hey, it's Soldier," called Chesson as Leaf was saying, "Via! Look how he's togged out!" Slade wore a Steward's tunic, blue-green with silver piping. It fit him no worse than the garment he had worn to the House.

"Fried potatoes with your breakfast?" asked Pretorius. He shook the skillet.

"Via, yes," Slade said as he sat down beside the fourth chair at the table. He took the plate the foreman handed him. Raw fries, nothing processed about them, gleamed beside a filet of shallotte or some similar fish. "You guys teaching potatoes to swim, then?" the tanker asked. There was certainly no garden plot at the station, swept as it was by tides on an average of once a month.

"My wife grows them," said Chesson as he took another mouthful. "Well, we both do every other month when I'm off, but I can't take much credit."

"No trouble at the House, then?" Leaf asked.

"Yeah, what did the Mistress say?" Chesson added

as he recollected the circumstances in which the big man had ridden off in the truck.

"Let the man eat his breakfast," said Pretorius. He took his own place at the table. Even in the foreman's eyes, however, were questions dancing to be answered.

"There was a bit of trouble," Slade said. Instead of eating, he eased his chair back and looked across the other three men. "Nothing that couldn't be handled. What happens this afternoon, though, that's going to be harder. They're going to give Bev Dyson guardianship of the Slade Estate."

Unexpectedly Leaf said, "I wasn't but a boy, not so much as Chessie's age." Chesson, who was a good thirty years old, bridled but did not interrupt. "The storm of 161 it was, the Great Storm. You remember that, Piet?"

Pretorius shrugged. "Before my time," he said.

Leaf nodded as if to pump up his memory. "There was never anything to match it," the old man said. "Fifteen days of wind and waves. There wasn't a let-up till the end. The eye missed Main Island altogether, just curled through us like the blade of a circle saw. But you know, lads—it did pass. Master Teddy is of age in two years?"

Chesson and the foreman were nodding slowly in agreement. Slade said, "If Bev Dyson takes over—" he raised his left hand, palm up and fingers extended— "in six months, Teddy will be in a fish's belly." The hand clenched with the suddenness of jaws snapping.

The three other men looked at Slade, at the fist and at the face set as hard as that fist. "This planet's been run a certain way since the Settlement," the tanker said. "Some mightn't like it, but it seemed to suit most pretty well. If Dyson takes over, the system isn't going to change, not really ... but the way it's applied won't ever be the same. The Council Islands'll toe'the line set from the Main, from Slade House or Paraclete, whichever Bev decides should be his capital."

Slade's voice was getting louder, but he did not move from his chair. "Councilors won't decide anything but who they screw on a given night. And all right, that doesn't bother you or me either. But the rock-hoppers, the independants, they'll all be pulled in and settled if they'll come—or hunted down if they won't, you *know* Bev Dyson. And when there's nowhere to run, he'll start squeezing every laborer on Tethys ... and he'll squeeze you the worst, my friends, because he hates every soul and thing that ever wore Slade Blue."

The clenched fist opened again as if it bore the future on a platter.

Pretorius shook his head with a look of sad wonder. "*I* can't leave, Holt," he said. "Maybe you can go back as a mercenary, but they wouldn't have me at my age. And I wouldn't have them! This is the life I want, right here. And if that means Dyson and all the things that *Dyson* means, then it'll have to be that way."

"It's not what Mistress Slade wants," said the tanker softly.

"It's not what *we* want," Chesson burst out, "but what bloody difference does that make?"

"A good question," said Slade. He grinned as the pieces came together, working his fingers closed again without haste. "You know, I used to wonder why the Old Man put us so heavy into food production. There's ten stations just about like this one, right?"

"Sure, but that's business," said Leaf, watching Slade with puzzlement.

The tanker nodded. "Business, sure," he agreed. "The Slades feed most of the planet from these stations. But there's a lot more profit to cost of plant and maintenance in mining operations, which is why we've pretty well got food stations to ourselves. Right?"

The crewmen gaped or frowned. The economics of the situation had never consciously affected them. They were Slade retainers, and they did the jobs their forebears had done before them.

"Right," said Slade gently. "So what's the difference between mining and food extraction? *Besides* what you're trying to bring out of the sea?"

Pretorius saw where the conversation was directed. He said, "No."

The others looked at him. The foreman nodded to the weapons racked beside the doorway. "The mining rigs have guards, too. Any time you work men near the sea, you need sensors and guards."

"Right again," said Slade. It was good to be sure he could trust the men he was with. Trust them to think as well as act. "But a manganese dredge doesn't bring them halfway around the planet the way the juice does from your rig, does it? How many critters—how many monsters, they'd call them back at the House—have you put down, Piet?" He gestured. "Leaf? Chessie?"

Chesson snorted. "I remember my first, though not real well," he said. "It was when Pops was on this rig, so I must have been maybe five. He let me pull the trigger when a networm surfaced right under the platform."

"All right, friends," said the tanker as he rose to his feet. He stood, arms akimbo, facing the crewmen. "This isn't your job or that of the crews off-duty and at the other stations. But if it isn't done by you, it won't be done at all. For yourselves, and for the Mistress—and for Master Teddy, who can just maybe set things straight again, like they were when I was a kid. If he just gets a chance and a little help. Are you up to it?"

The pumps gentled the silence with their background of *hoosh, hoosh*. At last Pretorius spoke. "It's us you'll want to call the others, I suppose, Soldier?"

CHAPTER TWENTY-NINE

"Mark," said Beverly Dyson to key his throat mike. "Subiyaga, be *very* careful with that one. Take the detector down to aluminum spray if you have to to make sure he doesn't have a throwaway derringer. Mark."

"Mark," said the civilian-suited specialist responsible for the detection unit. "Yes, milord." Subiyaga nodded toward Councilor Dyson, halfway across the courtyard on the roof of his van. Dyson had moved the vehicle ostentatiously into the courtyard the night before when he was ordered out of Slade House.

A squad of Dyson retainers had been told off specifically to support Subiyaga. Besides them, representatives of five other Council Islands observed the detector. Coon Blegan glowered at the equipment on behalf of the Slades. The newness and tailoring of Blegan's blue livery could not disguise the old man's paunch; but the pistol beneath his left arm was to be surmised rather than seen with clarity. Whatever might be the instructions other Councilors had given their observers, it was quite certain that Blegan would object forcefully if anything irregular occurred during the weapons checks.

Councilor Dyson did not care. He and those of his retainers whom he chose to bring within the

Hall would submit to the same careful vetting as the others. For this mercenary from Friesland, however, the search had to be extraordinary.

"Bastard," Dyson whispered. The three men of his personal staff stood behind him on the van roof. They looked sidelong at one another in concern.

Ten Dyson retainers were playing music opposite the detection station. Danny Pritchard did not recognize their wind instruments. Allowing for local conventions, Pritchard did not think the musicians were particularly skillful, either. Certainly the pair of Slade Housemen who accompanied Pritchard to the Hall did not seem to appreciate the music any better than did the ex-mercenary.

In all likelihood, the musicians were there to divert attention from the indignity of search; for even Councilors and their families had to go through the detection loop.

As Danny stepped into the loop, he smiled at Subiyaga. The specialist's brief conversation with his master was easy enough to guess, though Pritchard had heard neither end of it. Subiyaga let the unit run its pre-programmed settings without result. Then he began to punch additional commands into the cabinet.

Pritchard watched the apparatus with professional interest. The unit was considerably bulkier than the best of Hammer's similar equipment, but it appeared to be fully as capable once it was set up. The subject within the ground loop was a dancing outline on the screen. A line swept up the image, then down again, for as long as it took the cabinet to run its program. The color of the sweep

varied according to the element which was to be
detected on a given pass.

Danny had deliberately worn a suit scintillant
with fine wire to determine how sensitive the apparatus might be. The threads of stabilized aluminum remained on screen as an orange glow across
his image after one of the sweeps. The circuitry of
his stylus, his mastoid implant, and the heavy
remote unit at his belt, were separate blotches.
Their greenish tinge on the screen reflected the
close mixture of metals within the electronic
mechanisms.

Nowhere on the screen was there evidence of
iridium; or significant amounts of iron; or a cylin-
drical blur of metal deposited to mirror a glass
weapons-tube.

Subiyaga ignored Pritchard's stylus. "Mark," he
said, so that his master could hear the details.
"Sir, what is this, please?" The specialist pointed
to a blotch on the screen, but his eyes were on the
back of Pritchard's jaw which the blotch indicated.

"That's an implanted radio link," the ex-mercenary replied. He tapped the spot with his forefinger. "Keyed to a base unit, it's very useful. On
Tethys, of course—" the smile became momentarily carnivorous— "and without the Regiment, it
serves no function. Except to fill the hole cut in
the bone to hold it."

"And—" the specialist began, his finger sliding
to the lower blotch.

"And this is a remote unit that *does* function on
Tethys," Pritchard said, almost anticipating the
question. He spoke with the cool good-nature he
generally maintained around things wearing crimson. "It's linked to the Port, where a message cap-

sule is already cleared for Friesland. Colonel Hammer wished to be informed immediately if anything untoward occurred during today's deliberations."

He turned. The clothing Pritchard now wore was nothing like the battle-dress he had doffed for good, two years before. No one could look at him at that moment, however, and doubt his military background. "Do you object to Colonel Hammer having that full report?"

"Mark," said Subiyaga, clearing his link.

The man who met Danny's eyes from the van across the courtyard spoke briefly, sharply.

"No, Mister Pritchard," said the specialist to the ex-soldier's back. "We have no objection. You may enter the Hall, sir."

"I appreciate your courtesy," said Pritchard as he faced the specialist again. Danny's eyes swept like gunsights across the retainers, noting their stance, their alertness; where they set or carried the gun cases which were their badges and power. "And in thanking you," Pritchard went on, "I speak for Colonel Hammer."

Pritchard strode toward the massive doors of the Hall. The Councilors and attendants whom the delay had forced to queue now began passing through the checkpoint as well.

Councilor Dyson stared at the empty doorway for some seconds after Hammer's man had passed through it.

"Mother!" said Edward Slade when he saw how Marilee was dressed. "It's—you know you can't wear blue, they'll say you look like a servant!"

His mother snorted. Teddy blushed at the patent absurdity of what he had just said.

Marilee's garment flowed from a loose-fitting stasis to follow its wearer's movements with its own slow grace. The garment's color was indeed blue, Slade Blue, but pulses moved up it with the inexorable polish of color in heat-treated steel. The pulses did not, however, so much change the color of the fabric as the saturation of that color. Marilee could no more have been mistaken for a servant than Slade House could have been mistaken for a mining station.

"Besides," the woman said, amplifying the rebuke she had not needed to voice, "there won't be any servants with us. Though—" a wrinkle flitted across her face as she recalled—"I did send two Housemen with Danny since he wanted to enter the Hall early. I suppose they may stay."

"Mother," the youth repeated, this time in irritation rather than surprise.

Teddy himself was a stiff ensemble in black and white. From his outfit, he might have stepped from a subordinate position in Late-Nineteenth Century diplomacy. Housemen in fresh livery glanced from one to another behind the youth, wondering how Marilee's statement would affect them. "I realize how you must feel," Teddy said without even considering whether his words had meaning or were merely sounds, "but we mustn't give in to frustration. We're Slades, and even if we're beaten we mustn't slink away into a corner. That is, I—"

Teddy's breath caught and strangled the next words in his throat.

That was by no means soon enough, but it halted the arm Marilee had raised to slap her son. The tall woman's face was white with blotches as the muscles drew back over her bones. "Will you say I am no Slade, *boy*?" she whispered. Her right arm slipped forward so that the fingers of her left hand could knead some of the tension out of it. "I was a Slade before you were conceived, Edward. Don't you ever forget it. *Ever*."

She looked back at the servants. "Get out of here!" she shouted.

The Housemen scattered down the corridor. There were more of them than Marilee had realized, at least a dozen.

"Edward, come in here for a moment," the woman said. Her voice trembled around expended emotion. Mother and son had been standing near the door to the Trophy Room. Now she opened the door and waved the nervous youth within.

The corridor had skylights and, along the baseboards, glow-strips. The Trophy Room's great window was vivid with ambient light and the sun reflected from the facade of the Hall. Marilee could have chosen to polarize the glazed expanse, but she did not. The light bathed her, and the warmth massaged the shuddering from her muscles.

Marilee looked at her son. He braced himself defiantly, but she was no longer angry. She had assumed that Teddy did not know how soon he was going to die, to be killed like his father. Now Marilee realized that the youth was not a fool and not too young to recognize that Beverly Dyson had made murder an instrument of policy. Edward was keeping up the appearances of the world in which his father had raised him to believe. The youth did so for the same reason that a drowning man finally breathes the water that will kill him: there is nothing else to do.

"Edward," Marilee said slowly, "I decided—about the Housemen—when we were discussing who we should put at the checkpoint to make sure that everyone was checked even if they wore red."

Her son nodded. He was relieved but still uncertain about his mother's change of tone. "Coon Blegan," he said.

"Yes, Coon," Marilee agreed. "Because there was no other member of this House we could really trust with that duty."

The woman sighed and put a hand on her son's clasped hands. "Something went wrong, Edward," she said. "Somewhere along the line. I think my husband would have been good for Tethys if he had been allowed to be. But not for Slade House."

Her voice rose. "Three times as many servants here as when I was married, and only one holdover that we can trust with our lives. That shouldn't be. All the bowing and sharp dress in the world doesn't make up for that, does it?"

Teddy squeezed his mother's hand. He took a deep breath. "I'm sorry, Mother," he said. He was neither willing nor fully able to state the subject of his apology. "We'll have to do something about the Housemen. As soon as we—can." It would not be their House after the Council met, as surely as the seas washed the shores. "But for now, I think we had best get to the Hall. We are Slades."

They walked formally, arm in arm, the few steps to the door. Edward then preceded his mother down the narrow, tightly-coiled staircase. His head was high, and his pace was as measured as if he had scores of attendants.

Marilee was close to tears, though there was nothing in her quizzical expression to suggest that. Perhaps if he ran? Fled Tethys, became—became a mercenary soldier, with his uncle easing his way in that alien culture, watching over him. And then in a few years, when it was safe to come home—

Don was right. It would never again be safe on Tethys.

As her feet patted against the stair treads, Marilee's face drew itself into a smile as taut as a tetanic rictus. Each tap of sole on stone put her and the House and the planet twenty centimeters closer to disaster. She should have hired the Slammers, curse the expense in all its meanings.

Dear Lord, she should not have ordered away Don Slade. Not now.

And not twenty years before, either.

CHAPTER THIRTY

The doors of the Hall were four meters high and proof against more than storms when they were closed and locked from the inside. The trunions on which they swung inward ran in trackways grooved into the base slab. Open, the doors gaped as wide as they rose in the concrete facade. For the symmetry of the occasion, the leaves were fully open now; but a solid line of Dyson retainers across the threshold made sure that none of those entering failed to go through the security check first.

Two of the red-clad men had stepped aside with perfunctory smiles. Councilor Roosevelt, his wife, and fourteen assorted members of his family and staff were passing into the Hall. The youngest child made a curious attempt to pat a crimson trouser leg. His nurse snatched him back immediately. The adults of the entourage preferred to act as if the guards did not exist.

At least that rascal Dyson had shown the decency to leave his squad unarmed. The remainder—almost fifty—of his men in the courtyard flaunted their cased guns with a particular relish this afternoon. The deliberations of the Council would be sealed by custom against interference; but there was only the single exit from the Hall.

"Passage, gentlemen," said a voice from within the

door alcove. The guards were bored and unprepared for someone who wanted to leave at this moment.

"I said," snarled Danny Pritchard, "get your butts out of the way, turtleheads!"

The line clotted as Dyson's men wheeled to face the ex-mercenary. Those in the queue waiting to be checked began craning their necks to see what had happened. The music tangled to a momentary halt before the leader of the musicians snapped his group back to attention with a nervous look toward Beverly Dyson. The musicians were supposed to cover, not join, awkward incidents of this sort.

Danny Pritchard stood with a sneer and his fists on his hip bones. He was not a scarred tough like many of the men he now faced; but he was a commander glaring at men who knew they were only vessels of power. The guards would be discarded without hesitation if they overstepped bounds of which they were only hazily aware.

"Subiyaga! Via!" shouted the leader of the squad on the threshold. Subiyaga was not even in the blurred chain of command, but he was the only one present with a link to the source of power. "Are we supposed to let people out?"

"Blood, McKinney!" Subiyaga said. "Are you crazy? Of course they can get out. What do you think you're doing?"

"Let him go! Let him go!" the shaken squad leader said. His men were already reacting like dollops of a fruit hit by a projectile. They were not there to alienate Councilors whom Dyson wished for the time to coddle.

Danny Pritchard strolled out with a nod toward the specialist. The guards at the detection cabinet had fumbled with their cases during the tension. It was only now, however, that they saw who the source of the incident had been.

"Hey!" called Ahwas, the leader of that armed group. "Mister! You got to go through the loop again before you go back inside!"

The man from Friesland grinned broadly. "I hear you talking," he said. He continued to walk toward the House from which he had come so recently.

Subiyaga watched him walk away. The specialist's face was troubled, but he could not be quite certain of what he saw.

The courtyard was not particularly hot. The bright sun which had been a caress in the Trophy Room was here a slap in the face. Perhaps that was because of the way the light danced with such frequency from crimson livery. There were numerous groups led by Councilors at one stage or another of their progress to the Hall. Even so, Dyson's retainers seemed omnipresent. The man himself stood on his van ten meters away, as if he were on a reviewing stand.

Marilee paused in the doorway. Behind the Slades, Councilor Picolo squeaked as her way was blocked by her hostess and son. Marilee murmured an apology to her, one of only two women who were Council members in their own right. As Marilee did so, she drew her son into the shade of one of the armored drones flanking the doorway. She needed to take stock.

"Mistress, I was told to escort you into the Hall," said the man who had waited patiently beside the same drone. "Told by Mister Pritchard."

His livery had blended well enough with the blue shade; and until he spoke he had been as motionless as the 10 cm gun above him. For that matter, Don Slade was no longer the flamboyant hell-raiser who had left Tethys twenty years before. Like the gun-drone, he was scarred and stolid now; but not to be ignored.

"You fool, you *mustn't* be here!" the woman said in a voice that was as much a curse as a whisper.

"Mistress," said the big man calmly. "I'm going inside as your escort. Nothing you say will have any effect except to call attention to—us."

"Mother, he *should* go," interjected Edward. "You said we had no one except Coon we could trust. Well, this man, this Holt, proved yesterday that he wasn't afraid of Dyson or Dyson's men. Didn't he?"

"T—," Marilee began. Then, "Edward, there are things you can't . . ." She paused again when she realized that this was neither the time nor the place to explain. Anyway, the explanation would not matter in any real sense.

Not when Don Slade said, "I *will* enter the Hall this day, Mistress." One did not have to know the big man as Marilee Dorcas had known him to realize that he would do just what he said, though it killed him. As this time it surely would.

"I think," said Marilee carefully, "that Mister Pritchard's own presence within the Hall will prevent anything—untoward. I—truly appreciate the solicitude, Holt, but I don't think it's wise under the circumstances."

She and her son could almost pass for sister and brother, Slade thought. His dry mouth made it hard for him to speak. He felt as if he were strapped in and waiting for insertion, desperately afraid as always. To those who heard him, his slow speech was only obsequious. Possibly Edward thought the speech was a symptom of a slow mind, the sort of mind that befitted a powerful body as his father might have said.

"Mistress," Slade explained, "Major Pritchard had other business to attend. He's left the Hall, and he's told me to accompany you." When the woman hesitated with her mouth open but the words not quite ready to come out, Slade added, "We're all adults, you know. We can't live any lives but our own."

"What?" said Edward.

"All right, Holt," Marilee said crisply, unemotionally. "You will follow us at two paces, and you will not speak unless spoken to."

"Yes, Mistress," the big man said. The bill of the cap he wore nodded submissively.

"Come along, then, Edward," the woman said. There were only a few people waiting yet to be passed through the check point. "It's almost 1500 . . . and I very much doubt they'll delay the door closing because we aren't yet present."

She glanced up as they began walking toward the Hall. "Of course," she added dryly, "we can be sure the doors will remain open until the President of the Council deigns to enter."

The man behind her kept his face blank, but Marilee's expression at that moment would have very well fit Mad Dog Slade.

"Them," said one of the men standing behind Beverly Dyson.

The comment had been as much as anything an attempt to drag a reaction, even a rebuke for speaking, from the Councilor. Dyson had not spoken for the past quarter hour, as the queue shortened and more and more people waited within the Hall for his coming triumph. Presidency of the Council was nothing. The Slade Estate was and always had been Tethys itself.

Dyson was erect behind the rail on the van's roof. He had intended to move the vehicle into the courtyard at this time even if—the Widow Slade—had not ordered him out of the House the night before. Now he rotated his head very slightly to watch the trio striding toward the Hall ... the youth fashionably archaic, the other pair in Slade Blue.

As Councilor Dyson wore crimson.

She understood, the bitch. What it meant to be a Council family, to share Main Island with the Slades, to be as wealthy as the Slades—and to be ignored, whenever a difference arose, because you were *not* Slade. Ever since the Settlement.

Until now.

"The big one," said the retainer. "He's the one ..."

"Baucom," whispered Beverly Slade as his eyes tracked those crossing beneath him, "shut up or I'll have you killed."

It could not be. Every man aboard every ship which landed was checked. Whether they were passengers or crew, whether they planned to disembark on Tethys or were only staging through. The gunman, Pritchard; *he* had been noted. A mercenary, very likely a courier from the Mad Dog. But not the man himself, not by a half.

Don Slade had not come home. There was no

such money in the galaxy that would preserve the man who took it to hide Slade on Tethys from Beverly Dyson. Everybody on Tethys knew that. And Slade, even the madman Dyson knew him for, was as sure of that as were any of the guards searching incoming starships. Don Slade would never even try to walk on Tethys.

And yet—

More or less audibly, the Councilor said, "I can't remember his face." The men behind him strained to catch the words, but the words would have meant nothing without a context thirty years in their master's past. "I hadn't realized that. When I try to remember his face, I see the wrench instead . . . and I see the wrench when I look at that—"

Dyson broke off. He had not realized that he was speaking aloud. "Baucom," he said. The brief tremor in his voice sounded dangerous to the men who stiffened to attention.

"Sir?" said Baucom. His eyes were wide, but he was deliberately staring past the Councilor.

"I was going to use the radio," Dyson said, again fully composed, "but I will not. That man, the large one."

"Sir." Marilee Slade had passed through the detection loop without incident. Her son was preparing to follow with an expression of cool indifference.

"I want you," the Councilor continued, "to take the squad leader—it's Ahwas, isn't it? At the cabinet?"

"Yes, sir."

"Take him aside before you join us in the Hall. Tell him that when that man comes out again, after the Council meeting or before, he is to be shot. Immediately. Is that understood?

There was nothing in the Councilor's voice which permitted any question. "Yes, *sir*," said Baucom.

As if he were a machine switching frequencies, Beverly Dyson said, "Mark. Subiyaga, I want that man with the Slades checked the same way you did the mercenary. Mark."

The specialist looked up and bowed toward the van. In Dyson's ear, his voice said. "Yes sir, I'm already doing that. There don't seem to be any weapons, but he has the same kind of communications device in his jawbone as the other one did."

The man, the Slade retainer—if he were a retainer—stood in the loop with his back to Dyson. He seemed to be oblivious of the hushed conversation of which he was the subject.

"Mark," said the Councilor. "Very good, Subiyaga. Carry on. Mark."

Dyson turned to face the trio accompanying him. "When they kill that one, Baucom," he said, "they are to avoid injury to Mistress Slade and her son if possible." He paused. In a measured voice, he continued, "I expect that mercenary gunman, Pritchard, to come out of the House carrying his weapon. If he is present when the—other—is killed, I want him treated the same way. Ahwas can pass the word among the other squads."

"Yes, sir," Baucom repeated. He was terrified that his master was about to add some final order which would be suicide for the retainer to execute personally. An order to personally provoke a confrontation with Blegan, for instance, to get the old gunman out of the way as well.

But instead, Dyson said mildly. "They think to threaten me with some jumped up mercenary

twenty Transit minutes away. Not here. Not on
my world."

Then he added, "Come. It's time for us to open
the meeting." Lithely, the Councilor swung down
the ladder to the ground.

CHAPTER THIRTY-ONE

The door leaves rang heavily against their stops. Then the crossbar slotted home with a sharper note, and the tension in the courtyard was released. The Council might think it was separating itself from external distractions. Those outside knew that they were temporarily preserved from the screwy whims of their employers.

All but a handful of the men in the courtyard wore crimson.

One of the exceptions was a kitchen assistant. He trotted from the House carrying on a yoke a pair of large insulated canisters. It was food and drink for the musicians. Their leader, Codell, had shown the foresight to lay on the refreshments ahead of time. There was no question of the musicians relaxing in the vans outside the walls which acted as barracks for most of Dyson's men. They were still on duty. They had put up their instruments and were openly belting on the sidearms which were to be part of their regalia henceforward.

Ahwas took off his gold-billed cap and wiped his forehead with his sleeve. The sound the gunman made reminded Subiyaga of the gurgle of recovery following a near drowning.

The guard leader looked around him. His own men were already uncasing their submachineguns.

Ahwas nodded approval. He motioned Subiyaga nearer to him and whispered, "You keep an eye on things here, huh? You saw Baucom give the word to me? Right from the top, that was. I got to go *talk* to some people."

The specialist grimaced. "Via," he said, "your goons aren't any business of mine. Do what you please, but leave me out of it."

Four of the men who had formally observed the checkpoint were now clustered a little apart. They were talking while their eyes roved nervously. None of them seemed disposed to notice the guns appearing all around them.

When the Hall closed behind Councilor Dyson, Coon Blegan stalked lumpily away from the detection cabinet. He stood now by the shaded south wall of the yard, not far from the outside gate. His arms were crossed and the sole of his right boot was planted against the wall at knee level. The old man was a brooding threat which drew Ahwas' eyes even though whispers could not carry that far.

"Well," the guard leader said.

Subiyaga had begun disassembling and packing his rig. The specialist had served on a dozen planets with as many different varieties of security forces. That gave him a professional familiarity with weapons. The ignorance of many of the liverymen around him was appalling. The sooner he had his equipment packed and had carried it out of this courtyard, the happier he would be. Incompetence could make the enclosure a killing ground, even without the orders Ahwas seemed so proud to be passing on.

"Blood! Look at that!" the guard leader said. In

case his tone were not demanding enough, he snatched at Subiyaga's sleeve to turn him toward the House.

The specialist bit back a curse as one of the sideplates rattled out of the groove in which he had just inserted it. Nervous fools with guns were dangerous enough without having their emotional temperature raised still further. "Well, I see him," Subiyaga said. "The mercenary, Pritchard. And if he's got a gun, it isn't anything as big as the one he backed you boys down with the other night."

"Don't matter," muttered Ahwas, "don't matter cop. We got him this time."

The guard set his cap in place firmly. He began trotting toward Dyson's van. There the liverymen who had blocked the Hall doorway were being issued their own automatic weapons.

Subiyaga paused for a further moment to watch Pritchard. The ex-mercenary had climbed onto the deck of one of the drones. He was relaxed, his arm resting loosely on the gun tube. Hard to tell his expression at the distance, but it did not seem to be too concerned. Too bad. Subiyaga liked to work with other professionals, but this time the few such around were all on the other side.

The detection loop was held rigid and a finger's breadth above the ground by its own internal charge. Subiyaga reversed the polarity with a pop. The loop collapsed. He began to reel it in. One thing Subiyaga had seen for sure: Pritchard still wore his remote unit, the one Subiyaga had thought he must have left behind in the Hall.

Or another one, of course; but why would the mercenary have carried two identical commo units to Tethys?

*   *   *

Ballenger was in charge of the van. He also acted
as Councilor Dyson's steward when the Councilor
was traveling. The pudgy man considered himself
a cut above Ahwas and the other gunmen, though
Dyson had never formalized lines of authority. Everyone in crimson livery was *Dyson's* subordinate.
The Councilor believed that lack of certainty beyond
that fact kept his retainers nervous and alert. It
also made it unlikely that Dyson's men would make
any major decision without personally clearing it
with their master, which suited his style very well.

The ten-meter van looked larger from the outside than it was within, what with the drive units,
the equipment that made it the Councilor's command station—and especially because of the squad
of armed liverymen now babbling in the main room.

"You have no business here!" cried Ballenger in
a powerful voice. It was a surprise coming from a
small man who looked soft from any angle. "Take
your—" he made shooing motions with the backs
of both hands, trying to dismiss the submachineguns he had just been required to issue— "things
and get back where you belong. I don't know *what*
the Councilor is going to say when he sees the filth
you've tracked into his compartment."

"Via, that's easy for *you* to say, piggy," said
Ahwas, still puffed with the orders he had delivered to the chief of the other squad. "*We've* got to
blast that merc and the other just as soon as they
come out of the meeting."

"Right when the doors open, Rag?" the other
leader asked. He was toying with the safety of his
own weapon in a way which would have terrified
anyone in the van with better sense.

"Well, I . . ." Ahwas began.

"Of course not, you buffoons!" snapped Ballenger. "Is this Slade going to be the first person out the door?" Several guards frowned in an attempt to answer the question. "Of *course* not!" the steward repeated in fury. "So if you shoot this one when the doors open, you'll warn the other, won't you? *Won't you*? So wait till the other one comes out of the Hall, then kill them *both*."

Ballenger paused, breathing hard.

"Right, that's just what the master told me to have done," Ahwas lied. He took off his cap and wiped his face again, darkening the bright scarlet with his sweat.

"Sir," called the driver who monitored the instruments from the cab. "There's a couple supply trucks coming in."

"That's correct," the steward said primly. "There's to be a celebration banquet in Slade House this evening. They'll be bringing additional specialties."

The armed liverymen were beginning to file out of the van. Ahwas watched them with a glum expression. "Won't help us a bit, though, will it?" he said. "Now that we aren't allowed in the House anymore."

Ballenger opened his mouth in an amazement that was only partially feigned. "That isn't a *problem* anymore, don't you see?" he said to the guard. "After the meeting, *we* own Slade House. We own *Tethys*. In just a few hours."

He continued to shake his head in wonder as the last of the gunmen trooped out of the van.

CHAPTER THIRTY-TWO

Even the Hall had shrunk, thought Don Slade. That was not because of how he had grown since his memories of the building, but rather because of what he had seen on other worlds.

The Council Hall was a ferro-concrete A-frame thirty meters to the roof peak and a full hundred meters along that beam. It had been designed to hold the original population of Tethys—had done so for a day and two nights during the Swarm of Year Three. The Hall remained the planet's largest building now because it was an anachronism—and in his youth, Slade had found very little use for anachronisms.

Communications among the estates scattered across the planet were excellent and trustworthy. Physical assembly of the Council was needless. Because it was also relatively dangerous, the practice had been abandoned by the time the twins were born. Slade's father had reinstituted the practice on an occasional, ceremonial basis. Tom had apparently amplified ceremonies for his own reasons. The Council, with increasingly little of substance to debate after the life and death decisions of the first generations, was willing and more to fall in with the practice.

Beverly Dyson would have seen to it that this

occasion was face to face, no matter what had been the practice of the immediate past. His triumph demanded that.

"Mistress," said a Slade Houseman. He bowed low as he never would have done under other circumstances.

Don's father had filled the great room with auditorium-style seating at an expense the Old Man had sneered at. All that was gone, now. It had been replaced with wooden benches and wood-paneled enclosures to waist height. The panels separated the areas assigned to the various Council Islands, formalizing a practice which had some historical support.

The wood, however, was a matter of insanity rather than nostalgia. What Tom—it must have been Tom—was thinking about was wholly beyond his twin. The only trees on Tethys were those carefully nurtured from imported stock, and the gravelly soil tended to stunt even those. Every scrap of these fittings must have been shipped from off-world. Gold would have been cheaper. Sea-mining at least produced an indigenous supply of gold.

As the Houseman straightened, he swung inward the low gate of the enclosure and collided with his fellow. This was not the sort of thing they had practiced often enough to get right. The whole business was a little pathetic. The Slade enclosure would have seated two hundred. The five of them were lost in it.

Some of the other Councilors had as many as forty in their present entourage, but even those enclosures looked empty. The day for which the Council Hall was built would never return. If Don Slade had more affection for the old barn than he ever in youth had thought probable, it was because he now realized that he too belonged in the Settlement, two centuries before his birth.

The Houseman looked askance at Slade when he followed Edward and Marilee into the enclosure. The big man smiled at the liveried pair and asked, "I believe you boys have something for me? Major Pritchard left it with you."

Marilee looked back to see why Slade was not immediately behind her. The servants had started to whisper to one another. One promptly turned to the woman and said, "Mistress, your guest left a, an object with us which this—person—says is for him."

"Well then, *give* it to him," Marilee replied in a venemous tone. It was the first evidence Slade had seen that she was tight as a cocked pistol herself, ready to blast petty officiousness for fear of the real dangers that had drawn her so taut.

The Housemen scrambled to obey. They collided once more and almost got into a tug of war over the remote unit, hidden under one of the empty benches.

Marilee looked puzzled. The object was nothing she recognized. Edward was not so much bored as anesthetized by—fear was too blunt a word, but fear would do to describe the emotion.

"Yeah . . ." the big man said, "thanks."

His head still felt light, airy, as he hooked the unit onto his belt. There was a surge of warmth also, however. Slade had grasped a floating spar; and while that did not itself preserve him from the maelstrom, it at least made preservation conceivable. He was beaming as he sat beside Marilee on the front bench of the enclosure, facing the podium across another low wooden barrier.

"What is that?" the woman whispered. "Holt?"

"Oh," said Slade. "A, well, commo unit, you'd say."

He could have carried the remote unit into the Hall himself; it was genuinely no more of a weapon than was his mastoid implant. It was barely possible that somebody would have recognized the object, however. If there were trouble, it was best that Danny be the one to field it. His status as representative of Friesland did not give him total immunity, but it would carry him further than anything Don Slade had to offer.

The doors shut with the solidity of a natural force. A riffle of air was driven before them into the Hall.

Whispering by less than a thousand people could no more fill the Hall than sunlight could fill a bucket. Still, hushed voices hissed and quivered between the slanted concrete slabs which were roof and walls in one. Through the whispers rapped the boot heels, Beverly Dyson's and those of the three men in lock step a pace behind him. A squad of crimson liverymen guarded the doors they had just closed from the inside. Twenty more men rose to their feet in the Dyson enclosure. These retainers were unarmed, at least in so far as the detection cabinet had shown; but they were scarred, solid men.

When Dyson's own men stood, there was a hasty clatter throughout the Hall. Rising for the President had been no part of the plan. The Council was by history a gathering of equals—in form. But no one wanted to be the last to honor Beverly

Dyson, especially when the toughs in the Dyson enclosure were turning to stare back into the Hall.

The two Slade Housemen popped to their feet from where they sat by the çentral aisle. Marilee held to an icy indifference. Her eyes were on the podium and the President's chair only two meters in front of her. Edward caught the movement, however. His face blotched angrily and he started to lunge toward the servants.

Don Slade touched the youth's shoulder and held him down without effort. Slade was smiling at the Housemen. One of them glanced around surreptitiously. He saw the smile and edged back onto his bench. The first servant tugged at his fellow's sleeve. The other man looked back in surprise. He also sagged as if shot, just as Dyson strode down the aisle past him.

Slade released his nephew.

Someone began to clap. The sound was nervous in the great building. Dyson's liverymen did not take it up, and the attempt collapsed save for its rustling echoes.

Beverly Dyson mounted the four steps onto the podium with stiff-backed grace. It was four paces more to the President's chair, off-set as it was to the Dyson side of the aisle. The three liverymen of the Councilor's personal staff looked clumsy by contrast as they followed their master onto the podium. They arranged themselves behind the chair, standing formally as they had before on the roof of the van.

A handsome bastard, Slade thought as he watched his enemy sit down. Cold as iced steel, but with the sort of slim good looks that aged better than fuller features did.

Dear Lord, who stood with our forefathers through storm and beasts, be with us now.

Beverly Dyson laid the commo-control board across the arms of his chair. He touched a switch, his own, the red one second from the upper left corner of the forty possibilities. Staring past the Slades and out over the Hall like a hawk sighting prey, he said, "As President, I call to order the Council of Tethys in this, its third formal meeting in the two-hundred and twelfth year of settlement."

Dyson's voice rang out through over a hundred speakers mounted overhead on the sloping walls. The lag between the nearest speaker and those further away created a dynamic echo throughout the Hall. Because the units were in phase, however, the result was clearly audible and not cacaphonous.

"The business before this Council today," the man in crimson continued, "is the choice of guardian for the Slade heir until his majority. No other business will be considered at this time."

It was one of the paradoxes of formal Council meetings that the Hall was too big for face to face contact and hugely too big for unaided speech. When they were scattered across the planet, the Councilors could see each other and speak simultaneously, using satellite relays and large split screens. In the Hall, Councilors could only be glimpsed when they chose to rise. All discussion was channelled through the board in the President's lap, which in turn fed the speakers overhead. Marilee and the thirty-eight Councilors, all but Dyson himself, held short batons. Thumbing the end of a baton would set a corresponding switch in the President's array alight. Not until the President threw that switch, however, would the baton glow and the Councilor's words be broadcast to the Hall.

There was one exception to that general rule.

"I will now entertain a motion on the stated question," said Beverly Dyson. His words marched through the Hall with the sonorous majesty of a coronation parade.

Marilee was furiously pressing her baton. Dyson looked directly at her for the first time since he entered the Hall. He smiled and said, "The chair recognizes Councilor Hauksbee."

Clipped to the left epaulette of Slade's tunic was what looked like a standard microphone/loudspeaker, the sort of miniature unit issued to troops where the expense of mastoid implants was not justified. It had a simple mechanical key which Slade clicked home as he stood.

Who the hell did they think had *built* this place, anyway? Dysons?

"By custom of this Hall," the tanker said, "the first speaker on any question is a Slade. That's what my grandfather taught, and I never heard anybody call the Old Man a liar."

His voice rolled through the building. There was no immediate consternation, for the audience expected words. The import of the words which came was not immediately absorbed. The Old Man had liked hardware. He never presided over a meeting in the Hall, but it was with glee that he had demonstrated to young Donald the override which locked out the commo-control board. The override had still been in the Old Man's room, waiting for Don's need with the pair of remote units.

Somewhere toward the back of the Hall, Councilor Hauksbee's unaided voice was being swallowed by the space around it. Beverly Dyson was stabbing at the control board. His expression was one of furious incredulity.

Slade swung over the waist-high panel before him. He cocked his right knee, then, and mounted the low podium without bothering with the steps.

The Hall came alive with nervous exclamations, but the big man rode them down with the amplifiers as he said, "Today I'm the first speaker. And if there's anybody out there who hasn't guessed by now—I'm Don Slade, and I've come here to get justice for my nephew Edward." He paused. Very faintly through the façade of the Hall came the sound of what was happening in the courtyard.

CHAPTER THIRTY-THREE

"Hey, what'd those trucks do?" demanded one of Ahwas' men. "Give us the slip and go round the back way?"

"Bloody well better have," said another with a nod back toward the north wall of the courtyard. The wrecked cars had been removed, but the gravel was still enlivened by scorch marks and bright debris. The van had been parked outside the complex until the present dawn. It was easy enough to imagine the effect another out-of-control supply truck could have on Dyson's expensive scarlet vehicle.

The gate squealed inward before the cab of a truck. The leaves scraped as the vehicle edged them open, but that did no apparent harm to the battered skirts.

"Thought those gates were supposed to be locked," muttered Ahwas.

He wished the Master would give an order about this.

Danny Pritchard's mouth was filled with a dry vileness, as if someone had stuffed a used tennis ball into it. He was too old for this. He had been a *curst* fool to give up the body armor which alone had been his chance of living through the next hour. He was a tanker, by the Lord, and he went into the battle wearing only tinsel that would burn like a torch when he was killed!

Blood and Martyrs. Dyson's liverymen were in scattered clumps across the enclosure. They were either still gossiping among themselves or watching a second truck follow the first through the gate. They knew the meeting would last a minimum of two hours. The only business had been transacted months before, and the formalization required only minutes. All the Councilors would speak, however, both to praise Beverly Dyson out of fear and to hear the sound of their own voices in public.

There were forty-five Dyson liverymen in sight, plus one or more additional within the van to Pritchard's left front. The five observers were still loosely grouped where the detection cabinet had been set up. The specialist was wheeling his gear toward Slade House at something more than a normal pace.

There was Coon Blegan; and Danny Pritchard; and the Lord be *praised!* men in blue coveralls were climbing out of the back of the leading truck as it halted near the gate!

No rest for the wicked. Danny gripped the safety switch at the back of the gun housing. He swung it live in a hundred and eighty-degree arc. The drone quivered in a puff of dust and gravel as its systems came up. Pebbles pinged the skirt of its mate across the doorway. No one noticed because of the commotion at the gate.

Pritchard stepped away from the quivering drone. It was already beginning to drift because its drive fans were out of alignment. A bit of rock spanged from the second drone and rapped Pritchard's instep. He ignored it as he jumped to the second drone's back deck and threw its safety also. Then he dropped to the ground again as the air around the House doorway filled with grit and the sound of fans.

Somebody had noticed after all. Subiyaga flattened himself beside his equipment, twenty meters short of the House and safety. Pritchard did not have to see the specialist's expression to know it for one he had worn himself often enough, when it was about to drop in the pot and you could only hope the splash would miss you.

Both supply trucks were disgorging men, dozens of them. Each man gripped the bulky rocket gun of his trade. Liverymen who had started toward the trucks in curiosity now scrambled away. Submachineguns were being pointed from all around the yard.

When the drones were switched on, Danny Pritchard had no reason to stand in the open. He gripped the yoke handles of the remote unit, knowing that the hologram display it threw up for his eyes would be the same whether he stood in the courtyard or behind the concrete facade of the House.

But what the Hell. The drone to his right moved as he twisted the controls. The orange pipper on the display skidded across a monochrome landscape to its target. Don Slade was home, but a lot of Danny Pritchard was home again also.

Ballenger flung open the side door of the van. "Hey!" he cried. His loud-hailer had a remote link and belt hooks, but he had not taken time to arrange them. "You *fishermen*," his voice boomed.

"Get those filthy trucks out of here at once! Don't you realize that the Council will be processing through here in—"

The anti-tank gun on Pritchard's drone ripped the van the long way.

The cyan flash was narrow and intense, but its reflection seemed to fill every angle of the yard. The high-intensity 10 cm gun could knock out the heaviest tanks. On Tethys, it had been used for single-shot kills on creatures large enough to be mistaken for islands when glimpsed from the air. Like any powergun, it liberated most of its energy on the initial impact, but the charge was heavy enough that a hole puffed in the back wall of the van even as the cab exploded in the flames of its own vaporized components. The fireball pitched Ballenger onto the shingle. The skin of the Steward's back was unharmed, but his hair and livery were afire.

"Now listen up," roared the loudspeakers on the drone. The vehicle slid away from the spot in which it had been parked for a generation. There were occasional sparks where the left skirt continued to drag the gravel. "All Dyson servants, drop your guns. You will not be hurt. Drop your guns at once."

Several cases of ammunition in the van went off. Seams leaked blue-green light for an instant as the walls bulged. Then the rear of the vehicle sucked itself flat so abruptly that even the fire in the cab was beaten down for a moment. Subiyaga swore and began to scuttle toward the moaning steward.

The gun drone pivoted on its axis. "You will not be hurt," the loudspeakers repeated dissonantly.

The muzzle of the cannon glowed white. Heat

waves above the barrel rippled the image of Slade House. The station crewmen were as surprised by the steel monster as were the Dyson retainers they had come to fight. The blue-suited crewmen were moving cautiously to keep the supply trucks between them and the drone.

As the gun rotated past him, Ahwas saw the ex-mercenary standing fifty meters away in the entryway of Slade House. Ahwas did not recognize Pritchard's voice through the drone's cracked amplification, nor was he fully aware of what Pritchard was doing. Still, he knew enough, and cowardice was not one of the guard leader's failings. Ahwas lifted his submachinegun and thumbed off the safety.

Coon Blegan fired twice from the gate leaf against which he braced his pistol. The second round was from training, not present need, because the first had blasted Ahwas' cap and skull. The head shots were deliberate because the submachinegun was already aimed.

Ahwas spun. His weapon raked the House facade. The window of the Trophy Room dissolved into hair-fine slivers that winked and danced in a cloud drifting down on the courtyard.

"Dyson servants, drop your weapons!" the drone snarled as it threw itself sideways at the pace of a fast walk. The dragging skirt bumped against Ahwas' body, then lurched over and through it. "You will not get another warning! Slade men, prepare to gather up the weapons."

Men were throwing down their automatic weapons. One guard stripped off his crimson tunic and flung it away as well. Like sheep, others began to pull off their livery also. Crewmen strode forward

with burgeoning enthusiasm, slapping at one another with weathered hands as their nervousness
dissipated.

Then the second drone, the one Danny Pritchard
did not control, pulled away from the doorway. A
frozen bearing screamed as it galled its shaft, but
the heavy vehicle continued to gather speed. Subiyaga was trying to carry the injured steward to a
place of relative safety beside the House. The drone
swivelled around them, dragging its skirts instead
through the molten wreckage of the van. As the
drone continued, a trail of blazing plastic followed
it toward the armored doors of the Hall.

"This man is an imposter!" Councilor Dyson
shouted in a voice that only the handful nearest
him could hear over the pandemonium in the Hall.

Slade turned. "Bev," he said, "you know me."
He gestured with his left hand, palm down and
fingers splayed. Again his amplified voice rocked
through the high-pitched clamor. "But there doesn't
have to be any trouble."

Dyson flung away the useless control board as
he jumped from the chair. "Get him!" he screamed
as he backed through his retainers. "Get him!"

Baucom hesitated, then lunged as the big tanker
glanced down at the remote unit he gripped with
both hands. Slade slammed his left elbow into
Baucom's chest, hurling the liveryman back with
cracked ribs. His fellows grabbed Slade from either side.

Instead of leaping to the podium himself, Edward Slade caught the nearer liveryman by the
ankles and jerked. The man squawked as he fell,
banging the point of a hip on the edge of the podium.

Marilee chopped at the liveryman's eyes with the top of her baton. "Come *on* you bastards!" she screamed at the Slade Housemen. She had no leisure to notice that one of the frightened servants actually did clamber onto the podium to face the score of men swarming from the Dyson enclosure.

Slade kneed the third of his immediate attackers in the groin, then shrugged loose from the crumpling man. He looked up from the hologram display. Beverly Dyson was five meters away, flattened against the outside wall. His hands were raised against the wrench which shimmered in his memory. Slade grinned and squeezed the trigger built into the right handle of his remote unit.

The doors of the Hall rang like a god's anvil when the ten-centimeter bolt struck.

The doors were built to be proof against the largest and most vicious monsters that Tethys spawned, but it was only the thickness of the crossbar which kept the anti-tank round from penetrating the Hall as a jet of directed energy. Instead, the great room lighted with a white flash that painted sharp shadows across the wall beyond the podium. Blazing steel and a plasma that had been steel bulged across the squad of Dyson retainers still hesitating near the doors where they were stationed. None of them had time to scream as they shrivelled.

"Don't *move!*" shouted Slade and the speakers as the echoes crashed.

Half the crossbar still sagged against the door beneath the glowing cavity in the center where the leaves met. The other half had been ripped from its bracket by the gout of gaseous metal. The powergun bolt had no kinetic energy of its own, but its impact created enormous secondary kinetic effects.

"Don't move!" Slade repeated, wheeling on the Dyson liverymen whose rush the flash and blast had frozen. The armored drone Slade controlled slammed against the doors, breaking the fresh welds which sealed the panels when the bar was shot away. The doors recoiled open. The fighting vehicle waddled into the Hall.

Husks of liverymen near the door powdered as the skirts touched them. They whipped around the drone as bitter smoke.

The aisle was wide enough for the drone's deliberate passage, but the long-ignored running gear required more than an inertial guidance mechanism to keep the brute in a straight line. When Slade looked up from his display, the drone's back end swung enough to splinter panels of the Hauksbee enclosure. Not, perhaps, the least fortunate of accidents.

"All of you, back out of here," Slade ordered. He gestured with the remote unit toward the red-suited retainers who now cowered at the edge of the podium or just beneath it. The drone had no turret. The whole vehicle rotated in the aisle to enforce Slade's will with the muzzle of the gun.

A number of the liverymen were ducking so that they could no longer see Slade. It was a common misconception. Its converse made drones difficult to manipulate. Slade's own line of sight did not control the cannon's fire. The pipper on the remote display did, and its sending unit was part of the gun mount. Slade and Pritchard had decades of experience guiding heavy armor with no view but that from remote pick-ups. Handling the drones was second nature for them, as it would have been to a settler of the first generation.

Edward Slade stood to his uncle's left, Marilee to Don's right. The Houseman who had jumped to the podium was now standing upright and wondering what to do with his hands. Dyson retainers slunk away from him and from the podium. The broad lighting strips in the roof still seemed dim after the fireball which had blasted clear the doors.

"This isn't a place for people anymore," said Don. The drone slid to the end of the aisle. He grounded the vehicle there, almost touching the podium. Its armored skirts sang and sparked as they settled on the concrete. "We'll go outside— Via, we'll go to the, there's room for forty in the Trophy Room and we can talk—"

"Don!" screamed the woman to his right.

Edward was fast, very fast for a youth with neither training nor experience. He jumped to-ward Dyson. But Don Slade was the pro, the Mad Dog, and he was fast enough to catch his nephew by the arm and fling him out of the killing zone.

Beverly Dyson was still backed against the wall three meters away, but his hands no longer cov-ered his face. He aimed a glass derringer, the only metal in it the atom's thickness which mirrored the interior of the barrel.

Not a military weapon at all, Slade thought fleetingly, but neither is a man a tank. Aloud, forgetting the link that threw his voice out over the speakers, he said, "Go ahead, Bev. I don't think you've got the guts."

Slade's last thought before the derringer fired was how the Hell had he mistaken Dyson for a handsome man. The face glaring over the muzzle could have come from deep wat—

The bolt made a light popping sound in the air and a crash like breaking glass when it struck the middle of Slade's chest. The big man staggered backward. There were screams from several points in the Hall, though why, one more shooting on *this* day . . . ?

Dyson tossed the gun away like a man snapping a spider from his hand. The discharged piece was too hot to hold. It clattered against the wall and back to the podium.

A plate-sized patch had been burned from the center of Slade's tunic. Its edges were still asmolder. The breastplate of the ceramic armor beneath the tunic was blackened. Crinkle marks at the center of the pattern indicated that the plate would have to be replaced. It had been degraded to uselessness in absorbing the single bolt.

Guess I owe Danny for a chicken suit, Slade thought as he raised the President's chair in one hand. His laughter boomed out over the speakers and he added aloud, "And my life . . ." No one in the Hall understood the words, but by that point no one particularly expected to.

The chair was wooden, like the benches, and probably as uncomfortable for all its smooth curves. It weighed fifteen kilos, a clumsy bludgeon but a massive one. Slade poised it overhead. "Thirty years, Bev, hasn't it been?" he said.

Councilor Dyson turned to the wall. He began trying to claw and bite through the concrete.

Marilee touched Slade's shoulder, the left one, the one that held the chair poised. "Don," she said very softly. "No."

"He's faking that," said Slade and the speakers.
There was blood where Dyson's fingers scratched.
The sound of his teeth on the age-darkened con-
crete was more hideous than a scream.

Slade turned. He tried to set the chair down
gently, but his muscles failed him and let it crash
to the podium. "Dear Lord," he said. "Dear Lord."

Men and women had already begun to move
toward the door. They stepped gingerly or with
the set expressions of feigned ignorance as they
crunched through what had been the guards. Already the shadows of armed men waiting in the
courtyard darkened the doorway. Councilors and
their vari-colored retainers paused, trapped between death and uncertainty.

"Go on out," Slade called. "You won't be harmed.
No one will be harmed. We're men here on Tethys,
not animals."

Beside Slade, Beverly Dyson mewled against the
wall he was beginning to scar.

CHAPTER THIRTY-FOUR

"I'll have the Trophy Room readied," Marilee said. She took a deep breath in reaction to the past minutes. Even on this end of the Hall, the air was bitter with ozone and sweetened by death. "The House doors have probably been locked," she added wryly. "I don't doubt you can get in, but . . ."

Slade let the remote unit fall, as if his right arm no longer had strength for its burden. He clicked off the speaker control pinned to his left shoulder as well. "Yeah," he said. "I'll—be along. Have to take care . . ." His voice trailed off as he glanced back at Dyson.

"That's all right," said Edward unexpectedly. The youth had a long pressure-cut on his forehead. Both sleeves of his morning coat had ripped loose at the armpits. "You two—" He pointed at the pair of Dyson liverymen trying to creep off the podium. "Yes, you—Baucom, isn't it? Get back here and restrain the Councilor. We'll take him to the House medicomp. He needs treatment."

Edward turned to his mother and uncle. Marilee nodded very briskly. She scrambled off the podium and over the silent gun drone as quickly as she could. She wanted to prevent the fact that she was crying from being obvious to her son, no longer a boy.

The Houseman who had joined her on the podium now looked around. "I'm coming, Mistress," he called loudly as he bolted after the woman.

You never know, thought Slade as he walked slowly up the long aisle. You never know about other people, and you never know about yourself. Don Slade was anything on Tethys now that he wanted to be . . .

Many of the spectators in the Hall were only now beginning to leave. Shock and fright had kept them hunched behind partitions that would have been of no more account than farts in whirlwind, had the fighting really rolled their way. Now these folk ducked back out of the aisle or scudded ahead of Slade's progress with fearful looks behind them.

Home? Blood and Martyrs! But that would pass, and Don Slade was home indeed.

"I was getting ready to come look for you," said Danny Pritchard. The ex-mercenary lounged again beside the gun of his fighting vehicle. This time it was parked beside the shattered doors to the Hall, as still as it had been when day broke. "Marilee said you'd be along, though, so I figured I could wait."

He slid off the drone. "Here," he said, holding out one of the submachineguns gathered from Dyson's thugs. "You might want this."

Slade took the weapon, checking the load and safety by instinct. He gazed around the courtyard. The pool of orange flames and bubbling smoke took a moment to connect with Dyson's van. There didn't appear to have been the carnage he had feared and expected, though.

There was a crowd of what had surely been Dyson's guards in a corner between the House and the enclosure wall. Most of them had lost their livery as well as their weapons for some reason. Fishermen were pointing guns at their captives from the ground and from the roofs of the supply trucks. There would probably be accidents, but Slade was not disposed to worry about the despondent liverymen at this moment.

Chesson, atop one of the trucks, waved and shouted when Slade appeared from the building. "We got 'em, Soldier," he called gleefully.

"Just a little longer," the tanker shouted back. "By the Lord, it won't be forgotten."

"You know, Danny," Slade said to his companion, "I don't think I want this after all. Not right now." He handed back the gun he was holding. A stream of people was passing across the courtyard from the Hall, but only Council members seemed to be entering the House. Marilee had matters under control there already.

"Let's go talk to some people about the Slade Estate," said the big man mildly. "And about Tethys, I do suppose."

Together, the ex-mercenaries began walking toward the House. Danny Pritchard still cradled the automatic weapon.

"Everyone's gone upstairs, D-don," said Marilee from the bottom of the staircase. The name had come so smoothly from her memory that she stumbled when she paused to consider what she was saying.

Slade smiled. "I thought at least a few of the

Councilors'd figure the going was good," he said. "Marilee."

"They may be afraid of what you've got to say," noted Danny Pritchard from the political background which had absorbed him since Hammer took Friesland. "But they're going to be a lot more afraid of not being there when you say it."

He chuckled. In a different persona he added, "Want some company while you talk?" Pritchard did not have to gesture with the gun to make his meaning clear.

Slade punched him gently on the arm. "Hey," the big man said, "that's *my* line. I think—" He paused, then went on. "Upstairs I've got to handle myself. I'm the guy who's going to live here, right?"

Pritchard grinned. "Via, you're learning," he said approvingly. "Come back to Friesland and I'll find you a job in Admin. Hang in there, snake. I'm going to organize some of those people—" he gestured in the general direction of the hidden prisoners— "into a clean-up crew. Crispy critters are likely to offend the tender sensibilities of your peers."

Whistling, Hammer's heir strolled back toward the courtyard. Slade watched him for a moment. Then the big man cleared his throat and offered his crooked elbow to Marilee. "Shall we?" he said.

The woman's mouth quirked in a fashion that could have broadened into a smile. "The stairs are a little tight, aren't they?"

"Via, has it been so long?" Slade said with a chuckle that loosened his muscles and his taut, turbid mind. "Come on, my dear." His arm looped out to circle Marilee's waist. It was, he thought as they climbed in step made awkward by the wedgeshaped treads, a very long time. And it felt as good now as ever it had.

CHAPTER THIRTY-FIVE

Every Council member was standing, though there were seats enough in the Trophy Room for at least half of them.

The room's width between the trophy wall and the shot-out window was enough to keep the gathering from being cramped. No one wanted to be in the front, however. As a result, the Councilors were strung out along the window transom as if awaiting a firing party. Their faces bore out that suggestion, Slade thought as he strode to the center of the room.

"All right, now everybody move closer," Slade said. He raised his voice of necessity but avoided harsh modulations. "We're going to talk like human beings, that's all."

He had done this job before, many times before. Every time his troops set up in a populated area, the local leaders had to be called together. Frightened; the timid ones sure they were about to be shot, the smart ones aware that they *could* be shot at the mercenary's whim, whatever might be the orders of a distant headquarters. These faces were the same, though Slade recognized at least a dozen of them from his childhood.

The Councilors moved in from either end. Most of them shuffled, but two or three stepped firmly

and kept their shoulders squared. Jose Hauksbee
was one—still short, still pudgy, but willing to
meet Slade's eyes. Dyson had not chosen a syco-
phant, then, to move his triumph but rather a true
ally—or a foe, now broken to obedience.

"I returned from fighting," the big tanker said
as sullen faces waited in a shallow arc around
him. When he swayed, he could feel the skull of
the knife-jaw at his shoulders and the warmth of
Marilee beside him again. "What happened today
I regret, it's not what I came home to do. I didn't
come back to run the Slade Estate, either."

He paused and emphasized his words by staring
at the men and women around him. "That was for
my brother," he went on, "and it'll be for his son
. . . but right now, because you've decided Edward
should have a guardian for the next two years, I
think it might be a good idea it you appointed
me."

There was a hiss of conversation with one clear
voice wondering, "Where *is* the boy, then?"

"I move," cried a Councilor whom Slade did not
recognize, "that Donald Slade be confirmed by
acclamation as Councilor and heir of his father in
accordance with evidence presented at our last
meeting." The man who spoke was old and slender
with dissipation rather than health. His teeth were
perfect. Only the way his face moved when he
grinned suggested they were rotten.

"No!" Don Slade was shouting. Marilee's fingers
were tight on his left arm. What he heard was a
nightmare, a demon repeating words that Slade
himself had spoken only in his own mind, over
and over as he paced through the courtyard he
had won by force of arms. "No, I don't—say that.

Guardian for my nephew Edward, Councilor and heir of the Slade Estate. To his majority. That, Via, only that."

"So moved," said Councilor Hauksbee, "by acclamation." He continued to meet Slade's eyes.

There was a rattle of agreement and clapping, even some cheers. If there had been a formal second, it was lost in the noise . . . as the problem would be lost in the formal record.

"One other thing," said Slade, raising his voice over the babble that followed the action. "There's some problems at the Port. If you'll give me six months and a free hand, there won't be problems anymore."

"So moved!" cried the Councilor who had earlier tried to make Slade Councilor in his own right.

"Wait a minute!" the big man added as concern again blanked the faces of many of those around him. "The Port is an enclave, not part of the Slade Estate. Nothing's changing except that *everybody's* goods are going to be moving through again without screwing around." Slade raised his hands to keep the silence while his words marshalled themselves. "I don't want what you have. I don't even want what Dyson has. His estate will pass by law, wherever. But I'm Don Slade, people. What *I* have, I hold!"

The hush that followed was broken by Hauksbee's dry voice saying, "I second the motion of Councilor Gardiner."

The rattle of agreement which followed was again whole-hearted.

Slade put his arm around the woman beside him. "That's all I have to say," he remarked. The relief and elation he felt softened his voice. "I suppose whatever arrangements were planned for after the meeting are still on."

There were a half dozen cheers. Councilors surged forward to clasp the hand of the man from whom they had edged in terror moments before. Through the chorus of flattery and congratulation, Slade alone really noticed what Councilor Hauksbee was shouting. "Wait a minute!" the tanker roared. He raised his hands again. "Wait a minute!"

Hauksbee had not stepped forward, though he had been the nearest to Slade of the Councilors when the meeting began. With the background noise low enough for everyone now to hear him, Hauksbee said, "What happens to Dyson, Councilor Slade? What happens to the people who supported him? I was nominating him as guardian, you know."

And by the Lord! Dyson hadn't picked a coward for that task, Slade thought. Aloud the big man said, "Bev goes into exile. He can't be here and me be safe, it's that simple. Or any of you safe either."

Slade glanced sternly around the gathering. "Most of the servants he'd gathered up, they'll go too. Lot of them aren't from Tethys to begin with, and we sure as hell don't need them around. For the rest—"

There was a collective intake of breath from the Council. Even Hauksbee swallowed as he tried not to look away from the tanker.

"For the rest, I'm not asking questions and I'm not listening to tales. We've all done things in our past we don't want to be reminded of. Forget about—Via, the past twenty years on Tethys, if you like. I will."

"Why of course—" and "I always said the Slades—" were the only phrases the tanker could hear clearly in the sycophantic chorus. Hauksbee pursed his lips and nodded acceptance, not joy.

"Jose, all of you!" Slade said, using his voice to hammer its own path of silence. Men were grasping his hands. He did not snatch them away, but the slighter fingers fell away from Slade's scarred, powerful ones as he spoke.

"I'm not a saint," Slade went on in the new silence. "I've done terrible things." He swallowed.

Only a few of the faces turned toward Slade understood the sort of things he meant. The profession of slaughter, like others, has its arcana. No one could doubt Slade's sincerity when he went on. "I don't need to lie, people. If somebody's going to be shot, I'll tell you. Bev isn't, and neither are his boys."

There was another roar and surge of agreement. This time Slade responded to every hand, every enthusiastic greeting with the comment, "I appreciate that. You'll want to get down to your people right away and explain that the trouble's over."

He himself was walking slowly toward the door. Marilee paced just ahead of the tanker to boost Councilors to escape velocity with her own handshake and grim smile. *She* had not promised to forget.

Councilor Hauksbee was the last. "I owe you an apology, Mister Slade," the pudgy man said. He extended his hand but did not snatch at Slade's the way so many others had done.

"It was Don when we were kids, Jose," Slade said with a smile. They had not been friends, but each boy for his own reasons had a circle of enemies which often overlapped. "And you needn't apologize for honesty. Not anymore."

The handshake was a little more than formal. The trio poised by the door out of the room. "Not for being honest," Hauksbee said, "but for assuming you weren't. I—just wanted to be sure of the rules."

Slade nodded. His hand was now touching Marilee's again. "There's an Alayan ship in orbit," he said to Hauksbee. "The—Bev and the rest, they'll go aboard. Some may be released on Friesland, if Danny and the Colonel think they'd be useful. Most'll stay with the Alayans for—use." The tanker cleared his throat. How in the *hell* had the Alayans known there would be a cargo for them on Tethys? "They won't be mistreated, but they won't leave the ship."

"We'll talk later," Hauksbee said as he stepped through the door. When he was already out of sight of the anteroom, he called back, "I'm glad you've come home, Don."

"Are *you* glad, Don?" Marilee asked coolly. She stepped to the door to close it. She did not move back into his waiting arms.

"I came home because I wanted to be on Tethys," Slade said. He spoke as he would have walked through a minefield, slowly and with the greatest care. "For various reasons. And if you mean 'glad I came just now'—yeah, I suppose I am. Somebody needed to put things straight. I guess it's worked out as well as anybody was going to make it."

"Guns do make it easier to run things, don't they?" the woman said in the same brittle tone. She began to walk back along the trophy wall, skirting the man as she passed him.

"Listen, curse it!" Slade said. He paced behind the woman, fists clenched, the image of a carnivore at heel. "The guns were there before I was born. The only difference now is there's a *man* behind them again. I'm not going to melt down those gun-trucks, but they'll stay parked till they rust away for anything I do in the next two years."

Marilee spun. "Can I believe that?" she snapped. Her blue gown had not torn in the fighting, but there was a bruise showing already on her left cheekbone.

"Anything we've got left is an administrative problem," Slade said quietly. "I'm not real good at those, but I know how to recognize people who are. You don't use guns to solve admin problems."

He took a deep breath that trembled with the emotion he was trying to keep out of his voice. "But there's gun problems too, Marilee. Don't ever forget it. And don't blame me for seeing that there are."

She moved slightly, away from the wall. He saw the trophy that her body had screened as they walked back from the door. The argus larva was no more than the length of Slade's adult arm, but its spines still bristled with the vicious intensity of life. Old Man Slade had replaced each one of those which the boy's bare hands had shattered.

"I don't blame you," said Marilee as she extended her arms. "Welcome home, Don."

VENTURE SF FROM HAMLYN
PAPERBACKS

All these books are available from your bookshop or newsagent,
or you can order them direct just by ticking the titles you want
and completing the form below.

☐	1 WE ALL DIED AT BREAKAWAY STATION	Richard C. Meredith	£1.95
☐	2 COME, HUNT AN EARTHMAN	Philip E. High	£1.75
☐	3 HAMMER'S SLAMMERS	David Drake	£1.95
☐	4 INTERSTELLAR EMPIRE	John Brunner	£1.95
☐	5 THE STARWOLF TRILOGY	Edmond Hamilton	£2.50
☐	6 STARHUNT	David Gerrold	£1.95
☐	7 SOLD – FOR A SPACESHIP	Philip E. High	£1.75
☐	8 RUN, COME SEE JERUSALEM!	Richard C. Meredith	£1.75
☐	9 CROSS THE STARS	David Drake	£1.95

Postage (see below) _____

Total _____

_____

VENTURE SF, BOOKSERVICE BY POST, 84 SUFFOLK STREET,
BIRMINGHAM B1 1TA.

Please enclose a cheque or postal order made out to Andromeda
Books and send it to 84 Suffolk Street, Birmingham B1 1TA. Postage
rates for UK, Eire and British Forces: 55p per book, 20p for second
book and 12p for each subsequent book up to a maximum of £1.50.
Foreign: 75p for first book, 25p for second book, and 20p for each
additional book.

NAME ....

ADDRESS ....

....

Whilst every effort is made to keep prices low it is sometimes
necessary to increase cover prices and also postage and packing rates
at short notice. Hamlyn Paperbacks reserve the right to show new
retail prices on covers which may differ from those previously
advertised in the text or elsewhere.